Up For Grabs

The one individual facing toward me was a dumpy character, with small beady eyes and a large bulbous nose, and he looked as if he and the god Bachus were on friendly terms. He was dressed in a blue serge suit, and I could see that he felt uncomfortable, as if the suit was his Sunday best, and I am sure he would have preferred to be dressed in tee-shirt, jeans and sandals. Mentally I named him Wimpy, after a similar looking character, the ever scrounging fellow in the Pop-eye comic strip. His companion, on the other hand, was a far more sartorial specimen. He was slim and svelte, his suit, from what I could see of it, was of light cream material, free of creases and seemed to fit him well. He wore a canary yellow shirt with a green bow-tie, spotted I thought, for the distance made it vague, with small black dots. He was crouched toward his companion, but every so often, he leaned back and glanced furtively around, thus giving me the opportunity of getting a half to three quarter view. He never once faced me directly and I caught his face only in profile. It was a sharp featured face with a smudge of a moustache. He was of dark complexion and could have been Italian or Arab, or someone similar from those climes. Both their voices, however, were certainly South African. He must be the one called Jack.

For some reason I thought it prudent to imprint these characters firmly in my mind. I took careful note of their features and mannerisms and I knew I would recognize them if need be. The man I now thought of as Wimpy, asked, "Do you know how he operates this scheme of his?"

"Oh, he has been doing it for years," said Jack, "He is, as you know, Wilson, the chief accountant at the city treasury. I don't know the in and out of it, but apparently he found a way to rip off a percentage of the city employees pension funds. He is a trusted and well respected member of the municipal staff, and over the years has worked himself in a position of total control of the municipal finances, he is personally responsible for the disbursement of every one of the staff's salaries, and somehow he managed to cook the books and still kept the auditors happy all these years. I've been told that he is due for retirement shortly, and then of course, he will take his loot and cut and run. So if we are going to do anything about it, it had better be soon."

"Not soon enough for me," Wimpy interjected, "Have you any idea of the total amount.?"

"I believe he rakes off about forty grand odd a month, say about eighty thousand Rand a year. He has been busy at his scheme for something like ten years, so that works out to four million plus, and remember, it's all in cash."

Wimpy's voice cracked in excitement, "Wow! Really? It's all in cash and it's up for grabs. I can't believe it! And you say it's all in an unlocked cabinet, unbelievable! How did you tumble to all this, Jack, are you sure it's the truth?" Wimpy was rocking back and forth in his chair in his agitation.

"You better believe it, and I heard about it by the purest luck," answered Jack. "This Wilson character, I guess he is getting the forty year itch a bit late in life. He has been trying to get into the pants of certain little redhead that works in the filing department. So that he could impress her he started to boast how much he was worth, and just how clever he was, and how the municipality would throw a fit if they knew how good he was with figures. He told her they deserved what they got for not paying him according to his worth. What he didn't know was that this particular bit of fluff was my bedmate. She told me about his move on her, and how he had promised her a fabulous time and riches beyond her wildest dreams if she was good to him."

Jack went on to explain to his companion how he prevailed upon the redhead to play up to Wilson, and pump him for as much information as she could, about the whereabouts of all the riches he boasted about. Jack explained that Noreen, for that was her name, was a really beautiful, sexy and seductive woman, and once she got to work on Wilson, he did not stand a chance. Before long Wilson was trusting Noreen more and more, and confiding in her to a much greater extent. He hinted at the scam he was operating, and how he kept stacks of money hidden in a cabinet in a building nearby, because, he said, there might be awkward questions if he banked such large sums over and above his already substantial salary.

"Yes," concluded Jack, "I got Noreen to really play up to him. The stupid bastard, he thinks with his prick. He couldn't wait to impress her with his cleverness. It's amazing how an otherwise brilliant man can be fooled by a pretty face."

Wimpy could hardly contain himself, "All that money in an unlocked cabinet, I just can't believe it, the man's a moron," said Wimpy, who if I am any judge of character, was close to being a moron himself. "Hell Jack, let's go and get it, what are we waiting for?"

I sat there mesmerized; it was as if I was included in the conversation. Every word came across to me as if I was sitting at their table. My sumptuous meal was forgotten, I was agog for the next installment of this most incredible happening. I did not have to wait long.

"Not so fast my friend, maybe I exaggerated a bit, maybe the cabinet is locked, I don't know for sure. I do know, however, that it is a cabinet and not a safe, but it is still not going to be that easy," cautioned Jack," Since Noreen told me about the office in Nietrop building, I have spent a great deal of time following Wilson, so as to get an idea of his modis operandi. I know for instance, that every fourth of the month, or nearest working day thereto, he makes his way to Nietrop building during his lunch break with a stuffed briefcase, and I noticed that the case is always flatter when he comes out of his office again. If I'm not mistaken, unless he is carrying a four course meal, that briefcase is stuffed with money to add to his cache. But here is the snag; those offices are better secured than Fort Knox. Talk about overkill, there is only one door to the office, and it is so securely locked, and the door made of such material that a safe maker would be pleased to use. It will take a week to break in if one had the time, but during the day there are too many people about, and at night there is a security guard who patrols the floors."

Before Wimpy could interject, Jack continued, "Now I am working on a plan whereby I can get the security guard replaced. The man I want to replace him is you, O.K. I am not going into detail explaining how I intend to manage this; suffice to know that it can be done, but unfortunately, not before the end of the month. Once you are in, we will have thirty days before Wilson turns up on his monthly visit, and we will have plenty of time to figure out how we will handle the break-in. Now, remember this, my friend, no one knows about this except you and I, AND THAT'S HOW IT'S GOING TO STAY, UNDERSTAND—Mums the word O.K.?"

"Sure, sure," Wimpy nodded, "It's a great plan Jack. Yeah, you sure got the brains all right, Jack, you sure got the marbles all right."

"Yeah, Yeah, flattery will get you nowhere, now listen" finalised Jack, "We have a whole month, so in the mean time I want you to keep an eye on Nietrop building in case Wilson changes any of his plans or movements. I do not think he will, but you never know."

CHAPTER 2

I was earning enough as a jobbing builder, but the building trade had been somewhat depressed, and I had not been gainfully employed for a month or two, in fact, now that I came to think about it, I had not had a job for the last three months. I was not broke, you understand, I had about forty thousand in the bank, I owned a beat up Toyota truck with over one hundred thousand on the clock, but it was paid for and got me where I wanted to go. I had no family to support; I lived in a comfortable bachelor flat, I owed not a cent. No I was not broke, but four million odd, I could do with that. While I finished my sweet and coffee I ruminated on just how that four million could change my life.

"Will there be anything else?" The waitress was again at my table.

"No thanks; it was all very satisfactory, thank you." I settled my bill and tip and got up to leave. On my way out of the restaurant I had no conscious thought of acting upon the information that had so fortuitously come to my attention. I subconsciously reasoned that if the money was in fact fraudulently obtained, and if it was again stolen, there would hardly be a hue and cry and no police involvement. The original thief might make an attempt to regain the money himself, but he would have to know who was responsible for taking it off him in the first place, and where to find him.

I do not know when I decided to take a hand in the game, but suddenly I realized that I was paying more attention to the matter. By the time I had reached my flat, such thoughts as, 'they say opportunity knocks but once', and 'take the tide at the flood' were going through my mind.

My bachelor flat at Castle Court comprised a bedroom come living room with an attached kitchenette and a bathroom. There was a double bed, I had always hoped for a partner, two easy chairs, a table with a TV, a built-in cupboard that housed my meager wardrobe. The kitchenette also was also furnished with a table, two chairs and a dresser, and this I referred to euphemistically as my dining room. A draw in the table contained my writing materials comprising a writing pad, sundry pieces of paper, pens and pencils. In one corner of the kitchenette I stored my toolbox. The place was no great mansion, but it was home. I kicked off my shoes, switched the TV. on and threw myself onto the bed. My favorite TV. Show, a re-run of,'Everybody loves Raymond' was just starting. The wise cracks were as good as ever, Marie was being her usual busybody self, but that night the show did not even raise a smile from me. My mind kept straying back to the millions there for the taking.

I got up from my bed, took a clean sheet of paper and pen from the draw on the table and proceeded to draw up a list of points I had gleaned from the overheard conversation.

1—Nietrop building—I had worked on it during construction and knew every nook and cranny.

2—The office in question was on the fourth floor.

3—Wilson arrived the fourth of the month, assuming a working day.

4—Today was the twenty eighth of July, that means Wilson will visit the office on the following Friday.

5—Apparently, September month is Wilsons final trip to Nietrop building. A little over a month to get hold of the money, a calculated risk.

6—As money already stolen, hardly likely an alarm if money stolen again.

7—Immediate action needed to stay in front of the opposition. Jack said D-day planned for the fourth of September.

Upon reading these notes I finally realised that in writing item seven, I had committed myself. I was going to steal FOUR MILLION BUCKS.

On Monday the thirty first of July I was at Nietrop building, walking about, casing the joint as Wimpy would probably say, and also refreshing my memory of the layout of the building. As I moved about the details came back to me. I remembered the overall dimensions; it was a small block by city standards, only thirty metres by thirty metres. The main entrance faced Main Street, on the other three sides, going round the building in a clockwise direction, were Baxter street, at the back, Service road, and on the other side, Caxton Street. Down the center of the block, on the Service road side, was the fire escape. The street level of the fire escape, contrary to all regulations, was locked off by a grill mesh cage. I remembered that in the center of both side walls was a service shaft built into the building which housed all the water and sewage lines that serviced the various offices. In these shafts, the wall opposite the one carrying all the pipe work had steel rungs let into the surface to form a ladder to allow for the inspection of the pipe work. Entrance to both these shafts was by means of service doors on the ground floor of the building. The layout of the ground floor comprised the doorman's office immediately on the right as you entered the building. On the left was a bank of public telephones, next to them was the ladies public restrooms, followed by the service door to the shaft on that side of the building, after the service shaft door was the nightwatchmans cubicle. Moving round to the back were store rooms and continuing to the opposite side were the men's public restrooms and the other service shaft, and then one was back at the front of the building. The center of the building housed the elevator shaft, and around the elevator was the stairs to the upper floors. The three floors above contained the office suites, each of the floors having the same layouts. As one stepped out of the elevator on the first floor you faced a floor to ceiling glass wall. This glass wall continued right up the face of the building. Immediately to the right and left were two of the office suites. I remembered they comprised a reception area, and leading off the reception area were two doors leading to separate offices, and on the opposite side was a door to private toilet and ablution facilities.

There were four suites of offices on each of the upper floors, each identical to the one described. The previously mentioned service shafts ran up the back of the two adjoining toilet facilities servicing the two office suites on each respective side of the building, and on each respective floor. The outer wall of the shafts being on the street side, the two side walls forming part of the adjoining office walls. The four sets of offices were situated around the perimeter of the building, with the elevator and stairs commanding the center area.

I went up to the fourth floor to establish, if I could, the position of Wilsons office. I could find nothing with his name on, but I did find that the suite of the office at the right back on the fourth floor had an extremely robust door fitted with high quality security locks. There was only a number sixteen on the face of the door, but judging by what the man Jack had said about the security of the office, I assumed this was Wilson's office. I next cruised round the other offices to establish what types of business were in occupation. They were a mixture of legal firms and business consultants, with one lone electronics firm on the third floor. There was one empty suite on the first floor with a notice stating the rental agent's name and phone number.

Yes, the layout was the same as I remembered it, now I just had to wait until Wilson paid his monthly visit, which would prove to me that it was not just a pipe dream of Jacks. Also I would be able to confirm Wilsons actual office. The man I had dubbed Wimpy would also probably be in evidence, but as he did not know me, it should not prove a problem. In fact to know what he was up to might be to my advantage. After Wilsons visit I would have a month in which to put a plan into operation, because, judging from the conversation between Jack and Wimpy, they were greedy enough to wait until Wilson's last deposit had been made in September. I felt confident that with my knowledge of the building, and with an early start, I had a distinct advantage. I returned to my flat well satisfied and ready to begin working out my plan of action.

After considering various alternatives, I finally decided that the best and simplest plan was to gain access to the service shaft to Wilson's office, climb up the shaft and, using my knowledge of the layout and construction of the building, and my expertise as a builder, break through the wall of the office, collect the cash and exit the same way. This way there would be no alarms and excursions at all, unless Wilson decided to make public the robbery on the occasion of his next visit. Something that was hardly likely to occur. It all seemed extremely simple, no one would be suspicious of work being carried out in the service shaft, the assumption would be that it was routine maintenance work. The only hurdle that I could see was to convince the doorman of my legitimacy for being in the service shaft.

That night I slept very badly, my mind was in turmoil. My thoughts ranged from my plan of action to the life I would lead once I had obtained the money. I fantasized about the woman I would have, the car I would buy, the exotic places I would travel to, maybe even a sea going yacht. The possibilities were endless. Normally I was a steady sort of person, not given to wild excesses. Women, well I had often imagined a dream girl, but had not met anyone yet. Suddenly my mind was filled with extreme ideas and fancies never before envisaged. I rolled and tossed on my bed until I fell into a fitful sleep and woke in the morning with a thick head.

I staggered out of bed, switched the coffee percolator on, and while it bubbled and squeeked, I took a shower Later, sitting at the table sipping the hot coffee, I remembered I had promised to look at my landlady's faulty washing machine. 'Damn,' I thought, 'just when my mind is filled with this other thing, I have to remember my promise to look at a faulty washing machine.

My landlady was a sweet old lady, always pleasant to me, always fussing and worrying about my diet, and lack of balanced food. She regularly complained that my diet, of hamburgers and TV. Dinners I usually ate during the week, was not suitable for a hard working man. In spite of the fact that I explained that once a week I splurged on real healthy meal at Francesco's, she still insisted that I come up to her flat for a good healthy dinner on a regular basis. She certainly was very good to me and I felt obligated to her, so when she asked me to look at her washing machine I felt I could not refuse. But not this morning, it was just too bad, but I didn't feel like the continual chatter she would maintain while I was trying to fix her machine. 'I'll attend to her machine some other time, 'I thought,' I have too much to think about at present.'

The fourth of August had come and gone, I had seen Wilson visit his office, which was the number sixteen I had earmarked, and it all went exactly as the man Jack had described it that fateful evening. As I had expected, I had noticed Wimpy also ensconced on the fourth floor when Wilson arrived.

Wilson and I had travelled up on the same elevator together, and I had, had time to study him. He was a man about sixty years old, with a very open and serene face. He had a full head of wavy, silver gray hair, brushed straight back, and with his good looks, he reminded me of a film star, rather Lionel Barrymoorish, if you know what I mean, Than the accountant I understood him to be. He was fairly tall, I estimated him to be five nine, or there about, athletically slim and impeccably dressed, the sort of man who would be very attractive to most women. Wilson unlocked his office, glanced rather apprehensively, I thought, toward the lurking Wimpy, who certainly did not give the impression of an entirely disinterested bystander. I hoped that I was not that obvious. In any event he hardly glanced at me as I walked past him, and passing Wimpy in turn, I entered the next office. The offices I entered happened to be those of Carruthers and Steimetz, attorneys at law, and the décor of the office left no one in doubt that one's bank account had better be substantial and in good standing, if you hoped to receive any legal advice.

The receptionist looked up as I entered, and I could see that her experienced eye had categorized me as a non paying customer. Nevertheless she managed to pin a professional smile on her face as she asked me how she could be of assistance. I asked if I could see Miss Benson, hoping that there would be no Miss Benson, either on the staff, or visiting.

"I am sorry," apologised the receptionist, "we have no Miss Benson on our staff."

I tried to look suitably flustered. "No," I said, stalling for time, as I did not want to exit these offices until, hopefully, Wimpy had disappeared, "She is not a member of your organization, but a client, and she asked me to meet her here at two o'clock. I am sorry but I am a bit early."

The receptionist glanced through her appointment book, looked up and replied, "Sorry, no appointment has been made by any Miss or Mrs. Benson for this afternoon."

I could think of no further reason to prolong my stay and I retired as gracefully as possible. Wimpy was still there as I exited the offices into the passage. He took a hard look at me as I past him on my way to the elevator. So far so good, everything checked out and I felt I could proceed with my plan. Just to be certain, I lingered about the entrance of the building to make sure that Wimpy made no untoward move, and that Wilson left the premises as was usual.

CHAPTER 3

I spent the week-end polishing my plan and obtaining a few props. On Monday morning the seventh of August, suitably attired in a khaki dust coat and wearing a hard hat and tinted glasses, I approached the doorman at Nietrop building carrying my toolbox. The doorman was a black gentleman dressed in a light gray uniform with gold piping at his sleeve cuffs, collar and shoulder lapels. There was also gold piping down the outside of his trouser legs, his peaked cap was equally bedecked. He was certainly an imposing personage.

"Good morning," I greeted him with what I hoped was a winning smile, "I have come to carry out some maintenance work in one of the service shafts. Where can I find a key to the gates, please?"

"Good morning," he greeted, "First give me your copy of the works order, so I can enter it in my log book."

"Works order?" I repeated, acting surprised, "They didn't give me a works order."

"No work gets carried out here without a works order from Fuller and Clark. They have the maintenance contract, and they know very well that they must send a work order with their workmen."

Seeing that I was completely put out, he took compassion on me and said, "O.K. I'll phone them and ask for your order number so I can give you the key. But don't forget to bring the order tomorrow when you come back here to work."

The last thing I wanted was for him to phone Fuller and Clark, so I said hastily, "No, don't bother, thanks all the same. There are probably some balls up as usual. The job I was supposed to do would be finished in a morning, so I wouldn't have come back in the morning anyway. I'll go back to the works and check on it, see you." And I hurried off.

'That really blew it, 'I thought,' Oh well, back to the drawing board'. Now what? Obviously I was not going to be able to wangle a work order, and even if I did, the doorman's curiosity is now piqued and my original idea of gaining access to Wilson's office via the service shaft was truly scotched. Then it came to me. I could still use the service shaft as a means of entry. I was a builder was I not? I had suddenly remembered the vacant office on the first floor I had noticed when carrying out my inspection of the building. If I could break into Wilson's office from the service shaft, I could also break into the shaft from the vacant office in the same way. I remembered the vacant office was situated on the first floor directly under Wilson's office on the fourth and thus utilizing the same service shaft. I would lease office number two.

A little later that day I returned to Nietrop building, but this time dressed in a natty black pinstripe suit, collar and tie, my best actually. Looking like a successful businessman I re-approached the building. This time I had no hard hat or spectacles and I was reasonably certain that provided I did not stop and chat to him, the doorman would not notice me among the passing traffic. I waited just out of sight and when I noticed a reasonable flow of people going in and out, I slipped amongst the crowd and easily made it to the stairs, up which I hastily ran. I wrote down the name of the agent and phone number, and then high tailed it out of the building. When I phoned the number I found that the agents Friedman and Schlebusch were situated in Saker buildings right across town. I was glad of this, as I did not want a letting agent close by who could be breathing down my neck at inconvenient times. What I needed was privacy. I asked for the agent whose name appeared on the notice and made an appointment to see her.

The agent I met with was a Mss. Jean Scott. Neatly coiffured, neatly dressed in a white blouse and black pencil skirt, silk stockings and high heels, she neatly dealt with my enquiry. Yes, number two Nietrop building was available at one thousand Rand per month, water and electric deposits and usage was for the tenants account. Number two comprised unfurnished offices and reception area, private ablution and toilet facilities. She would be delighted to show me the suite at my convenience. Right now? Certainly let me just find the keys.

After going through the motions of inspecting the layout of the offices, which, of course, I already knew perfectly well, I expressed my satisfaction. We then repaired to her own office once more to finalise the lease. She said she would attend to the electricity and water connections on my behalf and would have the offices cleaned first thing tomorrow morning. I thanked her, and asked if I could in the meantime, borrow a key, so that I could plan my office layout and furnishing. I promised to return the key when I brought my first rental payment tomorrow.

I think I mentioned earlier that the building was twenty years old, what I needed to do was test the plaster work to check how hard it had become over those years, as this was pertinent to the success of my plan, and the speed at which I could proceed with the work. Once alone in the office I chose an unobtrusive corner and knocked a thin screwdriver through the plaster. I wriggled it about a bit and found I was able to extract it easily without breaking the surface plaster other than leaving a six millimeter hole. The screwdriver went through the wall with comparative ease, and I was certain that it was soft enough not to offer undue resistance to my attempt to break through the walls. I dampened my handkerchief under the tap and wiped up the small amount of plaster dust from the floor and rinsed it off in the basin. I decided my plan was feasible and decided to rent the office and in so doing, become a legitimate member of the building's population. This would allow me to come and go as I pleased, and behind the closed door of office number two, I could break into the service shaft at my leisure. Once in the shaft I could create a scaffold system that would allow me to reach the fourth floor, and finally gain access to Wilson's office. 'An altogether professional approach, even though I do say so myself,' the four million plus seemed to me a certainty.

I realized that the thousand Rand a month, and I would have to rent the office for a reasonable length of time to avoid any suspicion, would be a considerable slice out of my capital. However, I rationalized that it was a small enough investment for a big and fast return. I withdrew seven thousand from my account, which should be enough for six months rental, plus sundry expenses such as light and water deposits etc. and I returned to settle up with Mss. Scott. I leased for six months with an option for a further year. Miss Scott was curious as to my type of business. I managed to curb her curiosity by saying that I was in assaying and research for mining houses. The payment for six months rental in advance went a long way to make her lose further interest in my affairs. I had given my name as Jack Wimpy, which appealed to my sense of humour. The advance payment settled everything; Miss. Scott never even asked to see my I.D., which was the usual thing these days. It is amazing how flashing large sums of money can simplify matters. I received my office keys once again plus an additional key. Mss Scott explained that there was no doorman on duty after five p.m., only a night watchman. She said that if I wished to enter the offices after hours I must make myself known to the night watchman. Getting the building entrance key was a bonus, and her remark about being in the building after hours started a new train of thought. I might be able to do some work at night.

"Hullo," she greeted, "I see you are off to a job, it is good that work picking up again. By the way, I hate to be a nuisance, but you haven't forgotten about my washing machine, have you?"

"No, not at all, Mrs. Walker. I hope to be free on your wash day so that I can see what happens during an actual washing cycle. I hope that will be suitable to you?"

"Of course, of course, anytime that suits you, I'm just ever so grateful for your help, you know. It is always so difficult for women who are alone. I am really grateful to you, thank you."

I honestly meant to help her, she was a good old soul and I liked her a lot, but I really had to attend to this other matter first. Those waiting millions exerted a strong attraction over me, and the fact that the two men who had been instrumental in getting me interested in the first place, were themselves making plans to make off with those same millions, did nothing to ease my mind. In spite of Jack mentioning September as their date when they planned to take action, I could not stop the nagging worry that they might act sooner.

Back at the truck, I first drilled two holes each at the one end of each of the timber boards and that was all the preparity work I could do at present. The rest of the cutting and drilling would be done on site, where I could measure accurately. I reloaded all the goods on the truck, then I walked to a liquor outlet to buy a bottle of Brandy with which I proposed to cement Cotteral's loyalty to me. I had done all I could for the moment in preparation of my night's work and now I had about four hours to kill before I could take my material into my office. The thought entered my mind that now might be a good time to have a look at Mrs. Walker's machine. It was a good intention, and I was about to go in search of her, when the four million plus loomed up in my mind. I suddenly decided that I did not feel up to fiddling about with a washing machine.

That evening it took me three trips to move all the material and tools to my office. I accomplished two trips while Cotteral was busy with his first round of the night. I deliberately left the last trip until Cotteral was back downstairs. I approached him and asked if he would be good enough to help me carry some stuff to my office. He willingly agreed. Cotteral gazed interestedly at the timber and tools. To settle his obvious curiosity, I told him about the shelves I intended constructing to house my rock and earth samples.

"Rocks and earth?" He looked at me blankly.

"Yes, I am an assayist and I have to analyse samples the mines send me to check the gold bearing value of their seams." It sounded good to me; I hoped Cotteral would be as convinced. To try and further convince him I told him the name of my business was 'Water @ Earth Analysis @ Research'—'W.E.A.R.' That seemed to satisfy him and he returned to his cubicle. I was fairly confident that he would not worry unduly about the noise I would inevitably make when I started knocking holes in the wall.

A little later I followed him there and invited him to join me in a nightcap, producing the bottle of brandy I had purchased earlier and two glasses. I could see by the way his eyes lit up that I had judged him aright, Mr. Cotteral would prove no trouble to me.

I said, "Nothing like a snort to while away a long night."

I poured him a stiff drink, which he almost snatched from my hand. I poured myself a moderate tot and raised my glass.

"Down the hatch," I toasted him. Cotteral's drink disappeared like magic.

"Another?" I suggested, proffering the bottle.

"Thank you kindly, sir." He said taking the bottle from me.

"Well, I suppose I had better get back to work. Keep the bottle." I went back to my office content that Cotteral had been taking care of, and would not be heard from again this night.

It was eight p.m. That night the ninth of August that I started to break through the wall between my office and the service shaft. At first I was alarmed at the noise the angle grinder made in the still of the night. I stopped and listened, all was quiet, no one appeared to be raising complaints. I chided myself, Cotteral would hardly react, and who else would be there to complain, other than the guard. I attacked the wall again and cement and brick dust welled up around me. I had deliberately left the window closed to minimise the noise factor, and to avoid dust clouds swirling out the window and maybe attracting attention. However the dust clouds were overpowering me and I was finding it difficult to breath, so I was eventually forced to open the window. I pulled the venetian blinds aside, and stood at the open window taking deep breaths of fresh air and generally cooling down. All was quiet on the street below me. I went downstairs to check on Cotteral. He was dozing comfortably. I was thus assured that the noise I was making was less obtrusive than I had thought, and this gave me confidence. I made a mental note to purchase a dust mask and a spray bottle to dampen down the dust, although most of the dusty work was complete, at least until I reached the top of the shaft and started upon Wilson's wall. Then all the dust and litter could fall down to the bottom of the shaft and not cause as much of a problem as had been the case in my office.

Returning to my office, I stood at the window once more savouring the cool night air. About to move to the bathroom to get a drink of water before starting work again, I became conscious of a car pulling up in the street below. I quickly dropped the venetian in a cloud of dust, and peered through the slats. A police car had parked at the curb and a man in uniform got out, looked around at the building, then tried the front door. A second policeman emerged from the car and joined his partner. A sound of loud knocking reached me and I heard a voice shout, "Open up, Police." I hoped Cotteral, in a drunken state, would not stagger to the door and complicate matters. I raise the venetian blind and called out, "Up here officer."

A torch shone in my face, "We had a call to investigate noises and breakages, open up please."

"O.K., I'm coming, I am just busy carrying out some office alterations."

"Please open the building," reiterated the officer.

"O.K.," I answered again, "Give me a moment to come down."

I rushed to the bathroom, took off my dust coat and brushed as much dust as I could out of my hair, sluiced and dried my face. A glance in the mirror showed a worried and tired face, and fortunately free of excess dust, although traces remained on my shirt collar. It would have to do. I rushed back to the office in which I had been working, dragged the timber, my skill saw, hammer and measuring tape through into the adjoining office, and locked the first office door. That was the best I could do in the circumstances, and hoped I could bluff my way out of trouble.

I set off down the stairs, the elevator being switched off at night, a fact that I was glad of, as using the stairs would in some way account for the delay in coming down. I arrived at the entrance the same time as the bleary eyed, half asleep security guard, who had obviously only just woken up. I opened the door.

"Good evening officers, what is the problem?"

"There has been a complaint about loud noises coming from this building. Can you explain the disturbance, Sir?" Asked the first officer.

"Your name, address and I.D., please," interjected his companion.

I apologised for having caused a problem and explained that I had recently hired offices in the premises, and was busy carrying out fixtures and fittings before opening for business. One cop thought it strange to be working at night, and asked if I had good reason for doing so? I told him that I worked at night so as not to disturb or to inconvenience the other office tenants.

"Yers, I can vouch for that. The gentleman has been very busy." Cotteral contributed.

"Who are you?" Queried the second cop.

"Night security guard, sergeant Cotteral at your service," said that worthy, pulling himself up into an erect and proud posture. The second cop turned back to me and again repeated his request for my name and I.D. I hesitated a moment, wondering if it would be wise to mention the name Wimpy. They would certainly check it out, and in any case I had no identity document in that name. I apologised profusely, saying that I did not have my I.D. with me as I did not think it would be needed. I said I was trading as Jack Wimpy, Water and earth analysis and research. I added that they could check with Friedman and Schlebush, the letting agents. I gave them the agent's phone number helpfully. The first cop finished writing notes on his pad and demanded to see my office, and so we all trooped upstairs.

The cops glanced at the material lying about and asked what I intended doing. I told them about the shelving I intended to erect to house all my many rock and earth samples, a story I was coming adept at telling. Cotteral, who had attached himself to the group, nearly sabotaged me by saying that," Cor' with all the noise I'd a thought that you had done more than this!" And I thought he had been sleeping!! My heart lurched, would the police react to Cortteral's remark? This was not the case, however, and all the officer asked was how long I intended to be working at night? I explained that I had only started that night, and as I had to erect dry walls as well as shelving, I thought I would be busy for at least two weeks or so.

"Ja, I see," said the cop, "When did you say you moved in?"

I had not said when I had moved in, only that I started on the shelves that night. However, I was not about to argue the point, I told him that I had signed the lease earlier in the week.

"Well, sorry to have disturbed you sir. We will probably call again to see how you are getting on. In the mean time try to keep the noise down. Goodnight sir." With this veiled threat they took their leave. Cotteral saw them to the door and locked up. I wondered if they had swallowed my story. The fact that they had intimated they might call again was of concern to me. Then again it was their job to be suspicious of everything. I settled down to work again, and with a knife and screwdriver, I scraped out a fair amount of mortar from between the bricks that were visible in the area I had cleared of plaster, and which I had undercut with the angle grinder. With a few taps from the hammer the bricks loosened and I could remove them from the wall. I had opened a space of roughly eight hundred millimeters square, sufficient room to crawl through into the service shaft. I was satisfied with the evenings work. I spent another hour cleaning the walls and floor meticulously. The bulk of the waste I threw down the shaft. I decided to call it a night. I locked up, and bidding Cotteral goodnight, I let myself out of the building and returned to my flat and a well needed shower. Tomorrow I must not forget to purchase a few more items, and dust masks and a spray bottle.

CHAPTER 4

10 August

The items I had to purchase were a table or desk, a chair, a bookcase and a carpet to give the office some semblance of authenticity. I also bought a small tin of black paint and sign writers brush in order to paint my business name on the door. I remembered to buy the spray bottle and dust mask I had promised myself. I decided to move these items into the building in broad daylight as obviously I couldn't pretend to be in business unless my office was furnished, and there were bound to be curious people amongst the other tenants on the first floor. I hired a casual labourer to help me get these items to my office. The largest items were the desk I had managed to get cheaply, and the bookcase, and the carpet. These the labourer and I deposited outside my office door as I did not want him to get sight of the work being done within. Maybe I was being ultra cautious, but I felt happier with fewer people knowing what I was about. I paid the man ten Rand and did the final moving of all the pieces into the office on my own.

I was pleased to find that the bookcase fitted nicely over the hole in the wall, effectively hiding the area. With the carpet on the floor, and with the desk and chair in place, the whole aspect of the office changed for the better. I reminded myself to borrow a picture or two from my flat to hang on the walls, and to buy some second hand books to place on the bookcase shelves, not too many as I would be pushing the bookcase away from the hole in the wall on a regular basis, and I didn't want it to become too heavy. Next I carefully painted W.E.A.R. on the door, followed by my phone number and, 'by appointment only', which, I thought, was a nice touch. I hoped that the, 'By appointment only,' would limit interruptions completely. Obviously only people who knew the meaning of the letters W.E.A.R. would phone, and that should translate into zero calls or interruptions. I hoped that these few props would prove sufficient in masking my true intentions.

I sat at the desk and rested for awhile, this was getting to be a costly and tiring exercise. I'd invested twelve thousand Rand in the lease, bought material and furniture, spent long hours in the evening working. I was constantly on the watch for a surprise move by the other party during the day. It better be all worth it. I could not even conceive of the possibility that I might yet be beaten to the punch. A cold shiver worried its way down my spine. I jumped up, shook off my depressing thoughts and decided to check the fourth floor once again, just to settle my anxieties.

Then I had another idea. If there was a presence on the fourth floor more or less continually, then Wimpy and Co. could hardly attempt to force open Wilson's door. With that thought in mind, I donned my dustcoat, collected my ladder and toolbox, and took the elevator up to the fourth floor. With my knowledge of the building it was an easy matter to locate the electrical switchboard for that particular floor. I switched the circuit breaker that controlled the passage lights, off, and established myself at a light fitting that afforded me a clear view of Wilson's door. I made myself comfortable on top of my ladder and proceeded to dis-assemble the light, and pretended to be carrying out repair work. Every so often people would walk around my ladder busy with their own affairs and perambulations; no one took the slightest interest in me I kept watch on Wilson's door.

An hour and a half later I was still watching from the top of my ladder and nothing had transpired. It dawned on me that I was becoming paranoiac, although keeping watch on Wilson's door was sound in theory, I could not spend every day on top of a ladder, it would prove soul destroying. Besides which, how long could a man spend fixing a light before someone eventually remarked upon the fact. I had to think of some other way to monitor my competitors' movements. I had heard Jack make September as their target date, but my own suspicious and subconscious mind would not let me accept that fact, I had the uneasy feeling of an imminent move on their part. I chided myself for being overwrought about Wimpy and Jack's imagined movements. I re-assembled the light fitting. Switched the power back on, and whilst I moved my equipment back to my office, I kept telling myself that surely they would not change their plan, they had no reason to do so, the fourth of September, that was the date to worry about. I repeatedly reminded myself,' fourth of September, you have until the fourth of September'. I sincerely hoped that would be the case, but who knew.

I suddenly realized that I was feeling peckish, and with that mundane thought overruling my paranoia regarding the opposition, I looked at my watch and noticed it was already the lunch hour. Fish and chips and a bottle of coke was sufficient or me. I felt a lot better after I had eaten. I decided to do some daytime work to keep my mind off negative thoughts, and with renewed energy, I pushed the bookcase aside and took up my measuring tape. The hole I had made was at right angles to the ladder rungs let into the outside wall. In order to reach the rungs I had to push a board across the gap. To allow for a firm positioning of the board at the rung end, I perforce had to saw a forty five degree angle off one end. I used my skill saw to do this and it made one hell of a racket. I held my breath. After a minute or two, since there were no irate knocks on my door, I proceeded to place the board in place. Taking up a length of rope I crawled gingerly out upon the board finally reaching the end at the ladder rungs. I tied the end of the board securely. I measured up the distances required to fit two boards upon the rungs and across the gap to the wall that carried the pipework, and crawled back to my office to prepare these. I prepared these boards just fifty millimeters longer than the gap between the outer wall and the wall on my right-hand side which carried the pipe work, so that they would wedge firmly. All this crawling in and out and measuring and preparing was a slow process and it was five p.m. by the time I had all prepared for the evenings work.

Back at the office that evening I made my contribution of brandy to Cotteral. Surprised and grateful, the brandy immediately became the centre of Cotterals' attention, and I went to my office secure in the knowledge that I would have a few hours of undisturbed work.

My first order of business was to fit, the batten which I had previously prepared, along the rung and projecting out on either side. I lashed this batten firmly in place, and then maneuvered, slowly and carefully, the two boards I had cut to length, so that they each rested upon the batten on the one end and wedged against the wall at the other end, next to the pipe work, I crawled to the centre of the diagonal board, and hammered the two wedged boards firmly into place, thus creating a firm base almost covering the gap of the shaft from end to end, and from which I could launch my attack up the other three floors.

The rungs were only there to allow for the inspection of the pipe work. The wall with the pipe work was situated two metres away, and at right angles to the wall I intended to break through. This meant I would have to erect a scaffold across the gap at each floor level at the extent of the reach of my three metre ladder, and so, step by step work my way up the shaft until my goal was reached. The intermediate scaffolds need only consist of one timber board each, just wide enough to place the foot of my ladder firmly at each level. The lengths of timber required to bridge the gaps at the various levels were the same as the last two I had cut for the first floor scaffold, except that, as I only required one board at each level, I could slip one side of the board onto a rung and simply wedge it fast against the opposite wall, instead of having to drill and fasten extra battens. I cut the balance of the timber to suit and drilled holes to accept fixing ropes. All this took a while to carry out, and it was after ten o'clock that evening before I had finished. I decided to call it quits for the evening. From this point on I felt it would be prudent to work at night in future, as my work would be carried out at other floor levels, and strange sounds emanating from the shaft during the day at those floor levels may cause comment and enquiry.

This meant I had another fruitless day to get through. I showed myself at the office just to add credence to my fake business. I sat around the office for awhile, and the idle time began to play havoc with my subconscious mind. One again the irrational feeling that Wimpy was up to something sprung to my mind, and I felt I just had to check Wilson's door again, in case it had been tampered with by the opposition. I could not imagine what the shock would be if I had found Wilson's door actually broken open, when my own efforts were only beginning.

The constant worry that the opposition would change their original plan, my own niggling guilt at what I was up to made me nervous, and it all tended to make my movements and actions all too suspicious. Fortunately most people in the building were too occupied with their own little problems to pay much attention to my loitering around the fourth floor. The actual fact of the matter was that Wimpy and Jack did not know of my existence. It was my own guilty conscious that kept me forever worrying about a possible threat from them. I belatedly realized that I probably ran the greatest threat from the two policemen and Mss. Scott, should they decide to pursue their enquiries into my actions. That thought stopped my in my tracks for the moment. "What did it matter what I did in my own office?" I asked myself in an effort to settle my nerves, and still this new worry over Scott and the two policemen persisted. No matter how much I tried to bolster my confidence, I still had the tendency to keep looking over my shoulder. With these thoughts jumbling through my mind I peered closely at Wilson's door as I passed along the passage. There was no sign of attempt to break through the lock. 'You unutterable clot,' I thought to myself,' of course neither Wimpy or Jack would be such fools as to tamper with the door and leave evidence of their attempt for other tenants to raise an alarm. The whole essence of their plan was to rob Wilson quietly, because they relied on the fact that Wilson, having embezzled the money in the first place, could not raise an alarm and thus raise awkward questions as to his legitimacy regarding the huge amount of money concerned. 'There was only one conclusion I could draw from that line of reasoning, and that was that I could rely upon them only making an attempt upon Wilson's person himself when he appeared on the fourth of September. Once again I silently berated myself for my irrational imagination that kept me in a state of constant anxiety about the oppositions possible early move.

I returned to my office and made myself a settling cup of tea. I sipped the tea, and consoled myself that I was still ahead in the race. Based upon the work I had carried out the previous evening, I figured that I should reach the fourth floor by the third evening, in other words the thirteenth of August. I could possibility break through into Wilson's office on the fourteenth. After that all I had to do was to rebuild the hole in my office wall, plaster and paint the office, and no one would ever be the wiser. The six month paid up lease would give me ample time to disappear.

CHAPTER 5

11th August

Evening arrived at last and I could proceed with my work once more. In spite of my earlier reasoning, I still had a continual feeling of losing my advantage for some reason. I could not give any substance to the thought, except that I felt the urgent need to get a move on.

I crawled into the hole once more, dragged the ladder in after me and placed it into position, thus gaining a means of climbing up to the second floor level. My idea was to attach a rope to a board, climb up to the second floor level, hoist the board to that level and manoever it across the shaft, and firmly tie it in that position. At the second floor level I heaved with all my strength, the rope cutting painfully into my hand. The board swung free from the bottom scaffold and the full weight suddenly jerked me sideways, hurtling me across the shaft, fortunately toward the narrower side. My left shoulder crashed into the wall most painfully and I was unable to keep a grip on the rope. The board and rope went crashing down onto the lower scaffold with such a blow, that it shifted one of the supporting scaffold planks sideways, almost upsetting me completely. It then slipped between the lower scaffold planks and continued down to the ground floor and the bottom of the shaft. I hung onto the ladder, shivering from shock. Eventually I managed to carefully push myself and the ladder into a more upright position, and ease myself slowly down to my floor level and crawled back out of the hole. I sat on my chair and drew in some deep breaths and steadied myself. It was not going to be as easy as I had at first thought. I hoped the falling board had not made too much noise hitting the bottom of the shaft, at least not loud enough to cause alarm. I went downstairs to confront and assure Cotteral that all was in control. All was quiet, Cotteral was nowhere to be seen, he must have been on his rounds of the upper floors.

Now, what to do? I had no equipment to fish for the fallen board. The only answer was to buy a replacement. I had the other timber I was to use at the additional floor levels, but I would need the extra board when I finally reached the fourth floor. In the mean time I must devise a way to lift the boards quietly, easily and safely. I required some sort of mechanical assistance. 'Blast! Was there no end to the preparations? When was I going to make reasonable progress? Once again I had the irrational feeling that Wimpy and Jack were wasting no time in effecting their plan. After all my efforts and expense, I simply could not let that happen. I locked the office and went home in a decidedly depressed state of mind. I had a whole week-end of inactivity to get through, or could I take a chance and work on the week-end. I thought I had better not, such energy and over time would be unlikely in a businessman such as I was supposed to be.

Monday the fourteenth of August dawned bright and clear, a new day, a new week. I was feeling much more relaxed. I still had time on my side, I assured myself, and the thing was to keep in control of my emotions. I realized that I could only work at night, in case of falling timber, or other noise making catastrophes. I must not panic and persuade myself I would make up time by working by day, the risk was too great.

The first item on the agenda was to obtain equipment for the handling of the timber safely and quietly. A light block and tackle would answer the need. I settled down with the yellow pages of the telephone directory, searching for a supplier of rigging equipment. Half hour of phoning produced no useful results. All the firms listed handled only heavy duty equipment, far in excess of my requirements. There surely must be light block and tackle equipment available somewhere? Next I tried hire firms, all this effort took time, time I could I'll afford, and a whole day had passed before I made any progress. One firm suggested I try the boating people, and at long last, Hanks Marine Services could build up a suitable tackle for me. I had to advise them of the weight of the lift, how far, or how high the load was intended to be hoisted, or hauled. I told them the weight would not exceed one hundred kilograms and the lift would not exceed four meters. Hanks marine calculated I would require one of two sheave cheek block and one of three sheave cheek block, twenty five metre of ten millimeter woven roven cord. I became agitated and cut short the technical lecture saying that I only required the price and delivery time. They said the blocks would cost One hundred and twenty Rand and three hundred Rand respectively, The woven roven sheeting at thirty Rand per metre. A total of one thousand and twenty Rand with tax. Cheek blocks? Woven roven? What did I know, except that it was more money down the drain? What was I thinking, I must stop being negative, so what was another thousand when the outcome would result in millions. I pulled myself together,' Stop being a negative fool, press on regardless, gung ho and all that.' I drew the money from the bank and travelled to Hanks Marine, which was situated in the harbour area. Not a very salubrious area to be walking around with a thousand Rand cash in your pocket, but need be when the devil drives. All this time wasting searching for the tackle had resulted in two days of my schedule being lost, I must make up time tonight.

The night of August the sixteenth I tried out my new block and tackle and found that I could lift, if need be, two boards at a time with ease, if somewhat slowly. The use of the tackle allowed me to work in relative silence and safety, and although slow, I was amazed to find that I accomplished more work than I had hitherto managed. I had reached the third floor level and had established three levels of scaffold from which to work, Even with the mechanical advantage it was hard an exhausting work, and I was totally exhausted by the end of that nights work. One last stage to go, and, though the spirit was willing, I was just too tired to go any further that night. In any case, in the course of my frantic search for a block and tackle, I had completely forgotten about buying the additional board to replace the one that fell down the shaft. It was the first thing to attend to tomorrow morning, I reminded myself as I locked the building front door that night.

I was excited about my progress the night before, and in the morning I hastened to purchase the extra timber. I decided to purchase two boards instead of one. With the block and tackle it would be an easy matter to lift two boards, and I would be more secure with a decent platform from which to work when I tackled the business of knocking the hole into Wilson's office.

I was walking through the foyer of Castle Court when Mrs. Watson accosted me.

"Morning Dearie, It's wash day," She yodeled, "You will look at my machine today won't you?"

'Oh damn,' I thought' that bloody washing machine again. "No, er, that is, I mean no, no I haven't forgotten Mrs. Walker"

She asked, "Are you all right, Dearie. You don't sound your usual self. Not in any trouble, I hope?"

"No. No trouble Mrs. Walker, I'll be right with you. Give me half an hour, three quarters tops and I'll be there. There's something I have to do first." I answered and escaped through the door to buy my timber.

Once back at Castle Court I searched out Mrs. Walker, and together we sorted her washing for the load. At first the machine oscillated correctly, but after a moment or two it started to vibrate alarmingly with an accompanying dull clanking sound occurring every revolution. I switched the machine off, and with a sad shake of the head I explained that it sounded like the suspension springs that supported the drum were fatigued and would require replacing. I explained that I unfortunately did not have the jigs necessary to fit new springs, and that she had better contact the agents. Mrs. Watson was disappointed that I was not able to help her further, and seemed at a loss as what her next step should be. I explained that she should look up the name of the washing machine in the phone directory, or look under washing machines in the yellow pages to find a repair centre. So the matter stood for the moment, and I was relieved to be let off the hook. Now I could devote all my attention to the work in the service shaft.

Keeping to my policy of attracting as little attention as possible, I decided to wait until evening before taking the new boards into the office. I did however; go to the office as a matter of routine. After all I was supposed to be a businessman and should keep office hours. It was just as well I did. Waiting for me at the office door was Mss. Jean Scott. I cannot say I was pleased to see her, even though she was a vision in her smart form fitting, low necked green dress. The skirt of which was just short enough to show off her silk stokkinged shapely legs,which in turn ended in feet shod with matching green shoes. With her hair in place, as always in a very attractive style, she made a delectable picture.

"Good morning Mr. Wimpy," she greeted me, "I'm glad I caught you. Is everything going well?"

"Yes, fine, though I am still busy with fixing the place up before opening officially."

The office was clean. I had placed the bookcase over the hole, and with the other furniture in place, there was some semblance of respectability, so I was not averse to inviting her in.

I apologised saying that I was sorry there was not much to see, but that I would soon have it fixed up and businesslike.

"Not at all, I understand Mr. Wimpy, I have just popped in to tell you I was most concerned to have had a visit from the police who were making enquiries about you. They told me that you had been working here during the evenings."

I told her that I knew all about the police and had in fact giving them her address as confirmation of my legitimacy as regards to being in the building. I agreed that I had been working at night and again offered, as my excuse, my not wanting to disturb other tenants during the day.

"Most considerate of you I am sure," she said in an unbelieving tone. "Just how far have you got?"

I indicated the pile of raw timber off cuts that were lying about the inner office, saying that so far I had only been cutting the timber to size.

"My goodness," she exclaimed, "What on earth are you doing with all this heavy wood?"

What could I tell her? "Er! You see, my samples, er, that is the commodities with which I deal are really bulky and heavy," I stumbled. I then repeated the story I told Cotteral. 'The mining houses send me earth and core samples, which I analyse as to their gold bearing properties. The samples are of necessity rather bulky and rough. That is why I must have robust shelving and worktops."

"Surely they have their own chemist to deal with matters like that?" Mss. Scott was most disbelieving, and I felt I was creating a great web of lies from which I would not be able to extract myself.

"Yes," I replied quickly, "That is true but, you see, I was fortunate. Whilst once working as an analytical chemist for Consolidated Investments, I stumbled upon a process that was much more accurate than the system that was that time in use. I realized the importance of my discovery and set out in business for myself. So here I am" I finished lamely, fervently hoping that she would swallow my story.

I could see from the expression on her face that she was not entirely convinced and I was about to blunder on, when suddenly her cell phone erupted in a riot of musical clamour. She retrieved the phone from the depths of her bag and answered.

"Jean Scott. Yes, yes. No, at Nietrop building. Yes with Mr. Wimpy. All right, right away. Bye."

Returning her phone to her bag, she turned once more to me, "I have another appointment, I have to go now. Thank you for your time Mr. Wimpy, good bye."

"Goodbye Mss. Scott, and don't worry, I will have this place looking fine and attractive. Once I've finished painting and varnishing, you won't know it's the same place." I blathered on inanely. She was gone, my last words echoing after her. I was wet with nervous perspiration. I wondered if she would take the matter further. I feared that what I had thought was a grand cover was not, in fact, very convincing after all, but there was nothing I could do; I was at the point of no return, almost in sight of my goal. Only one more floor to go and I would break into Wilson's office, take the money and disappear.

CHAPTER 6

The seventeenth of August saw Jack Rose, for that was his full name, in consultation with his henchman, the man nicknamed Wimpy by Grey, but whose real name was William Broad. Rose had just informed Broad that his night watchman job had been approved, and that he, Broad was to meet the existing watchman that very day. Rose told Broad that Cotteral was to be transferred to another building, and that he was to meet with Cotteral and learn from him just what his duties entailed.

Broad met Cotteral at a nearby bar, and over drinks, which needless to say, were paid for by Broad. They discussed the routine of the job and in the course of conversation Cotteral mentioned a Mr. Wimpy who worked in his office at night. Cotteral told Broad that Wimpy was a real gentleman and gave no trouble. In fact, hinted Cotteral, that, if Broad ever felt thirsty during the long night hours, if Broad knew what he meant, then Mr. Wimpy was just the man to help. Broad did not like the news of this Mr. Wimpy working at night. It might be nothing at all, nevertheless he thought he had better check it out. He arranged to meet Cotteral that evening at Nietrop.

When Wimpy of W.E.A.R. arrived that evening he was disconcerted to find the other Wimpy in Cotterals company.

"Good evening Sir," greeted Cotteral, "This here is Mr. Broad ; He is taking over from me at the end of the month." Turning to Broad, he said, "this is the kind gentleman I was telling you about William."

'William Broad, so at last I have his right name,' Grey thought to himself,' his name suits his build, so it should be easy to remember. It is just as well I have his name; otherwise it could get confusing with my calling him Wimpy and going under the same pseudonym myself.'

"How do you do Mr. Broad," Grey greeted him.

"I do fine Mr. Wimpy," Broad replied, "Mr Cotteral here tells me you work here most nights?"

"Yes, I am building furniture into my office." Grey informed him.

"Is that so ! I would have thought a gentleman businessman such as yourself would employ a shop fitting firm to do that type of work for you?" Broad came back at me somewhat sarcastically.

I could see Broad was not an easy pushover like Cotteral. I remembered ruefully, that when first seeing him at the restaurant, I had labeled him moronic, and a drinker. I was obviously wrong. He was by no means the fool I had at first thought him to be. I could tell him to mind his own business, but the last thing I wanted was to antagonize him. I explained that the simple type of shelving I required hardly justified the expense of hiring professional people, so why waste money.

"True," he answered, and then persisted "It's just that most business people I know would think such work beneath them. How long do you think you will be working at night, then?"

Grey responded, "Oh, maybe a week or two, that is all."

Broad said, "Then I won't be seeing you when I take over at the end of the month, will I?"

"I certainly hope not," Grey answered fervently.

And so the matter rested for the moment. I took my leave and retired to my office. Broads's presence was not unforeseen. Ever since I had decided to go after Wilson's cash, I had, had this continual fear that Broad, a.k.a. Wimpy, and Jack were likely to appear on the scene. I had hoped to have beaten them to the punch and been long gone before they made their attempt. Now it seemed as if they were gearing up to make a move. Once again I was letting my irrational subconscious overrule my better judgment. Broad had no idea that I knew of Wilson's millions, he was probably just worried I would be in the building when they decided to tackle Wilson and his cash. The way my plan was progressing, if they knew how advanced I was they would be the ones to worry. Perhaps this meeting was all for the best, at least I now knew for certain that I was ahead of them, and I had at least till the end of the month to complete my plan.

I thought that I should not work in the shaft that night in case Broad took it into his head to come knocking on my door. If that happened while I was in the shaft, I would not hear his knock. He might think it strange if I did not open to him. I idled away an hour, luckily I had brought today's newspaper with me, so I had something to help me pass the time. When I came down again on my way home, I found Broad still with Cotteral. I bad them goodnight and went on my way.

———————————

That same night Broad reported to Jack Rose what he had learned from Cotteral, and of his meeting with a Mr. Wimpy.

"I don't know what you think Jack, but it seems suspicious to me. I mean why would a businessman do his own dirty work, and at night especially, I ask you?"

"It does seem strange, "agreed Rose, "but how is it possible he could know about Wilson? In any event, what would a man building office shelves on the first floor have to do with Wilson on the fourth?"

"I don't know, except that Cotteral told me that Wimpy had just moved into the last vacant office in the building."

"Even so," persisted Rose, "How could he possibly find out about Wilson's cash hidden in that fourth floor office? And supposing he had found out, what has that got to do with building shelves."

"Again, I can't say. Unless, unless," Broad hesitantly broached a thought, "your little redhead has someone else she is talking to, huh Jack? You think that may be possible, huh Jack?"

Rose jumped up in a flaring rage, "Yeah, Yeah!! That must be it, I'll kill the bitch, that's for sure, I'll kill the bitch."

"Women," grumbled Broad, convinced he had hit the nail on the head, "They are nothing but trouble. You can never trust them. Now what do we do?"

Rose, fuming, walked agitatedly round the room, cursing and generally working himself up.

"That bloody woman! We can't let anything stop us now, and we cannot take the chance that this Wimpy shit, whoever he is, may be on to us."

After a while Rose calmed down. He asked Broad if it could be arranged for Wimpy to have an accident. Nothing permanent, just take him out of the picture for a while. Broad gazed at Rose blankly.

"Don't be an idiot. You know very well what I mean. Arrange an accident for him, not kill him, you understand, we don't want the cops all over the place. Just hurt him a little, just enough so that he is out of the picture long enough for us to complete our heist."

"Yeah, well o.k., I reckon I can come up with something. Leave it to me" Said Broad, relishing the prospect. He liked nothing better than a bit of violence. He could dish it out all right, just so long as it could not be traced back to him. It meant that he would have to keep close tabs on Wimpy to establish his daily movements, until he found a way to create a plausible accident. It would be preferable in some public place, not in Nietrop building, but maybe on the street outside. Accidents are taking place all the time in East Bay City. Yes, that would be the way to go.

Rose meanwhile was fuming about the supposed duplicity of his redheaded girlfriend,' The fucking bitch, I'll show her she can't fuck with me. I've spent thousands on her, wining and dining her, giving her a good time. So this is her gratitude, the bloody shit, I'll show her. So far I've only given her entertainment powder just enough to keep her happy. Now she is for it, I'll up her dose of cocaine, maybe put her on heroine. I'll get her spiked just like my other girls. When she is good and hooked, I'll put her on the streets with the other lot, and then we will see how clever she is. No one, but no one fucks with Jack Rose and gets away with it, that's for sure.'

Rose stormed out the door.

CHAPTER 7

I looked at the calendar, August the eighteenth, time was passing. I hoped that tonight would be free of interruptions, and that I could finish the final stage. However, before I could even consider attempting onto the final stage, I had to get through the daylight hours. Eight a.m., time to go to the office, make my usual daily visit for the sake of appearances. I never knew when Mss. Scott or the police might turn up unexpectedly.

With nothing to do, the daylight hours passed slowly. I decided to patrol the fourth floor, not because I really thought there would be something to see, but more to assuage my continual fear that Rose and Broad would win the race. More so now that Broad was officially on the premises. I suppose really it was simply an excuse to pass the time. The elevator doors opened at the fourth floor and I stepped out, and almost into the arms of Broad. We were both shaken to say the least. Broad gave me a hard look, he said.

"Now I know where I've seen you before. A couple of days ago you were also on this floor. I remember you went into Carruthers and Steinmetz. I remember because your visit was so short, in and out like a jack in a box. I thought it strange at the time. Don't tell me you are on another short excursion to the lawyers?"

What could I say, other than, "As a matter of fact I am, if it's any business of yours." And I pushed past him. The last place I had intended visiting was the offices of Carruthers and Steinmetz, but with Broad watching me, I had no option. I walked into the office of the intimidating receptionist. The receptionist looked up, and I could see, by the look of astonishment on her face, that she recognized me as the idiot who had pestered her recently about one or other fictitious person.

"Yes?" she enquired. No polite good morning greeting. Her antagonistic attitude immediately put me off balance, and I could not for the life of me, remember the name of the person I had asked for previously.

"I know this must seem extremely strange," I stammered, "but you see the lady I was expecting to meet me here the last time, assured me that she would be here today without fail. She asked me expressly to be here on time. Would you mind if I sat here and waited?"

"Just exactly who are you?" Snapped this very agitated lady.

The name that immediately sprang to mind was that of Wilson, probably because my whole existence centered on him at the moment. I said, "Wilson, er Ted Wilson."

"Well Mr. Ted Wilson," the ice maiden squeezed out, "I do assure you there is no lady waiting for you, nor do I anticipate any lady appearing shortly. I have no appointments booked for this day at all. If you do not leave immediately, I will have to call security."

"No. Please, she did say he would meet me here," I bleated desperately, wishing the floor would open up and swallow me. I needed to gain some time. I was sure Broad would be waiting to see if I really had an appointment this time round. I said, "You see, once she arrives, we hope to see, or make an appointment to see an attorney."

The receptionist, turned ice maiden now morphasised into a firebrand, "Mr. Wilson," she fired at me, "These are the offices of the respected and august firm of Carruthers and Steinmetz, Attorneys at Corporate Law. Not a public waiting room, nor a circus. We deal only with companies of repute, and not individuals. Do you understand?" This last word was hissed like fat crackling on a griddle. She finished her tirade with the words "Now please leave."

I could see no way to prolong my stay, I beat a hasty retreat.

Broad was still there when I came out, and as I passed him he muttered "Another short visit. Huh?"

I chose to ignore him and made a bee-line for the elevator. When the elevator arrived Broad joined me and we travelled down together in silence. I getting out at the first floor, and he continuing down to the ground floor. I quickly ran down the stairs until I could view the foyer. Broad was in conversation with the doorman, and while I watched, he took his leave and disappeared outside the building. I worried what this second meeting would bring about. The fact that Broad had been on the fourth floor meant something I was certain. Would our two chance meetings cause him any suspicion? I couldn't see why, but his facetious remarks regarding my short visits gave me some worry.

Against my better judgment I decided to work during the rest of the day and not waste any further time. I promised myself to be ultra careful and quiet and donned my dust coat, which was getting pretty grubby by this time. I climbed through the hole and worked my way as silently as possible up to the third floor level and switched on my lead light that was suspended where I had left it previously. I realized that I still had to hammer fast one end of the board against the wall at the pipe end, and tie it fast. I could not use the hammer during daylight hours for obvious reasons. I smiled to myself wryly; just imagine the expression on the face of the ice maiden of Carruthers and Steinmetz if she experienced hammer blows echoing through her sanctum of sanctums. There was no way round it; I would just have to wait until tonight to hammer the board home, what a waste of time and energy. It was my nagging fear that Rose and Broad would get ahead of me that had made me act so irrationally and hastily. I must really get control of myself and think things out, instead of rushing like a bull at a gate. I climbed down once more and out of the hole. It was frustrating to be so near and yet so far, but there was no way I could hasten matters, I would just have to be patient and kill time until it was nightfall once more.

At seven p.m. that night I was back in the shaft, climbing and hoisting the ladder after me stage by stage. I hammered the board fast and tied it securely against the rung. I crawled onto the board then hoisted the ladder up once more, and placed so that I could climb to the fourth floor. I reached the fourth floor a little after eight fifteen. It was a slow process each time to climb up to each level, hoist the ladder after me, place it in position, then climb once more, and repeat this process until the desired level was reached. In spite of the number of nights I had been repeating this process, I still found it very tiring.

At the fourth floor level I hooked the tackle onto one of the rungs let into the wall, let out the slack until the lifting hook was at my floor. Then I climbed down level by level until I was also at my floor. I collected the necessary batten I would require to lash the two boards against the rung, climbed up once more and lashed the batten along the rung as I had done at the first scaffold. Wearily climbed down again and fastened the two boards onto the tackle, and once again climbed stage by stage back to the fourth level. I hauled the boards up to the extent of the tackle, climbed down my ladder a short way until I could lift each board into place. Hammered and tied the two boards fast so as to allow me adequate and safe working space for my final stage of breaking through Wilson's wall. I tested them for steadiness then climbed from the ladder onto the boards. I measured and marked off the section I wanted to break open. Again I had to climb down to fetch my angle grinder, an additional short extension lead and two way plug, cold chisel, spray bottle and water. These items I placed in a plastic bag tied to a rope suspended from the top of my ladder. Placed a dust mask in my pocket and went through the process of climbing up once more.

Whilst going through this slow and tiring business of setting up for the major work of the night, it dawned on me that, even at this late stage it would be worth my while to invest in two more ladders and fix them at the intermediate floor levels. It would make climbing up a lot faster and easier, and certainly less tiring. 'Why wake up to that fact at this late stage when the job is so to say completed,' I chided myself. Then thinking rationally for a change I realized I would probably need the extra ladders when I climbed down with the money. Five million odd would require more than one trip I was certain.

I settled myself comfortably on the fourth floor scaffold, fixed the dust mask upon my face and proceed to cut into the wall. It made a devilish noise, and I worked at the cutting spasmodically, as I did not want a continual harsh sound to cause Cotteral to investigate. I had timed my work so as not to be cutting when Cotteral was on his inspection rounds, and I hoped that the sound I was making would be sufficiently dampened by the distance between the fourth and ground floors. After I had completed the cutting of the sides of the hole I intended to knock out. I climbed down once again to check if Cotteral had been disturbed at my activities. I crept down to the foyer and peeped toward the night watchman's cubicle. Cotteral was blissfully and unconcernedly lacing his coffee mug from my latest brandy donation.

Up on the fourth floor scaffold I made the final cross and vertical cuts across the area I had first demarcated. I did not want to break completely through the wall at this time, as I was not sure that I had enough time this night to complete the cut through the wall and also remove the money The wall was not load bearing and therefore only one hundred and fifteen millimeters thick. Of that thickness ten millimeter would be plastered on the office side. I therefore made all my angle cuts one hundred and five millimeters deep. This would leave the plaster whole, and the office side of the wall appear undisturbed. The net result of all this undercutting was to leave a series of brick protrusions, like stalagmites, but growing sideways instead of down. These I would easily break off with my fingers, thus leaving only the plaster layer. The plaster layer I could easily and gently tap out at my leisure. Of course all this activity with the angle grinder made it necessary to use the spray bottle regularly to dampen down the rising dust cloud and I was thankful I had taken the trouble to invest in one.

It was eleven o'clock when I finished for the night, the latest I had ever worked, and I think it was the nearness of my goal that pumped the adrenalin through my body, that kept me going. Back in my office bathroom I looked askance at my image in the mirror. I was covered from head to foot in a reddish gray sludge. My dust coat was smeared with the mess, my face, ears and neck were plastered and streaked with the stuff. I could, and did, wash a good bit of the muck off in the wash hand basin available, but it was only a superficial job. I made the best of a bad job, but even with my dust coat off, and my face washed, I looked a mess. Thank goodness it was late at night and I could slip home without being noticed. I had only to slip quietly past Cotteral. I did not want him to witness my condition, and perhaps mention it to Broad.

There he was, nodding away in his cubicle, clutching his bottle. As far as he was concerned, even if he noticed me, I would probably only register in his mind as his personal Genie, who regularly granted his ever present wish for the golden liquid, and the happy dreams it brought him each night. I slipped quietly past and out of the building.

Again I was tempted to work on the weekend; I was keen to make an end to it, to get those millions at last. Then caution and wisdom prevailed, the only thing I did do, was purchase the two ladders I had decided upon the night before. On that quiet Sunday evening I slipped them into my office.

CHAPTER 8

When Wilson deposited his takings for August in the filing cabinet, they were considerably less than usual, and that was to be expected. He had started his phasing out programme. When He retired in eighteen months there had to be no way his successor could find any trace of his clandestine activities over the past ten years. Nor, hopefully, would anyone else realise that any money had disappeared from the system.

His scheme resulted in the leaching out thousands a month into his own pocket, this by creating an army of fictitious council workers, who came and went over the years. Some of whom, according to his false records, had actually received tokens of appreciation for supposedly good and faithful service. Others were listed simply as casual workers. The heads of the various departments of sanitation, water, electricity, parks and dozens of other peripheries of the great metropolitan council were blissfully unaware of the number of fictitious employees on their respective payrolls. It was Wilson's responsibility as treasury chief to make up the monthly payroll, and he was respected as a highly efficient, diligent, brilliant financier, and an honest official of many years standing. With his skill in money matters, it was an easy matter to create, and operate this phantom work force, and to ensure that the monies due to them ended up padding his own briefcase each month end.

He smiled to himself as he thought how he was busy at present slowly bringing to an end the various careers of these fictitious personnel, as he wrote them off his books as fired or retired, as the case may be. How elated the council will be with his successor when their annual budget improves to the tune of sun four hundred and eighty thousand Rand! Yes indeed! He was quite proud of his ability to hoodwink the great city to the tune of some forty thousand Rand per month. Of course his system had to have been foolproof to have withstood the last ten years of continual embezzlement. He had created a number of files, listing resignations, firings, sick leave, casual employment. Bonuses paid, salary increases and so on. These files were cross referenced, back listed, forwarded, refiled and so convoluted that it would take auditors many, many months, if ever, to sort the wood from the chaff. Wilson was certain, when the auditing staff saw the mountain of work that would be involved, that it would be easier to remember his glowing career, and simply accept his paperwork.

Wilson never minded the huge amount of paperwork he had created. He was a financial wizard, an expert with figures, and he enjoyed the challenge. After all it was worth it, he would be a very wealthy man when he retired. Yes, he had been meticulous all these years, even his establishment of the offices in Nietrop building as a depository of his takings had been done with deliberate care and aforethought. He did not want raised eyebrows by depositing this extra money in a bank, over his substantial salary cheque. Opening bank accounts involved other people, and the fewer people who knew of this additional money the better. Better to simply stash it under a mattress, as it were, and no one would ever know of its existence. There was no cloud on Wilson's horizon as he locked his office on that August day and returned to the municipal buildings just a block away.

All his working life as city treasurer he had devoted to perfecting, streamlining and implementing his scam. He was a good looking man, and carried himself well. He had an engaging smile, twinkling eyes, cleft chin, and long combed back wavy silver hair. Many of the female staff of his age, he was sixty years old, and even some of the younger girls, had tried to inveigle him into a liaison, but to no avail. He was totally and exclusively engaged in perfecting and carrying out his embezzlement. The rewards were too high and the risks too great for him to be sidetracked. However, now that he was winding down his scheme, he was finding more time on his hands, and for the first time in years he began noticing other staff around him. He came up, as it were, for air, and was suddenly aware for the first time of an extremely beautiful redhead, with a figure no red blooded man could resist. This ultimate in men's fantasies, wore the shortest mini-skirts and the most revealing cleavage, and what was more, went out of her way to be enticingly interesting. Wilson was captivated, where had he been to have missed this vision? For the first time in ten years the flame of lust filled his soul. He introduced himself and asked if she was new in the filing department. She said she had been hired by him exactly one month ago, and didn't he remember? Wilson became flushed, blushed and stuttered his apology. How was it possible that he could not remember such a ravishing beauty? He really must have been blind at the time. Anyway, if he had hired her, and he must have, she would not have got the job unless she was capable. He marveled at the fact that he had been so involved in his own little world that he could have gone through the motions of hiring genuine staff without registering the personality or individual. He wondered just how many of the actual staff that worked in the municipality he had been responsible for, and how few he actually knew. Probably a great many of them, and they, in turn, probably thought of him as a stuck up and aloof prig, for all his friendly manner and charm.

At first his approaches were politely deflected by the redhead, silly man, he was old enough to be her father. She was only thirty years old, and he was sixty if a day. Wilson was not to be denied, he was besotted, and for the first time in ten years, he thought of something other than his acquisition of money. He started lavishing her with gifts and flowers. He dangled first night theatre tickets before her.

Noreen, for that was her name, was nothing if not if not mercenary and she accepted the gifts with alacrity. The flowers were later consigned to the waste paper basket, and offers of a night at the theatre politely turned down, these were not a premium in her lifestyle. Noreen preferred clubbing and drinking with her steady boyfriend Jack Rose, besides Jack could always be relied upon to provide a snort of cocaine when she felt the craving.

It was a night of dining and dancing, she had worn the jeweled watch that Wilson had given her. Rose noticed the watch and queried where she had got it? She told him about the old fart at work, as she called Wilson behind his back, and how this Wilson bragged about his riches, and how much he loved her, and if only Noreen would put out for him, he had promised her she would have no regrets.

Rose was not concerned about this suitor in his girlfriend's life, he knew he had her firmly hooked on drugs and he could use her as he wished until he tired of her. Then he would consign her to the rest of his gang of prostitutes. Jack Rose was a small time drug pusher and pimp, but he was also a man who could seize an opportunity when he saw one. He instructed Noreen to go all out to hook this fish. Once she had Wilson firmly on a string, she was to pump him subtly about the whereabouts of this money he boasted about. Maybe engineer herself into a position of getting her hands on it, or find out if Rose could hijack it somehow. Rose's wish was Noreen's command, and so Wilson became aware of a subtle change in her attitude toward him.

She suddenly became more amenable to his advances. When they passed one another in the somewhat restricted aisles of the filing room, she deliberately rubbed against him, and his blood ran hot in his veins. On one occasion she could clearly see his erection straining against his trousers, and she carelessly allowed her arm to brush against his extended member. This was too much for Wilson; he grabbed her and tried to kiss her. She broke free and slapped him across his cheek. He was instantly remorseful, and it was then that Wilson made the error he had schooled himself never to make during all the past years. He grabbed Noreen's arm thus preventing her from pulling away, and gabbed out his innermost secrets. He told her he was much richer than his position at the council would indicate, that he had millions in ready cash over and above his more than satisfactory bank account. All this could be hers, he promised her, he told her that he loved her more than life itself, and only if she would give him a chance, he would lavish her with anything she desired, she would live like a queen.

Noreen was a practical woman, she had no illusions, and she had heard it all before. A man would do anything; waste enormous sums of money to impress a girl and would make exorbitant promises whilst in the heat of the chase. But once he had had his way with her, he would soon cool off, and after awhile she would find herself alone once more. She knew her business; she flirted outrageously with him, made erotic promises of the paradise to be experienced within her arms. She went just so far and no more, and Wilson was beside himself with desire.

In a quiet corner of the filing room, she would embrace him and respond to his kisses, and when Wilson was in the heat of passion, and his breathing became short, and when he clutched at her breast, then she would ask in a breathless whisper, "Tell me more about this wonderful money. Do you really have it lying about in cash?"

"Oh yes," he would reply, "It is all there in a cabinet in offices I have in Nietrop building. All ready for us to pick up when I retire in eighteen months time."

Noreen continued to work on the poor besotted man, and he became as putty in her hands. After a while he trusted her implicitly and confided all his secrets in great detail. All this information Noreen faithfully passed on to Rose, who rewarded her each time with a line of cocaine.

The rest of the municipal staff was amazed at the change they saw in Wilson, and there were many conversations around the coffee urns about there being no fool like an old fool. Like offices around the world, there is nothing better than a juicy office scandal. There were also a few spinsters among the staff who were jealous of Noreen's success, and bitter about their own failure in hooking the handsome catch.

Wilson was blind to all the gossip and innuendo, and for all his brilliance as a bookkeeper, was an absolute babe when it came to social intercourse. Noreen was certainly taking him for a ride in more ways than one, was the general office consensus. The gifts, flattery and devoted attention pleased Noreen's vanity, but a promise of a life of ease and luxury some eighteen months hence was nebulous as far as she was concerned. Noreen had never had any real money, she spent every penny she earned, and lived only for the moment. A life of riches and idle luxury were just fairy tales, and never happened in real life. She faithfully carried all the information back to Jack Rose, who was the real anchor in her life at present. No airy, fairy promises about Jack, he was a sexy lover who was lavish with money when he had it, and wined and dined her equally as well as Wilson could. In any case Jack understood her needs and satisfied them. She knew that if she helped Jack get Wilsons money, then he, Jack would be as generous as Wilson ever would be. Noreen was happily having her cake and eating it at the moment. She was not mentally equipped to think and plan for the future; she only lived for the here and now. However she was a realist and knew that in spite of the hectic nightclub rounds and lavish social life with Jack, he was only interested in her as a sexual trophy. Jack had never suggested or hinted at marriage, nor for that matter had Wilson. Without a marriage contract in the offing, a girl had no security, but as long as Jack supplied her with cocaine she was his, and was content. It was the source of cocaine that kept her clinging firmly to Rose, and slowly and firmly her increasing dependence on the drug made her more and more Rose's slave.

Just the other day she had been able to inform Jack of Wilson's move to close his scam, and that he was due to make his final deposit at Nietrop building on the fourth of September. This bit of information resulted in Jack giving her an extra line of cocaine as a thank you present, such a reward was worth more than all the gifts and promises Wilson could make make.

Then Jack had suddenly turned on her and accused her of telling someone else of Wilson's cache. She was stunned and indignant in her denial. She was devastated when Rose refused to believe her, and slapped her into tears before leaving in a rage. If it had not been her dependency on Rose for her fixes, she would have left then and there.

The night of August the eighteenth Broad and Rose we're having drinks at Rose's apartment. Rose was angrily telling Broad about his meeting with the redhead Noreen, who had vehemently denied telling anyone else about Wilson's hoard.

"I'll get her back, I'll show her she can't fuck with Jack Rose. I'll stoke her full of cocaine and maybe heroin and meth's, the whole bang shoot. She won't know what hit her, and then I'll put her out with the other girls who work for me.," ranted Rose viciously, referring obliquely to his other interests of selling drugs and pimping prostitutes.

"Anyway," Rose continued, "We can't waste any more time worrying about breaking Wilson's door down. What we'll do is nab him as he unlocks his door and enters his office, knock him unconscious, gag him and tie him securely, then lock him in his office and leave with his keys. We won't be able to remove such a large amount of money during daylight hours, it would be too obvious. So what I want you to do, is when you are on duty that night, and during your rounds, you go back to his office and take the boodle and bring it to me, where I will be waiting outside in the car. Then go back to the doorman's office while he is not around and leave the keys with a note, a note that says that Wilson would be pleased if someone would open his office and free him. He won't be able to say anything about the money, or explain why there was such a large amount in cash in his office without being caught out himself, so it should be safe enough. Once you've done that you join me in the car and we'll be A for away. How does that grab you mate?"

'That's fine with me, the sooner I get my hands on the loot the better," said Broad, "but we had better get rid of Wimpy first, not so?"

"Yes, that's another thing. When are you planning to do something about him? You are certainly taking your own sweet time about that." Grumbled Rose.

"O.K. keep your hair on. I'm working on it; I should be able to bring it off any day now," Broad answered, "I just have to catch him when he arrives at the office in the morning. I've been keeping tabs on him and he always arrives just before eight a.m., before the office rush starts and there are only a few people about. I figured you wouldn't want an incident in the building, besides an accident is always easier to arrange in a busy street."

"I don't want to know about it, just do it quickly. Just remember no killing; we don't want murder complicating things."

The plan Broad formulated for the removal of Wimpy relied on specific timing. Half a block up the street from Nietrop building was the city main Post Office, and Broad had noticed that a military dispatch rider made a daily stop of about twenty minutes at the Post Office at about the same time as Wimpy usually arrived at Nietrop building. Broad had spent some time watching the movements of both Wimpy and the dispatch rider, until he was certain their times of appearance overlapped regularly. Satisfied of the fact that these two occurrences took place on a regular basis, Broad was ready to put his plan into action.

CHAPTER 9

Grey was about to leave for the office when his cell phone rang. Mss. Scott again, she said she had forgotten to ask for his I.D. when he had negotiated the lease. She apologised, her fault entirely, but she needed it for their files, and could she ask that he drop it off at her office soon, so that she could make a photocopy. She was very sorry for the inconvenience.

It was something I could not avoid, of course, and it would mean awkward explanations about my giving a false name originally. I hesitated a moment, thinking of a way to stall her until I had completed my heist. I asked her if it was extremely urgent, or could I bring it in a day or two, when I happened to be in her part of town. Certainly she informed me, no real hurry, it had to be done of course, but a day or two would not matter much. She asked, if she was not around when I called, would I ask the girl at reception to make a copy for her. Mss. Scott rang off. 'Quite a change of approach,' I thought, 'I wondered what had caused her to become so friendly. 'Maybe she had bought his story after all; He certainly hoped it was so, anyway, for the moment he had bought some extra time. 'In a day or two I would conveniently forget my promise. 'I thought. I figured I had about a week before Mss. Scott took it into her head to contact me again. By that time I should have completed my task and been long gone. 'I went out to my office.

That evening I set about installing the extra ladders at each floor level. What a difference it made. My miserliness had precluded that I spend the extra on ladders initially, what a fool I had been. The extra ladders made it quicker, and easier, and less tiring to climb up and down the shaft. I settled myself at the fourth floor and proceeded to break out the sections of brickwork remaining. I had to work carefully as any rough, or careless movement, might break through the plaster skin before I was ready. The day or night that I made my final move I had to be sure I had everything ready to complete the operation. I did not know how long it would take to empty the cabinet, nor did I know how big a load four million Rand was or how many bags I would need to pack the load. Once packed in the bags how long would it take to transfer the money down to my office? On the day or night I decided to break through I wanted to start early, and have as much time as possible, so as not to rush and make a mess of things.

I finished breaking the last of the brick pieces out of the wall section; at last I was ready for my final assault. I packed up for the present as it was quite late. Tuesday the twenty second of August would be my D-day. The day was finally arriving when I would realise my dream, the day I would begin to live the life of 'Riley.' I was well inside the time limit, I had beaten Jack and Broad to the punch, so what if I missed on Wilson's last deposit, there was more than enough boodle for me.

The following morning I was preparing a stack of plastic refuse bags I had assembled to hold the money, plus some soft wire lengths to tie the bag tops closed, and generally preparing for the last scene of my venture, when my cell phone demanded my attention. It was Mss. Scott again. Surely it was not about the I.D.card so soon. She never mentioned it, she had phoned to advise me, as she was doing for all the tenants, that the owners of Nietrop building had decided to upgrade the floor covering of all the passages leading to the office suites. The work was due to start that

day and would continue for three weeks. In order to finish the contract
as soon as possible, the work would be carried on throughout the day
and until ten o'clock in the evening. The contractors were starting at the
ground and first floors initially, and she had been instructed to inform
the various tenants of the situation, and at which time the workmen
would be busy on their respective floors. She hoped I would understand
and bear with the inconvenience, It was lucky, she said, that as I was not
yet open for business, it should not affect me as some of the others on
my floor.

What could I do but agree, and not show I was in any way alarmed. I
could not be seen walking out of my office carrying bags of money whilst
the place was overrun with workmen. I wondered how long they would
be busy on my particular floor, and I wondered what Rose and Broad
would make of this development. True Wilson would be using his office
for a long time yet, but what change could this new development bring
about in Rose's plans? Any delay or interruption of the status quo meant
danger for me, but I could do nothing but wait out this latest hurdle to
my plans. I desperately hoped that they would soon finish at my particular
floor. The work on the upper floors would not affect me; in fact it would
prove a bonus. The racket the workmen made would afford me a chance
to work with impunity during daylight hours. Looking at the problem in
retrospect, I realized that the contract work would prove an advantage for
me. I felt a lot more at ease.

The next few days I was like a cat on a hot tin roof. I was in and out
of Nietrop building continuously, to check on the progress on my floor,
and to check if Broad and Rose were in any way active. I must say that
as far as the contractors were concerned, I was pleased to note that they
were professional in their approach. To a layman, I supposed it looked
somewhat chaotic, with piles of tiles here and there. Tapes and cones
seemingly haphazardly placed, but forming demarcated areas, interspersed

with drums of adhesive standing about. But to a trained eye such as mine, I could see method in the layout, and could understand the planning so as to minimize delays. I appreciated their efficiency, but nevertheless could see that no matter how fast they worked; there was no way the first floor would be complete in under a week at least. That meant I would not have a chance to complete my break in until the twenty eighth or twenty ninth. The time factor was becoming critical. From the very outset I had, had delays and interruptions. Each step of the way I had, had the intense anxiety of being near and yet so far. The strain was beginning to tell, even Mrs. Walker had remarked that, in her words, I was looking peaky and on edge. If only the contractors would get off my floor and start their work upstairs, and so allow me to continue.

On Friday evening the twenty fifth, I looked in on Cotteral, primarily to hear if he had any news of Broads movements. Naturally I did not forget to take him his expected bottle. He was his usual effusive self, fawning around me as if I was the returning Messiah.

"God love you sir, for thinking kindly of old Cotteral, it sure gets thirsty especially now with all this dust. I don't know what I'd have done without your kindness, sir," he blathered.

"Glad to be of help," I said insincerely. "By the way, have you had Broad for company at all lately?"

"He has been only once, it was last Wednesday, he came to have a look at all this flooring business. He didn't stay long. He asked after you sir, wanted to know if you were still working in your office. I told him I had not seen you these last few days, I told him maybe you was finished. I hope I did right sir?"

"Yes, As a matter of fact I am nearly finished, and I hope to open for business as soon as these flooring people are finished. That's why I popped in this evening, just to see how far they were. It looks as though they should be clear by this week-end."

"The foreman told me they would finish the first floor by Monday morning, and move all their stuff to the second floor in the afternoon. Can I offer you a drink sir?"

"Thank you," I replied, "Just a quick one, I must really be getting home."

We drank in companionable silence, then slapping Cotteral on the shoulder, I bid him goodnight and made my way home, content with the news I had received.

No later than Tuesday the twenty ninth would be my final day as a tenant of Nietrop building. A feeling of euphoria crept over me. The drink I had had with Cotteral lay pleasantly warm in my stomach and, as I drove toward my flat, I suddenly felt like celebrating. I drove instead to Francesco's and spent a pleasant half hour with the jovial company in the bar. Half an hour was enough; I did not want a heavy head on the morning of my penultimate day of my plan. As I drove home I was thinking how much more attractive the city was after dark, when one did not notice the paper packets and plastic and spilt refuse, that marred the view during daylight All the neon signs, the bright show windows of the shops, the street lighting, even the traffic lights helped to pretty up the otherwise drab and forlorn streets of the daylight hours. I found myself happily smiling; the world looked a better place. Soon, I would be rich. The drinks I had consumed tended to make me soporific, and I was not long in going to bed and falling asleep, in spite of my excitement and anticipation of the morrow.

CHAPTER 10

The information Noreen had obtained for Rose had placed him in a position of acquiring more money than he had ever envisioned in his life. To conduct the robbery of Wilson's money was easy pickings for the likes of Jack Rose, but he also knew that, due to his far from blameless life, the police as well as certain criminal elements knew far too much about these activities. There would be endless difficulties should he suddenly appear more than usually affluent.

To overcome these possible shortcomings he would have to set up some sort of money laundering, to filter the money safely and without trace to himself. To create this infrastructure would take time; he had originally thought he would have eighteen months to set everything up. Noreen's latest bulletin regarding Wilson terminating his scam, and therefore the cessation of further money deposits had curtailed his long term plans. Then there was this other worry of Wimpy turning up on the scene, personally he didn't think Wimpy posed a threat, but Broad seemed certain he was a danger, and Noreen's too vehement denial also tended to cause some doubt in his mind. He had to change his plans accordingly. 'Without a doubt', Rose thought,' it was now an urgent matter to get the money as soon as possible. The unforeseen appearance of this Wimpy character might present a major problem, or it might not! His crucial appearance just at this time, and his peculiar habit of working in his office at night was very strange. 'Rose wondered what he could be doing during those evening hours. In any event it was too great a risk to ignore. Matters were coming to a head and he could not let this once in a lifetime opportunity slip through his fingers.

Rose's initial attempt to set up a conglomerate of sufficient legitimacy was proving an expensive drain on his limited capitol, plus the embarrassing self knowledge that he was mentally deficient in any of the a skills required to set up or manipulate such an enterprise. He had to come up with a simple alternative.

Rose's back up plan was more in tune with his capabilities. He would ship out of the country as a deckhand on one of the many vagabond round the world yachtsmen that came and went through this port city. His priority was to get a passport. His history of tax evasion and his criminal record precluded his simply applying for a passport through the normal channels, but Jack Rose had one thing, that was contacts.

Mr. Vuysuli of home affairs was one of these contacts, and he met Rose over a drink to discuss Rose's dilemma. The outcome of this meeting was that for a sum of three thousand Rand and two passport photographs a passport could be made available. Rose agreed to have the photographs and the money ready the next day. He would just have to threaten his girls to be more active and pick up more Johns to make up the three thousand Rand. It was nothing, a bit of rough handling would solve that problem.

The next item on Rose's agenda was that of a suitable berth on some yacht. He would have to hang around the docks for a while, chatting up such cruise yacht owners as he could find. Someone was sure to offer him a berth, especially if he offered to pay his way. All this preparation was time consuming, and he was unable to keep tabs on the doings of Wilson or Wimpy. He had to rely on his dogsbody, Broad, to do this

Broad's future, nor that of his girlfriend, featured high on Rose's list of priorities. Broad had been a faithful hanger-on, and useful in carrying out odd jobs for him from time to time. His usefulness would come to an end once they had finished with Wilson. He would send Broad on some fools errand once the job was done, and while he was away, he, Rose would do his bunk. Noreen, his bedfellow and clubbing partner, would also become excess baggage once he had the loot It would be a simple matter to hook her good and solid on the drugs, she was halfway there already, and while she was heavily drugged he would simply walk away, just as he would with the rest of his girls as he liked to call them. They were only too ready to prostitute themselves to qualify for the drug fixes he had hooked them on, they relied on him and would be in a bad way once he had left. That was just their tough luck, they would be left to their own devices, he was finished with all that, the millions he was about to pocket would see to that.

Now that he came to think of it, it was about time he removed Noreen from Wilson's influence in case she had a change of heart, and blabbed to Wilson about his plans. He would start at once and give Noreen one or two really good fixes, it would not take long before she was hopelessly hooked and totally at his mercy. She was really a beautiful woman, and not yet ravaged by the drug. She would be worth a good deal on the streets, and before he actually got his hands on the money, he could see he would be faced with additional urgent expenses. Noreen could contribute to these quite adequately.

There was something else he had to think about. If he was to leave the country, he would have to change the money into a more international currency, say like dollars. The rate of exchange on the black market was prohibitive, but what alternative did he have. He would have to grin and bear it, damn, there was still so much to do.

Broad, on the other hand, saw the cache of money merely as a means to an end. The money was there just waiting to be taken, and once they had achieved that, why, it was just a matter of spending it, and living lavishly and in style. Broad's mind was uncomplicated; he could not understand his partner's worry over the handling of the money. All this business of laundering the money and so forth was, in his estimation, just a waste of time and expense. Money was money wasn't it? You tried all manner of ways and means to get it, and once you had it, you spent it; it was as simple as that. Thank goodness Jack had at last decided to act, the more they delayed the more difficult things became. Take this Wimpy business for instance, all this nuisance of having to find a way of taking him out of the picture. Jack wanted no killing, so now he was faced with having to come up with a plan of getting rid of him, or disabling him. Much more difficult than simply putting a bullet through his brain

The whole week Broad had watched for an opportunity to remove Wimpy. Throughout the week Wimpy had not kept to his usual eight a.m. arrival. Instead he had arrived at odd times during the day and did not spend a great deal of time in the building. Broad was about to give up on his original plan of running Wimpy down with the purloined motorcycle, when on Monday morning the twenty eighth of August, Wimpy resorted to his usual time table and arrived at seven fifty five a.m. Broad thanked his lucky stars, there was Wimpy pulling into his usual parking place nearly opposite the entrance to Nietrop building. The soldier had arrived just a moment before, and broad lost no time in annexing the military green, Harley Davidson motorcycle and side car combination.

I drove into my usual parking place and was in the process of locking the truck when I heard the roar of an approaching motorcycle. Instinctively I knew I was in danger and I looked hastily toward the noise. I saw a motorcycle, sidecar combination bearing down on me at speed. I tried to leap over the bonnet of my truck and almost made it, but the sidecar caught me at the hips and I was thrown over the truck and came crashing down on my chest, hitting the edge of the curb, knocking the breath from my body.

I fought to catch my breath, and at each heave of my chest I felt a severe stabbing pain, which in turn left me gasping again. The dizziness slowly faded away, and my eyes began to focus once more and looked at a forest of legs, some flannels, some jeans, some stockings. I looked up and saw a sea of anxious, curious and interested faces peering down at me.

I heard a voice say, "Call an ambulance."

Another said, "Don't move him, call a doctor"

Whilst a third called for the police.

The mention of police galvanized me into speech.

"NO, no," I protested, "I'm all right, just winded."

I knew that I was more than just winded, but I certainly did not want the police or doctors around. I tried to sit up, eager hands reached out to help, in spite of one agitated voice crying out for me not to be moved in case of internal injuries. With the help offered I managed to stand and lean against the side of the truck. Between my gasps at the stabbing pain I convinced my persistent would be helpers that I would be all right. I said I just needed time to catch my breath, and asked if my keys were still in the lock of the truck door. When this was confirmed, I asked for help into the passenger seat. Once settled in the seat, and provided I did not move, I was fairly comfortable. I realized that I had one or more broken ribs, and I could see my chance of claiming the millions fading away.

"I think you should see a doctor," a worried woman reiterated.

"I'll be all right," I said, "I think I have a cracked rib. A doctor can't do anything about that, it will just have to heal with time, that's all. I will have to take it easy for a week or two, and I will be fine. I will just sit here and rest for a while and I will soon be o.k., Thank you. Thank you all for your help and concern."

Reluctantly the small crowd moved off at last, and rejoined the flow of pedestrian traffic that had steadily increased as the morning moved on. I was alone, and in a few minutes it was as if the accident had never taken place at all. The world at large moved on unconcerned.

Accident? I wondered, it could have been of course, but I doubted it. In the few seconds I had noticed the oncoming motorcycle, I had also noticed in that fraction of time, that it was uncommonly close to my side of the street, and that there was ample space between it and the centre of the street into which it could have easily moved. It was deliberate, I was sure, and the rider had meant to kill me. I must have sat in the truck for half an hour before I felt I could try to move. I opened the truck door, swung my legs out and immediately tensed up as another spasm of pain coursed through my chest. I sat for what seemed an age before I ventured to stand. Holding onto the roof of the truck, and with my other hand pressing down upon the dashboard, I slowly, carefully, painfully and fearfully, inch by inch rose to an upright position. My first step almost brought me to my knees as a fresh pain flared up my left hip.

It must have taken me at least ten minutes to shuffle across to the entrance of Nietrop Building. Pedestrians flowed past and around me, all intent on their own affairs. One or two irritable glances came my way, but no one accosted me or offered to help. Typical city temperament, and although I would have welcomed some help at that moment, I actually preferred that I was not drawing too much attention to myself.

The doorman at Nietrop came out of the building and greeted me as I struggled up the few steps, asking if I was all right, and what had happened, and could he help? I told him I had been knocked down, just a bit bruised and winded. I shook off his proffered arm, saying I was quite o.k. and could manage. I went across to the elevator and eventually reached my office, thankful that the doorman had not been persistent in his concern and offer to help. I entered the office and immediately locked the door. It was as far as I could go at the moment. I sank down onto the floor and lay flat on my back. I felt very sorry for myself, frustrated and full of anger against Rose and Broad, who I felt certain, were behind the attempt to run me down.

I must have fallen asleep from shock and exhaustion. I don't know how long I had been asleep, but on awakening I could feel the cold of the concrete floor seeping through my body. I ached all over, was stiff and thirsty and hungry. I had to move somehow, again that searing pain through my chest as I rolled over and up into a kneeling position. I slowly crawled across to a wall and, using the wall as a crutch, I worked myself painfully upright. Supporting my ribs with my arm across my chest, and limping from the pain in my hip, I dragged myself to the ablutions and drank some water from the basin tap. The water refreshed me somewhat and I would have to be content with that, food was out of the question for the moment.

Although all I felt like doing was to lie down quietly and not move, I knew I was going to make some attempt at reaching the fourth floor. I took up my hammer and stuck it in my belt and staggered to the bookcase. Sliding the bookcase out of the way of the hole was a mission in itself, and after the effort I felt drained and weak and had to rest again. With difficulty I pulled myself together and called up a further surge of energy. I would let nothing stop me, there was no way I would let Rose or Broad beat me to the spoils. I was just about to let myself down upon my hand and knees in preparation for the crawl through the hole in the wall, when I remembered I had nothing in which to carry the money. I glance round to locate the plastic bags I had prepared for the purpose. I had no idea how bulky the money would be, but I was sure the bags would be suitable. I threw a coil of rope and the lengths of wire into one of the bags, and stuffed the lot into my shirt. I would need both arms to manage the climb up the shaft. I was ready.

My excitement at the nearness of the money pumped adrenalin through my system, and this somehow allowed me to overcome the pain and discomfort to a large extent. I still had to move slowly and carefully, and my painful hip gave me additional trouble in climbing the ladders, to say the least about the constantly jabbing chest pains. Perseverance and the gritting of teeth allowed me to slowly and painfully make my way up to the third floor.

How thankful I was that I had bought the two extra ladders. If I had, had to climb up using the one original ladder, and hoisting it up after me floor by floor, I know I would have failed in my efforts. Yes, these were factors on my side that gave me the confidence that I was going to reach my goal. The extra ladders were the one and the fact I had previously left my lead light hanging in position was another. Without these factors, there was no possibility I would have been able to attempt the task.

Finally I lay on the scaffold at the fourth floor. I was wet with perspiration and as weak as a baby. I rested away my tiredness. At least the effort of climbing had loosened my muscles that the injury, and my sleeping on the cold concrete floor, had caused. I rested until the sweat the effort had brought about had dried on my body, then I took my hammer and tapped away the last of the plaster that separated me from Wilson's office.

I crept at last into the fourth floor office, but this final effort proved too much for me and I fainted. How long I lay there I could not tell, but when I opened my eyes I could see it was daylight, and judging from the shadow the sun cast upon the office wall it was late afternoon. A glance at my watch confirmed the time as four fifteen, but I had no inkling of whether it was the same day or the next. All was quiet in the office and, except for the plaster dust that lay on the floor next to the hole I had made, looked undisturbed. The room I was in contained only a stack type partitioning screen as the only furniture. The door to the next office was closed, and if it was locked I would have to concede defeat. I only had my hammer with which to break down the door. Whilst feasible, I doubted if I would have the strength in my present condition. In any case the noise I would have made might be heard by others outside. I very much doubted whether the flooring contractors would have already reached the fourth floor.

A huge feeling of relief surged through me as the door opened to my touch. I slowly shuffled into the adjoining office, and there it was. It stood in a corner and was a standard four drawer cabinet finished in olive green, and contained the prize I had worked so hard to posses. Such was my relief and surprise, at seeing the cabinet in its reality, that I did not register the furnishing of the rest of the office. I was only vaguely aware of there being chairs, a desk and an oblong carpet, or rug on the floor, in a mustard shade. All I really saw was the long sought after cabinet. I reached for the top drawer, it was empty! I frantically opened the other three drawers—all empty. I could not believe it, was it all a practical joke after all? Had Wilson already cleared the money? Had Rose and Broad actually beaten me in the race? I was devastated, all the suspense, the expense, the hard work. All the scheming and planning, all the pain, all for nothing. An all consuming wave of depression swept over me and I sank down onto the floor. I felt totally dispirited. I would not have cared if Wilson, or the police, or anyone else had found me there. I had lost the opportunity and lost the will to live, utter despair.

Eventually I pulled myself together and struggled to stand. There was no way I could face climbing down the shaft again. I decided to check whether the door to the passage would open from inside the office. I hoped that that would be the case, and that I would be able to open it without a key and simply leave by that exit. In all the time I had kept watch on Wilson's door, and tried to work out how Broad intended to force an entry, I had never registered whether it was the type of lock that could be opened from both sides. I automatically assumed that this would be the norm. I turned round to face the entrance, and there, standing against the wall alongside the door, was another filing cabinet.

I caught my breath, my eyes opened in surprise, and in my eagerness I tried to rush forward and doubled over in extreme pain once more, and a wave of dizziness made the room swirl momentarily. When I came to my senses I found myself standing right in front of the cabinet with my hand clasped upon the handle of the top drawer. I wrenched the drawer open, and there it was, row upon row of stacked notes. I had never in my life seen so much money in one place, and I reached in and gingerly picked out a bundle of one hundred Rand notes.

So it was true after all. I was shivering once again, but this time with excitement. Weakness brought tears to my eyes as I gazed amazed at the sight. I had no idea how much was there, nor did I care, I simply stuffed the notes into my plastic bags. I did notice that some of the bundles were two hundred Rand denominations, and all the three drawers were full of bundles. The fourth drawer was however empty. Soon my bags were comfortably full. I stood back and hefted a bag. It felt about twenty kilograms, but in my weakened state I could not be certain; I was just pleased that it was a weight I could handle. There were ten bags full of money, four million Rand, Rose had said. 'So that was what four million bucks looks and feels like,' I said to myself.

The bags were bulky and heavy, and if I had, had any idea of what such a large sum of money weighed, I would have brought the block and tackle. In my present condition I could not consider fetching the block and tackle, there must be some other way I could lower the bags down to my floor. After some consideration, I lowered the rope I had brought to check its length. I was pleased to note that it could reach twice as far and more. This discovery led me to think of a plan that might just fit the bill. I sincerely hoped it would be successful, after all the hard work and pain, there was no way I would leave any of this haul behind.

After puzzling at the problem for awhile, I came upon the solution, but to carry it out I needed a knife which I did not have. Then I hit upon the idea of pulverizing the rope with the hammer at the points I required to cut, and eventually the rope would separate. I marked off the lengths I would need, and placed the section I needed to cut first, upon the exposed brickwork of the hole. The work was most uncomfortable and, with my chest pains stabbing me with every stroke of the hammer, it took a long while and with many stops in between to catch my breath and recover. Finally I separated two short one meter lengths, the remainder I cut in two. Each of the short lengths I tied to the four corners of the oblong office rug. Thus tied, when I placed money bags in the centre and lifted the two ends, I had a serviceable sling. The two long lengths of rope I tied to the centre of the loops formed by the ropes fixed to the rug. The opposite end of one of these ropes I tied to the top rung of the ladder. The other I looped round the ladder rung and let it hang down the shaft. I loaded a bag of money onto the rug and pulled it up to the hole. I pulled the slack of both ropes round the ladder rung and into the room. Thus I had created a purchase that would allow me to lower the bags one at a time down to my floor scaffold level.

I carefully maneuvered the rug sling with the first load of money through the hole in the wall and onto the scaffold. I pulled in the slack of the long ropes, and holding firmly onto these, I used my feet to ease the sling off the edge of the scaffold. Hand over hand I slowly let the twin ropes run over the top rung of the ladder, and equally slowly the sling with its load was lowered down to the first floor. Although the bag and rug, together with the ropes, could not have weighed more than twenty two or three kilograms, my injuries and weakness made it an exhausting exercise. Once the load had reached the bottom scaffold it was simply a matter of releasing the rope, that was not tied to the ladder rung, and letting it fall down the shaft. Now all I had to do was pull the rope that was tied to the ladder, up back to me and as the mat came with it, it would tip and deposit the money bag onto the first floor scaffold. Now all I had to do was repeat this exercise until all the money bags had been lowered to my floor level. It was a relatively simple operation if slow. Lowering ten bags down the shaft took a long time, exacerbated by the rest I had to take after each load down, and then again, once the rug was up to the top again, but at last it was finished.

I placed my first tentative step of my climb down the ladders. With much difficulty I reached the scaffold of the third floor. The feeling of success and elation that had buoyed me up thus far finally deserted me, I was shivering from weakness and exhaustion. For the first time I started to cough, and felt a bubbling in my chest. The pain was excruciating. I sat on the scaffold and rested once more. Then calling on my reserves of energy I lowered myself onto the next series of ladder rungs, I was determined to make it free with the prize.

Slowly, slowly. I crept down the ladder. Twice more I coughed up phlegm, which I spat down the shaft. Down, down to the second floor. Again I was forced to rest. Each time I stopped to rest I found it took longer to get moving again. Only one more stage then I would be on my own floor. That thought spurred me on, and I tried to hurry, but the final stretch was the worst. I was trembling so much that even the ladder was shaking. It took me at least twenty minutes to complete the last section. Every three steps I had to stop and cough and each cough was such agony that I almost lost my grip on the ladder. I was becoming short of breath and dizzy, and at each breath I could feel fluid in my chest. At last I reached the final scaffold and sank down once more.

The hole I had made on my floor was not very large and it was with difficulty I eased the ten bags into my office. Night had since fallen and, with only the reflected glow of my lead light shining down the shaft, the office was quite dark. I crawled into the office and lay on the floor panting and coughing; I wiped the back of my hand across my mouth and, in the dim light, noticed pink flecked spittle. With my last reserves I pulled myself up onto my knees and pushed the bookcase across the hole. The effort was severe and I fell flat on my face writhing with the most intense pain yet. I rolled in agony, finally ending up in a fetal position, clutching my chest and shivering from shock. I could feel myself getting weaker still, the chest pain over riding the hip pain into oblivion.

I had the money at last, I would just rest awhile and then—

CHAPTER 11

Broad parked the Harley Davidson on a quiet street and nonchalantly walked back to where he was able to hire a taxi, which he instructed to take him back to Nietrop building. The Toyota truck was still parked at the same place, and there was no sign of the driver, nor any other activity He went up to the first floor and listened at the door of W.E.A.R. All was quiet. He tried the door and found it locked. He wondered what had happened to Wimpy, he could ask the doorman, but thought it unwise to show interest and so draw attention to himself. The best he could do was to turn up that night and see if Wimpy's truck had been taken, or perhaps, better still, find out from Cotteral if Wimpy had been about.

The truck was still there when Broad returned that evening and nor had Cotteral seen Wimpy. The situation looked promising to Broad but he decided to keep on checking for a day or two to make certain that Wimpy was well and truly out of the picture, before reporting to Rose. For the rest of the week Broad monitored the building and there was no sign of Wimpy and Broad was at last confidant that he had removed him from the equation.

Broad reported the news to Jack Rose that Friday night that all was clear and Wimpy was no longer a threat. "There's been no sign of him for the last week, and during this period his truck has never been used, so I am positive I was successful in removing him from the picture," said Broad confidently.

"Good," answered Rose, "I've been checking through the papers as well, and there's been no mention of any accident or fatal injury, so at least you managed to take him out quietly. I suppose he is either in hospital or at home nursing his injuries. Good work William. He may never have constituted a threat to our plans, but it is better safe than sorry. At least we will have a clear field when we make our move on Monday.

Early Monday morning the fourth of September saw Rose and Broad sitting in a car, on the opposite side of the street from Nietrop building, awaiting the arrival of Wilson, and chatting idly of this and that. They had time on their hands as it was not yet midday which was Wilson's usual lunch time visit. A fire department truck pulled up and double-parked outside Nietrop building, then a short while later a police car parked behind the fire truck.

While they watched this unexpected event, idly wondering what had caused this activity, a plain clothed man placed some crime scene tape across the entrance to the building, effectively banning entry. Both Rose and Broad were dumfounded, what had happened to cause this intervention by the authorities. Time passed and a few more uniformed policemen arrived. Two of these took up positions at the front of the building on guard. Wilson arrived with his briefcase right on schedule much to Rose's satisfaction, and as they watched he was politely forbidden entry. Rose and Broad gazed in frustrated fury as they saw Wilson turn away and retrace his steps. Now there was no chance of proceeding with their plan of attack. Rose moodily let in the clutch and they drove dispiritedly away. They would have to re-assess their options and try again another day. Rose berated himself for starting Noreen upon the heavy usage of the drugs. She was becoming almost a Zombie and would be little use in abstracting fresh information from Wilson. He had been too hasty in getting her ready for the streets. Rose and Broad discussed the incident and could not imagine what had transpired to warrant the presence of the fire department and police.

CHAPTER 12

On Monday morning the office personnel and public, who were going about their various activities on the first floor of Nietrop, were conscious of an unbearable smell of death and decay. Phones rang at the premises of Friedman and Schlebush, the agents for Nietrop building, stridently calling for attention. Within minutes agent Jean Scott arrived at the scene. Holding a handkerchief, liberally doused with channel number five perfume, to her nose, she resolutely set off down the passage of the first floor. She was almost at the door of office number two when the overpowering stench caused her to convulse and throw up, adding the smell of vomit to the soupcon of decomposing flesh and channel number five. Jean Scott fled back down to the ground floor and contacted the doorman.

"I cannot be absolutely sure where the smell is coming from, but there certainly is something rotten," said she, stating the obvious, "I think you had better call the Municipal sanitation department."

The Sanitation department refused their services, as they held no brief for private property, and only dealt with municipal problems. Try the fire station. The fire department sent a delegation of four firemen, who in turn radioed their their headquarters suggesting the police and medical officer be summoned.

That is how detective inspector Harry Noble, of da Gama Precinct, Bay city Central, ended up with a case that was to prove unduly trying and difficult. Not that any of the cases da Game Precinct handled were easy, but the type of crime that prevailed in this sprawling port city of East Bay could generally be classified according to the area in which it occurred. For example, the district and suburban crimes tended toward housebreaking and burglary, which were relatively simple matters to control. Whereas the police division that covered the central and harbour area, were faced with prostitution, drugs and muggings in the main, which were an ongoing headache. At least that was how Inspector Noble perceived matters. The crimes that pertained to Central precinct always seemed involved and convoluted This particular crime was certainly to prove one of these.

Detective inspector Noble together with his partner, Blackie Swart, two members of the forensic team and a medical officer converged upon the offices of W.E.A.R. from which the overpowering smell was emanating. They forced the locked door and entered into an empty reception area, proceeding to the other offices, they found the one office also empty, but the other contained a desk and a chair alongside the window wall. A rug was laid out on the floor; a bookcase with a few magazines was against a further wall. In one corner was a toolbox and assorted tools. Almost in the middle of the room lay a bundled heap of a man, dressed in brown slacks, white shirt, and a dust coat. His clothes were dusty and dirty and smeared with reddish brownish coloured stains. Strewn around the body were ten full plastic bags.

The forensic team immediately set about marking the position of the body and taking photographs. Noble instructed his partner to radio for additional police, to man the four floors, and to have two at the entrance of the building. He instructed Swart to cordon the entrance off with crime scene tape, and man the entrance of the building, while waiting for the policeman to arrive. Thereafter Swart was to return to the office for further instruction.

Having seen to the immediate necessities, Noble stood back and let the forensic complete photographing the scene and dusting for fingerprints. Only when they had completed their tasks and returned to headquarters, did Noble venture to open a window and let fresh air in the office. Standing at the window, he suddenly realized he had been spasmodically holding his breath against the pervasive stench.

Meanwhile the gray haired doctor, a man well into his fifties, struggled to make his stiff knees bend to a kneeling position beside the body. Seemingly unaffected by the smell, he uttered a monologue to no one in particular while he carried out his examination, "Calliphora erythrocephalus, the common or garden maggot of the blue bottle fly. Hm,hm, a corpse, a warm ambient atmosphere."

"They lay their eggs in daylight, you know," he explained to Noble.

Noble interrupted this flow of words irritably, "Enough with the medical lecture, Doc. How long has he been dead?"

Undisturbed, the venerable doctor continued, "Yes, yes, they lay their eggs in daylight. The tiny maggot sheds its skin in between eight to fourteen hours. That's the first stage, they reach the second stage in two to three days, after five or six days they are really nice and juicy."

The doctor rolled the body over, revealing a fluidly mess. "Oh yes," he went on happily, "this condition occurs in about three to five days. In a cool situation such as found in this office, I'd say rather later than sooner, hm, yes, I'd say almost certainly between five, six days at most."

"O.K" sighed detective inspector noble, "Six days ago, a whole week, that puts it at about Monday or Tuesday. Any idea what caused his death?"

"You will have to wait for my autopsy report," the doctor replied, "Judging from the blood spots and dried spittle round the mouth, the marks on his shirt, and from what I could ascertain from my superficial examination, I would guess he died from a punctured lung. He certainly looks as if he had suffered a severe fall, or maybe beaten up. As I say, he definitely has a cracked rib, and probably a broken one as well, that caused the perforation of the lung. But for a clearer picture I will have to get him on the autopsy table, for a thorough examination and report." The doctor got creakingly to his feet, and stripping off his latex gloves, he turned to the mortuary staff who had since arrived and said, "I'm done here, you can scoop him into a body bag as soon as you are ready. "With his immediate work completed, the doctor left the building.

Harry pulled on a pair of latex gloves and carried out the unpleasant task of going through the corpses pockets. He found no identification of any sort. He dragged the plastic bags into the reception room pending later investigation. The men from the mortuary managed with difficulty to get the body into a body bag and removed it from the scene. Harry Noble was alone for the moment while he waited for Blackie Swart to join him. While he waited Harry inspected the contents of the plastic bags he had placed in the reception room. Then came the surprise of the day. Dead bodies are commonplace to the minions of the law, but never in his entire career had detective inspector Harry Noble seen so many one hundred and two hundred Rand notes together.

For a moment Harry was tempted. The forensic team had dusted the bags for fingerprints, then had taken no further interest in the bags, assuming correctly that, that was the investigating officers prerogative. The doctor had not even glanced at the bags. Nobody had taken any notice, Harry was certain that he alone was aware the bags contained money. Here was the opportunity of a lifetime. It was well known that the salaries of police officers were notoriously poor, he could not be blamed for being tempted. He could not stand looking at the hoard without wanting to fill his pockets, so Harry turned away, forced temptation aside, and waited for his assistant to return.

Once Blackie arrived they upturned the bags together, and bundle after bundle of notes spewed onto the floor. The money was counted, a total of four million eight hundred thousand Rand, which was then sealed in boxes and sent to the police station. At the police station the boxes were receipted simply as Nietrop evidence and placed in the evidence safe room. Harry had watched the boxes removed with very mixed feelings, had he lost the opportunity of a lifetime.

Finally everyone had completed their work and Harry was left to seal up the offices of W.E.A.R., whoever they were? The long tiring round of interrogations began.

Every one on the first floor was questioned, followed by further interrogations on the remaining floors. No—one had heard any sounds of violence or otherwise. No—one had, had contact with the tenant of number two, or had ever spoken to him other than the tenants of the first floor, who had one and all, merely greeted him in passing. Those who had taken particular notice described the man as of average height, probably one and a half to one and three quarter meter tall. Well built, with light coloured brownish hair, deeply tanned, with the looks of an outdoor man. It was assumed his name was Wimpy, no—one seemed to know just how they knew his name, which of course it was not, a fact that only came to light much later. All the tenants of the building, and the visiting public, who had been in the building on the arrival of the police, were finally interviewed and released to go separate ways. All the offices were visited, except number sixteen, which was locked. A check with the rental agents established that number sixteen was leased by a certain Mr. Wilson, who it was believed, was a municipal official.

The doorman who knew the dead man better than most, with the exception of the night watchman, Cotteral, decided on a policy of speak, see and hear nothing and one will not become involved. He had first decided on this policy when the first pair of policemen had made enquiries regarding Wimpy. He had thought at the time there was something not strictly kosher about the man in number two, and that it would be wiser not to be too inquisitive.

Cotteral on the other hand was much more vocal, but although voluble, all he could add was how kindly Wimpy was, and how he was busy fitting out his office prior to opening his business. Cotteral did not mention the free brandies received from Wimpy's hand.

Mss. Jean Scott was the only person who had, had any extensive dealings with Wimpy. She explained about the lease, and showed the detectives the relevant documents. Yes she had been very remiss about the I.D. but had arranged for the victim to bring his I.D. to the office. Unfortunately this tragedy had occurred before that could be done. No, she had not worried too much about the I.D., she knew it was policy, but as Wimpy had paid six months rent in advance, she could hardly see any problem. No, she had no idea why there should have been money lying about the office floor, and yes she did think it strange. But when you came to think about it, the whole thing was becoming strange.

"How do you mean strange?" Asked the interviewing detective.

"I mean, about the heavy timber supposed to be for shelves and counters and things," vouchered Mss. Scott, "What I would like to know is, where is that timber now? There is no sign of it, no shelves or counters either." Mss. Scott also told of the earlier police enquiry about Wimpy, and how the police had received a complaint from a man walking his dog that evening past the building, who had told about banging and machine noises emanating from the building. She explained Wimpy's statement to the police that his excuse for working late at night was in consideration of his possible disturbance of the other tenants of the building, had he worked during the day. The excuse that he had made to the police, and later confirmed to her, on the occasion of her visit to his office. That was when she had observed the heavy timber and tools which Wimpy was intending to use to erect shelves and counters. She also mentioned Wimpy's explanation regarding the samples he expected to receive from the mining houses. At a further question from the detective, she replied that she did not know the names or the numbers of the policemen that had visited her, they were just two policemen.

After receiving this statement from Mss. Scott, Harry Noble again questioned the night watchman and the doorman. The doorman again maintained his aloofness, and still claimed ignorance of the whole affair. The night watchman was again eager to help, telling how he had helped Wimpy carry tools to the office, and how Wimpy explained his intention of carrying out his own shop fitting. No he had not seen any actual shelves, or anything, just a lot of wooden boards lying around. He repeated the remark he had made on the occasion of the police visit about Wimpy having made a great deal of noise, but with there being little actual completed work.

Noble felt frustrated, he had nothing, not the victims confirmed identity, no worthwhile clues. No one seemed to know Wimpy, or have heard of the company W.E.A.R. As far as he could ascertain, none of the mining houses had ever heard of W.E.A.R. or of Wimpy. Consolidated Investments for whom, Wimpy had told Mss. Scott, he used to work, claimed they had never heard of him. So far nothing had come up except dead ends. It was a known fact that the first twenty four hours were crucial. If one could get a useful lead early on in the case, then there was a good chance of a breakthrough, leading to an early solving of the case, or an arrest of the perpetrators. How was it possible that a dead man could be found in a locked office suite in a prestigious building, lying amongst millions of Rand, having apparently died from injuries received from what or who knows where, without there being a clue that was worthwhile. Noble returned to headquarters to write up a very inconsequential report.

The media were having a field day; major newspapers carried lurid headlines to capture the public interest. The Daily News carried a padded and speculative story under banner headlines,' Decomposing body in Nietrop building'. The Evening Standard declared in a headline twenty millimeters high,' Lurid find in city office block linked to millions'. T.V. coverage showed an anchor man standing in front of Nietrop building and saying that a gruesome find had been made in the first floor offices of W.E.A.R. The anchor man also mentioned that the body appeared to have been lying in the offices for for some time, and that a hoard of money was found at the scene. He finished off by saying that police were following several leads and his station would be sure to keep the viewers informed. All this media frenzy had stemmed from the very barest information the police spokesman had released, however, it was the very nature of things for the press to prickle the public interest in the never ending search of material to boost circulation.

Of the public who followed the announcements mentioned in the papers and on the TV., Were four very startled and interested persons. Wilson was startled to attention upon reading of the matter in his evening news edition. Surely there could not be a connection, but it certainly seemed coincidental that a dead man with money strewed around him should be found in that particular building. He could do nothing about it until the building opened in the morning, and he hoped fervently that it would be open to the public and that there would be no police presence when he made his call. Wilson spent a very agitated night.

Noreen sat up, wide eyed, upon seeing the TV. coverage of the case. 'Could it be Jack? Had he tried to get the money and somehow murdered this man?' She jumped out of bed and phoned Jack's number.

"Sweetie, have you heard the news about Nietrop?" She inquired breathlessly.

"Yeah, I heard about it. So what?" Snarled Rose.

"You didn't have anything to do with it, did you?" Asked Noreen fearfully.

"Are you bloody mad," screamed Rose, "Anyway you just shut up about it, you hear? You don't know Nietrop Building, you don't know me, you don't know anything, you got it?"

"Yes but," ventured the now thoroughly alarmed woman.

"You heard what I said. Talk to no-one, and another thing, don't call me, I'll call you." Snarled Rose and he slammed down the phone.

The call had interrupted a heated argument between Rose and Broad. Noreen's call had inflamed Rose even more. He grabbed Broad by the jacket lapels and screamed at him. "You blithering idiot, I told you no killing. Now thanks to you, we've lost our chance to get the money, and on top of it all, there's cops all over the place. Now that stupid bitch is panicking. That's all we need, that she starts mouthing off as well."

"YOU stupid bastard," yelled Broad in turn, "You are the one that wanted Wimpy taken out. Anyway I never killed him. If I killed him when I knocked him down, how the hell did a dead man get into his office, huh? Tell me that."

"You must have killed him, you lousy shit, think logically. He must have got the money while you were pussyfooting around thinking of a way to do a simple job." Shouted Rose, working himself into a frenzy, "I don't know how he got into his office, and I don't care. All I know is you killed him and it's your fault we missed out on the money."

He flung himself upon the bigger man and they crashed to the floor, breaking a coffee table in the process, scattering used beer mugs and magazines on the floor.

They rolled and wrestled back and forth," I'll kill you, you bastard," hissed Rose, "you and your accidents cost us the money. I'll give you accidents, you bloody shit, how are we going to get the money now."

They grappled at one another frenziedly, with neither gaining an advantage. Finally Broad with his greater bulk managed to pin Rose down and fastened his fingers around Rose's throat. Rose thrashed about, his hands desperately pulling on Broads's wrists, his eyes bulging, his mouth gaping open, his lungs struggling for air. Rose's legs kicked against a glass fronted display cabinet, sending shards of glass and a cascade of Johnny Walker, Smirnoff and Klipdrift crashing to the floor in a splintering, slippery wet and sticky mess of broken glass, pungent liquor and blood from cuts they both received from the falling glass.

The police emergency number 1111 received a series of calls, some irate, some concerned, some fearful, but all complaining of the shouting and noise issuing from Flat 16, The Gardens on Gladhope road, Mountain view. Squad car responded and officers Booysens and Carter with guns drawn rushed to the flat door. Carter banged on the door with the butt of his pistol and called out their police presence. The fracas continued unabated, sounds of breaking furniture and grunts and yells filled the air, no—one responded to the police.

With a splintering sound of breaking wood, the lock was smashed and the door swung violently open, followed by the two officers, pistols ready as they crouched in the approved fashion.

"Break it up, break it up," shouted the police. Booysens holstered his pistol, pulled Broad off and flung him face down and handcuffed his wrists behind his back.

"You are being arrested for disturbing the peace and disorderly conduct," said Carter forcing Rose over. His face on the floor, gasping and heaving for breath, Rose was handcuffed in his turn.

"It's all over folks," announced Carter as they pushed the disheveled belligerents out of the flat and into the squad car. The curious thrill seeking crowd around the flat door reluctantly dispersed, as the squad car pulled away.

Noreen was worried, she was sure Jack was somehow implicated in the death of that man found in that office. She was the one who had told him about Wilson's money in the first place and she knew Jack had intended taking the money. She knew enough about criminal proceedings to know that she could be arrested as an accessory. Jack had forbidden her to contact him, and she had heard nothing from him since. Two days had past and she needed her fix to help her deal with the strain of uncertainty. She thought about going to Jack's apartment, but his express order not to contact him was fresh in her mind. Jack could be mean sometimes; if she disobeyed him he would smack her around. What could she do? She must get some powder somehow. The need for the drug began to take precedent over her concern over Jack's possible involvement in the crime.

Wilson had gone to the municipal offices to fetch his keys, and in walking across the entrance hall he met a colleague. The fellow had greeted him good morning and then remarked on the happening at Nietrop building. Wilson agreed that it was a shocker, then his heart missed a beat as he heard the man say jocularly," Nietrops not far from here, better check your staff, maybe someone is missing and your treasury funds with him. Ha, ha, ha" It was a poor joke, but it was too close to home, and at that instant Wilson almost choked.

"I say old man, "the other exclaimed, "are you o.k., Can I get you some water?"

"No thanks, I'm all right, just swallowed wrong." Wilson answered, recovering quickly, and they passed on.

Wilson had only one thing on his mind, his money. He rushed to Nietrop building, hardly noticing the police cars parked in front. He impatiently rode up in the elevator, burst into his office and came to a shuddering stop as he saw the open cabinet drawers. He knew the money mentioned in the papers came from here.

All his cleverness, all the years spent accumulating the money, all the years of stress and planning and scheming. The pain of failure was just too much to bear, all for nothing, ten years of his life thrown away. Who could have done this? He had always been so careful, told no—one, how could this have happened? His dream of ease wilted away, his dream of Noreen by his side—Noreen! No it couldn't; but could it? Wilson's shoulders sagged, his face crumpled in misery, 'All for nothing,' he thought, 'Oh Noreen, Noreen you bitch, you lovely bitch, how could you do this to me?'

Wilson was so dispirited that he never noticed the hole in the wall, nor did he wonder how Noreen could have entered the office, he simply turned and left, locking the door out of habit as he did so. Wilson did not go back to the municipal buildings, what was the point? Instead he caught a bus and returned to his small cottage in the suburbs.

About the same time as Noreen had been debating about what to do about Jack Rose. Wilson had taken from his desk drawer a point three two automatic pistol, placed the muzzle against the roof of his mouth and pulled the trigger. At least that was how the media explained the death in another flurry of banner headlines. This was the stuff to boost circulation. The daily Mail announced "Mystery death of respected senior municipal officer." The Evening Standard proclaimed, "Surprise death of senior treasury official." In the course of both articles it was mentioned it was a case of suicide and no foul play was suspected.

CHAPTER 13

Detective inspector Harry Noble was not pleased, this case was as dead as a Dodo, he could detect no sign of meaningful progress. Forensics had gone over the office thoroughly, not moving anything, but had painstakingly looked for any human hair, scales of skin, anything in fact that might explain the presence of a third party that might have brought about the bizarre circumstances that had resulted in the death of the man. The autopsy report had listed the corpse as having one cracked and one broken rib, a punctured lung and a severely bruised hip. The wounds were indicative of a severe fall or accident. Death had come about due to the punctured lung and shock. None of these facts helped Noble one iota as to where the fall or accident had taken place. Where did the money come from? Noble could not recall that such a sum had been reported missing during the last twelve months. Was the victim bringing the money into the building, or taking it out? Had he the money when he had the accident, and if so, how had the accident come about and where? If someone had brought him to the office, why was the money lying haphazardly about in bags ? Why had the money not been taken by him or them?

Where were the shelves and counters spoken of by Mss. Scott and Cotteral? Surely two such diverse witnesses could not be mistaken. What was more, that work had been done was borne out by the presence of the tools. Wimpy had rented the offices on the second of August for a period of six months why? He had proclaimed a non existing business named W.E.A.R.!! None of it made sense.

Harry sat in his office with his head in his hands. How thankless policing was. The press agitating for news of an arrest. The chief pressuring him for some action, and everything at a dead end. The money, he was the first and only person to discover the existence of the money, and he had been alone at the time. He could have helped himself and no-one would have been any the wiser. At least it would have made life more bearable, what a clot he had been. So ran Harry's thoughts.

Blackie Swart burst excitedly into Noble's office, "Guess what? I've just inspected office number sixteen, the one hired by Wilson. Who incidentally, was the same Wilson who committed suicide, and guess what I found?" Harry waited patiently for Swart to explain.

"The office had a hole knocked through the wall leading into a service shaft, and in the service shaft we found a series of scaffolding leading down to the office where the body was found. Also there is a mat or rug tied to ropes, and left hanging down the shaft. What's more, the rubble found in office number sixteen proves that the hole was knocked in from the shaft side, in other words it was the dead man who had broken into Wilson's office."

"How come we didn't find a hole through the wall in the first floor office ?" Asked Harry reasonably.

"Because it was behind the bookcase that had been pushed across to hide it," explained the excited Blackie.

"Great work, Blackie. Now we have something concrete to work with at last," congratulated Noble. They knew Wilson had been a municipal employee, so that was the next obvious step.

Noble paid a visit to the municipality, where he found the whole staff mourning the mysterious suicide of Wilson. He created a major panic amongst the financial staff when he suggested a link between the money, the dead man and Wilson. They could not and would not believe that a man of Wilson's stature was involved in any wrongdoing. Eventually Noble prevailed upon them to call in an unbiased firm of auditors to check the municipal books. It took some time for the auditors to reach consensus that, as far as the financial department books were concerned, there was no evidence of missing funds.

The council was relieved, it was hardly likely that they would admit to being embezzled out of four million eight hundred thousand Rand, which was after all public money. Any hint of a scandal would reflect badly on the Council, and as Noble could see for himself, the books balanced perfectly, as well they should under Wilson's careful administration. The Council was most indignant, Wilson had been a most honourable man, how could Noble suggest otherwise.

Harry reported his meeting with the Council to his chief and said that, in spite of City Hall being a powerful and almost sacrosanct institution, for the sake of a motive, he would continue to assume that the money originated from the municipal coffers. This reasoning would account for the money found with the dead man and also for Wilson's suicide.

An interesting point Harry discussed with his Chief, was that if the Council did not claim ownership, the money now packed in boxes in the evidence room, belonged to no-one. The Chief informed Harry that if the case was closed without ownership being established, the money would initially be locked up in the National Police Headquarters vault until the statute of limitations had run out, then it would revert to the state coffers. Harry clenched his fist, why, oh why had he let the opportunity to help himself to a couple of thousand slip through his fingers.

The City Council and municipal management arranged a valedictory service for Wilson, attended by all the staff at city hall. The Mayor read the eulogy, and praised Wilson for his experience, his efficiency and his many, many years of dedicated service and loyalty to the municipality, and to his fellow workers. Noreen Freebit, as a member of the filing staff, wondered if the Mayor would be so complimentary is she blurted out all she knew of Wilson's erstwhile activities, and his promises to her of a good life with him. 'That would sure get a good laugh,' she thought.

Rose and Broad had been locked in separate cells, and as neither had volunteered any reason for their behavior, they had been fined five hundred Rand each or thirty days. Thus far no bail had been forthcoming, and they sat sullenly silent in their respective cells.

If Harry Noble had only known that, languishing in the cells not far away, were two individuals who were the instigators of the crime that was giving him such a headache, and who could explain to his satisfaction the origin of the victim's injuries. Although they had not actually stolen the money themselves, these two individuals could throw light on many of the questions that were the bane of Harry's life at present. If Harry Noble had only known, but of course he was in complete ignorance of the existence of these two important links to his case.

An abandoned Toyota truck could also have helped Harry in his search for evidence, did he but know it, but it would be another day or two before it would be impounded by the traffic police. Even then it would be an outside chance that Harry would be aware of this fact.

Harry, in writing his report that day, did not know of these happenings, so far the case remained at a dead end. Harry made a list:-

1 Two offices linked by a service shaft, with entry holes broken through a wall in each case.
2 A dead man with broken ribs lying on the floor of the first floor office with money bags strewn around.
3 Cause of injuries unknown.

4 Four million eight hundred thousand Rand assumed taken from fourth floor office filing cabinet, as cabinet drawers found left open.

5 Fourth floor offices leased by one Wilson, now deceased { Suicide—no foul play suspected}

6 Wilson also erstwhile exemplary treasury officer of municipality.

7 Municipality deny any loss of large sums of money.

8 No other reports of money missing.

9 First floor offices leased by one Wimpy as reported by the rental agency.

Harry gazed ruefully at his list, plenty of facts, assumptions galore, but nothing to offer as proof. The Chief had, at Harry's request, allocated a large force to fine comb the area in case of the remote possibility of someone having witnessed an accident, or of someone having a closer relationship with the dead a man. This force of men were busy at the moment and it would be some time before they made their reports. His many years should by now have inured Harry of impatience, but he still could not rid himself of his irritation at delays.

CHAPTER 14

The landlady of Castle Court was somewhat concerned; the nice Mr. Robert Grey had not paid his rent. He was always on time, precisely on the first of the month, and here it was already the eighteenth, halfway through toward the next month already. Now that she thought about it, she had not seen Grey for; it must be a week at least. This was most unusual; she knew he had a job of some sort at present, and wondered if it was out of town. He was always so considerate and she was sure that, if he was to be away for a few days, he would have let her know. She decided to call on Mr. Greys neighbor in flat number five. The lady in flat five had been separated from her husband, and maybe if she had been lonely, she might have got to know Mr. Grey. Mrs. Walker was something of a romantic.

A moment or two after she had knocked, the door of number five opened.

"Good day Mrs. Walker, do come in," offered the woman.

"Hello Mrs. Noble," greeted the landlady, "Sorry to be a nuisance, I'm just enquiring if you had seen Mr. Grey lately? I haven't seen him for awhile, and unlike him, he is late with his rent."

"No Mrs. Walker, I haven't seen him lately myself. But please, do come in."

"Thank you; I'll only stay a minute." Mrs. Walker entered the flat and made her way through to the neatly furnished sitting room. "My," she exclaimed, "Those are lovely curtains, have you just bought them?"

"Not at all," responded the other with a laugh, "They are my same old curtains that I brought over from the house after Harry and I decided to separate, I've just had them washed and ironed, quite a difference is it not?"

"I would never have thought it," said Mrs. Walker, "By the way, I don't want to pry, but how are things going between you and Mr. Noble? I hope the separation is not going to end in divorce?"

"I really don't know," answered Mrs. Noble, "Can I offer you a cup of tea?" She changed the subject, obviously not wanting to discuss her personal affairs.

"No thank you dear," said the landlady, "I only came to find out about Mr. Grey really."

"Now that you mention it, I did notice his truck parked outside Nietrop building these last few days. I noticed it each time as I passed on my walk to and from work. It was only after I read about that ghastly business of the dead man found in the building, that it registered on my mind that it was Mr. Grey's truck that was parked there.," remarked Mrs. Noble.

"Oh, he hadn't said anything to me, but I suppose he landed a job there," said Mrs. Walker, and she went on, "Yes indeed, wasn't that business strange. What is the world coming to? A person is not even safe in his place of business. The paper mentioned that he was found with a lot of money. You would think though, if he had been murdered, the murderer's would have taken the money. As I say, a strange business. Anyway, I must be going. Good bye Mrs. Noble, I won't waste any more of your time." With a farewell wave, Mrs. Walker let herself out of the flat and waddled away.

Mrs, Noble softly closed the door and went to her bedroom to complete her toilet. She had been getting ready to go out when the landlady had called, and now she had to hurry or she would be late. The image reflected in the full length mirror showed a compact woman of about thirty five years of age. Her figure was well formed and firm and, as she looked herself over, she wondered, had she had the child she wanted so much, if her figure would have suffered. She and her husband being childless, she supposed that was the reason, had made it easier for their separation to come about. Her black hair, gray green eyes, soft creamy complexion was reminiscent of her Irish forebears. Together these features amalgamated into a very beautiful face, although, she thought ruefully, it took longer to obtain the effect nowadays.

She and Harry Noble had been married for ten years, but the long erratic hours, the lonely nights alone when Harry was on duty. Not knowing what he was facing at any given moment, not knowing whether he was in danger or not. The mood swings and stress suffered by her husband, and the unfair demands of his job as a police officer, had placed such pressure on their relationship that it had eventually proved too much. They had decided they had better try a break from one another. Their amicable separation was to be for six months initially, but had stretched to three years!! They were still friends, maybe even more than that, she could not decide. They still maintained contact, and had found that a monthly get together promoted a more sincere, passionate and loving environment, than they had ever had during their years of living together in the same household. Harriet, for that was her name, realized now that their façade of togetherness, gaiety and partying with their friends, was just that, a façade. The social whirl in which they were caught up in the old days, when they were referred to as H @ H and invited to every soiree, was only superficial, and grasped at by them to offset the strain of Harry's work.

Their intimate life was one of squabble and turmoil, of appointments cancelled, late homecomings, resulting in Harriet having to honour invitations alone, or to lie sobbing on her bed because Harry had forgotten their anniversary, and had decided to work late. Or else sitting alone anxiously worried if Harry was safe and wishing a dangerous assignment was completed.

No their separation had in fact consolidated into a really contented relationship as far as she was concerned. Because of their separation, she was not immediately aware of what Harry was involved with, and this allowed her to sleep at night. And when they did get together, the pent up longing and emotion for each other usually boded for a very pleasant, satisfying and passionate time, provided Harry could be persuaded not to talk shop.

'Did she love him, I suppose, if only he would take up some other profession,' was the thought that was constantly at the back of her mind. She put the finishing touches to her makeup, glanced at the clock, and reached for her bag. Harry would arrive at any moment.

Harry Noble was just as busy getting dressed for his date with his estranged wife. He loved her dearly and wished there was some way they could get together again. He was willing, but he knew that she would not again link herself to the strain of the wife of a policeman. He knew that his chosen profession could never offer the peace and security of a nine to five office type job. When he was young and full of dreams, he had imagined that his life as a policeman would be one of glamour and adventure and for a time it was like that. However, with time he had become very cynical. How often, after many hours of keeping surveillance in all sorts of discomfort, after many risks and dangers, finally an arrest was made, only to have the case thrown out of court by some clever, and sometimes, unscrupulous lawyer. If that was not bad enough there was the added insult of the low salary a policeman had to endure.

It was small wonder that they had problems; it was not only the stress and strain that had caused their breakup, he had been able to offer her very little on the salary he received. The bitter struggle to make ends meet made it very difficult for Harriet to create a relaxed home atmosphere. He thought back to the days when they had partied to excess placing an even greater strain on their limited budget, just to avoid facing the realities of life. Now he would have to be content with the monthly meetings that had become their norm.

Harry looked at himself critically in the mirror. He looked older than his forty years, but would not admit it to himself. "Not bad, not bad," he gave himself a mental pat on the back. True his blond hair had receded somewhat, but the resultant broader forehead gave him a greater look of intelligence, and his gray sideburns added a look of distinction. He was getting a little fat, he noticed, and involuntarily pulled in his stomach, his broad shoulders masked the thickening of his waist. He grunted in satisfaction, he was ready to go, tonight would be for her, no mention of his latest case, The damn thing was getting nowhere fast and would just put him in a bad mood.

They were to go to a popular Chinese restaurant, he would have loved to take her to that elite eatery on the beach front, but again his meager salary precluded such extravagance. 'If only I had some of that mystery money,' he fantasized.

They met at Harriet's door," Well Harriet," Harry greeted her with a kiss," You look absolutely gorgeous, dear,"

"You are not so bad yourself," she replied in kind "Tall distinguished and handsome, and so well turned out."

Harry was gratified, although he knew that she was just being kind. He had no delusions about his appearance. He had done his best, but even his best suit was a working suit, and since their separation, his clothes lacked the care they had once received from her. His look tended toward the crumpled style, Harriet, on the other hand, was elegant in a sheer, simmering evening gown of olive green, offset by a single string of pearls, just reaching the vee of her breasts, which were shown to advantage by the low cut of her dress. The gray green of her eyes were emphasized by the green of her gown, and the ruby red of her lips just offered enough contrast, she was ravishing. Harry's heart ached for her and he wanted to take her in his arms, instead he said, "How have you been, old girl? I see you are just as sexy as ever."

"Oh I'm just fine," she answered "and you, are you alright Harry?" They went out to Harry's car.

At the restaurant they ordered a bottle of cabernet sauvignon to go with their meal of sweet and sour pork. Strictly speaking, a white wine would have been more complimentary to the meal, but both Harry and Harriet were red wine buffs, and they were past the stage of trying to impress people by knowing what wine was correct with which dish. The evening progressed pleasantly, they spoke of this and that, laughed a lot and Harry strenuously avoided mention of his work.

They were getting to the end of their meal, and the last of their second bottle of wine, and there was a moment of silence as they gazed at the other diners and the few that were dancing. Breaking the silence, Harriet told of her landlady's concern for the missing Mr. Grey, her neighbor in flat number four.

"She's a lovely old duck," Harriet was saying, "She said she was concerned about his absence because he is unusually late with his rent. But between you and me, I think she has a soft spot for our Mr. Grey, and is missing him more than the rent he owes. It is really a bit if trivia and I would not have bothered to mention it, if it hadn't been for my noticing his truck parked at Nietrop building where that horrible business took place. The truck has been parked there for the last few days, and I happened to notice it on my way to work. Now with him missing like that, well I just wondered? You couldn't make some enquiries could you?"

"How did you know I was on that case? Asked Harry startled, "I haven't mentioned at all."

"I didn't know. Are you?"

"Yes," Harry admitted reluctantly, "How is it work always crops up? It's not my fault this time, you know."

"I'm sorry, it's my fault. Are you?"

"Yes."

"Well then, could you check it out, Harry, I mean it does seem strange that Grey has not been around for the last few days. It's not as though Nietrop building is a million miles from Castle Court, he could have walked if his truck was giving trouble."

"If it has any bearing on the case I will certainly check it out, but remember, only if it has any connection with what I am busy with at the moment. If there's no connection I won't have time to get involved with something else, I'm snowed up to my ears as it is with this enquiry at Nietrop. If you are worried about Grey, why not report him as a missing person officially then a docket will be opened and an investigation carried out."

"Yes, I suppose so," Harriet agreed contritely.

At eleven thirty Harry escorted Harriet back to Castle Court, and at her door he kissed her goodnight. He had hoped she would ask him in, but she did not and he didn't want to push his luck. As he drove home Harry thought it had been an extremely pleasant evening. The only time shop talk, the one subject that could have destroyed their date, had raised its ugly head was toward the end, and it had been an eye opener. This missing man Grey, and his struck being parked at Nietrop, can only be in connection with his case. Maybe it would be the crucial clue he had been seeking.

CHAPTER 15

The following day Harry found no truck parked near Nietrop building, it had been towed away as an abandoned vehicle. His phoned enquiry to the traffic pound confirmed the towing away of the truck. Subsequently, through Licensing, Harry established that the truck did indeed belong to one Robert Grey of Castle Court. Harry immediately arranged for the Forensic department to go over the truck to check if there was any connection between the truck and the corpse found in the office in Nietrop building.

That afternoon, an extremely fast response from Forensics, found that the D.N.A. of a hair found on the back rest of the seat of the truck compared ninety percent with the D.N.A. of the corpse in question. At last a factual clue, up to that moment all he had were a string of fictitious names, fictitious companies and hearsay evidence. Now he had the identity of the dead man, his ownership of the truck and the period the truck had been parked outside Nietrop building, and therefore the period Grey had been inside the building. The scaffolding up the shaft indicated that entry to Wilson's office was made by this means. He assumed the reason for the break-in was to steal the money that they had found with Grey's body. For the moment that was where his case came to a halt. He did not know if Grey was the person who had removed the money from Wilson's office, or if it was someone else that Grey had tried to apprehend, and lost his life in the process. The fact that the scaffolding led from the office rented by Grey to the office on the fourth floor, seemed to implicate Grey as the culprit. Harry knew however, that one could not rely upon assumptions, cast iron proof was necessary. Then there was the other snag, the fact that the municipality denied a shortage of funds, and insisted upon Wilson's impeccable honesty, made it difficult to prove ownership of the money. In fact, if it wasn't that the money in question was safely locked up in the evidence room, it would be difficult to convince anyone that there ever was four million eight hundred thousand Rand linked to the affair in the first place. But the money did exist, and the only thing that was absolutely clear was that it was the motive for all that had happened. The insatiable greed for money, didn't he know it, he had been sorely tempted himself.

Meanwhile Blackie and his team, having finished their work within the building, had started to interview surrounding businesses that were in the close vicinity of Nietrop building. They confined their enquiries to the time span from Monday twenty eighth August to the previous week-end, covering the period in which the man was presumed to have died. It was slow repetitive work, but to the detectives this was the reality of police work. They had done similar enquiries many times in the past, and their experience had taught them the right questions that would net them the most useful information. Most people were short and terse with their answers, not wanting to get involved, there were other, however, that would not stop talking, and often make up in their imagination what they thought they had seen and heard.

There was a Greek café on the opposite side of the street, and four doors down from the position where the truck had been parked, whose owner, a Mr. Christodoulos, could offer some useful information. Blackie himself undertook to interview the owner of the shop. He told Blackie he was assisted in the shop by his wife and two coloured girls. Yes they were busy every week, not so busy over the weekend no, but Monday to Friday was always busy. Had anything unusual happened between the twenty eighth of August and the first of September? Blackie wanted to know. No, the proprietor had said, it was just business as usual.

"What about on the street?" Persisted Blackie.

"No, nothing much." answered Christodoulous, "On Monday a man came in asking to phone for an ambulance."

"ON Monday you say. Why did he want an ambulance, do you know?" queried Swart.

"I don't know," continued Christodoulous, "We couldn't raise one anyway, I think maybe, it was something to do with an accident over by Nietrop Building. But it was not unusual, there are always accidents happening, jaywalkers, cars jumping traffic lights, always something, this is a busy street."

"This is very important," Swart insisted, "Do you know any details about this accident?"

"Yes, as a matter of fact, someone had been struck by a motorcycle. It was a man I think. He was lying on the other side of the truck. Lying in the gutter you know. There were people about and I could not see much."

"Did you see what happened to the man afterwards?"

"No man, I was busy you know, I must watch the shop. If you don't watch the shop they steal you blind. I just know a motorcycle hit the man and never stopped, hit and run, you know." said the Greek.

"You never got the registration number, I suppose?" asked Blackie hopefully.

"No, sorry, I just know it was a green one, you know, like what the army uses," the Greek concluded.

Blackie Swart turned to the other members of the shop staff and asked them if they could add anything, but to no avail. He returned to the owner and thanked him for his help.

"Anytime, anytime," beamed Christodolous," Can I get you gentlemen anything, a cup of coffee maybe."

Swart and his assistant accepted the offer, and sat at one of the few tables provide for customer use, and discussed the information they had acquired.

"Hit and run certainly makes it suspicious," Commented Blackie's companion.

"Strange vehicle to use though. An army green, I wonder, could it have been a military bike, do you think?" Wondered Swart.

"Come to think of it, army bikes are usually fitted with a side car, aren't they?" Commented his assistant, "If its army it shouldn't be hard to trace."

Blackie signaled to the Greek and asked him to come over. He asked him if he had noticed a sidecar fitted to the bike.

Christodolous hesitated," I am not sure, maybe, yes, now you say so, I think there was. I am not sure though, sorry."

"We'd better get on to it right away," said Blackie. Pushing his cup to one side, he stood up, thanked Chtistodolous for the coffee and the help he had given, and he and his companion left the café.

While Blackie followed up the motorcycle lead, Noble visited the landlady of Castle Court. Mrs. Walker was most upset to hear of Grey's demise. She sat sniveling into Harry's handkerchief, while Harry gently asked her what she knew of her erstwhile tenant.

"He was such a nice man, such a helpful gentleman, that's what he was, always polite and always most helpful. If I needed anything repaired, he was always most obliging."

"Did he seem strange in any way lately, Mrs. Walker? Did you notice anything different about him, or the way he acted?"

"No, not really, he was a little downcast about not having any work at the moment. He was a builder, you know, and what with building work being depressed and all. At least that is what he told me"

"What was strange," Mrs. Walker continued, "was that he was so late with the rent. That was not like him at all, he was always so prompt, even during this period of unemployment, he always paid up on time. He always used to say, never you mind Mrs. Walker, I may not have a job at the moment, but I've got a little put by, I won't let you down. But of course, this business of his death explains why he has not paid." At these last remarks Mrs. Walker burst into sobs once more.

Harry patted her shoulder awkwardly and asked if he might inspect Grey's flat. Mrs. Walker gave him a pass key. Passing Harriet's door on the way to Grey's flat, Harry reminded himself to phone her that evening and tell her about Grey. He hoped the call would lead to an invitation for them to meet.

The one item in Grey's flat that was relevant, was the list that Grey had made noting the actions of someone named Wilson, the dates, the note about the money being stolen and the last notation regarding the writers intention to stay ahead of the opposition. The reference to the office on the fourth floor and the fourth of the month were of particular interest. Noble took the notes back to Mrs. Walker to have her confirm that the handwriting was indeed that of Grey.

Blackie Swart had meanwhile found that a motorcycle had been stolen from the military, and that it was a sidecar combination. The police put out an all points bulletin, and before long a massive search was in progress. Blackie was certain that it would not be long before the missing bike would be traced. Such the matter proved to be, and the motorcycle was found abandoned in a quiet suburban road. The police obtained several sets of fingerprints from the motorcycle fuel tank, and by a process of elimination, one set of prints proved to be those of one William Broad, petty criminal and associate of a drug pusher named Jack Rose.

Noble and Swart were in the Captains office at Central Police station bringing the case up to date. Noble laid his considerable notes upon the

Captain's desk, together with the notes he had found in Greys' flat, and was paraphrasing for his chief's benefit.

"On Monday the twenty eight of August a hit and run accident took place outside Nietrop building involving a stolen motorcycle and a person unknown. On Monday the fourth of September we were called to Nietrop building where we found a dead man in a first floor office. On the floor of the office surrounding the corpse we found a number of plastic bags, each filled with a considerable sum of money. Subsequently Blackie established that a service shaft had been used as a means to enter an office on the fourth floor and it is assumed that the money came from this office. The man carried no identification. The building was immediately sealed off and a thorough interrogation of all occupants in the building carried out. Nothing came up that appeared to be connected with the dead man, or the first floor office. Steps were taken immediately to intensify the search of the building once again, plus the immediate surrounding areas." Noble paused for a moment, then continued, "On the first of September, while dining with my wife, she mentioned in passing, of a Mr. Grey that appeared to be missing from his home at Castle Court."

"How is Harriet, by the way?" Interrupted the Chief, who was very fond of Noble's wife and had been upset at the breakdown of their marriage.

"Fine, thank you sir," said Harry, "Anyway to continue." Harry explained how his wife had noticed the Toyota truck belonging to Grey parked at Nietrop, and how forensic investigation had established that Grey and the corpse were one and the same and that the truck belonged to Grey. He explained further how Blackie Swart by diligent and painstaking work had finally found a witness who had told of a hit and run accident whereby a man was hit by an olive green motorcycle. Further enquiries eventually traced the motorcycle to the military, and that it had been stolen. The motorcycle had finally been found abandoned in a suburban street, and amongst the fingerprints found on the bike was those of a petty criminal by the name of Broad. Broad had however as yet not been traced.

Noble continued his report saying, "It is assumed that the man who was hit by the bike was Grey. How Grey came to get to the first floor office of the business named W.E.A.R. is not known. The offices in question were leased for a period of six months from the rental agents, Friedman and Schlebusch by a man named Wimpy. The rental agency woman, a mss. Jean Scott, neglected to ask Wimpy for his I.D. in spite of the fact that it is company policy to have a persons identity document presented so the number can be recorded. So far we have not been able to trace this person Wimpy. The additional notes you have before you, were found by me in Grey's flat," Harry paused for a moment and sipped from a glass of water before continuing, "The notes mention a fourth floor office of a person named Wilson, and also it is possible, no probably the origin of the money. We have also not yet been able to trace this Wilson; however the suicide of a man named Wilson that took place this week, could be a connection. The suicide had been an employee of the East Bay City council treasury department. An investigation by me carried out at the city council offices elicited that Wilson had been head of the treasury department, and had been a much respected employee. Auditors had been called in to check the municipal books, and no moneys were found to be missing that could account for an amount as large as four million eight hundred thousand Rand. In conclusion, there is no proof of ownership of the money. It would appear that Grey tried to take the money from Wilson's office, but died in the attempt. Grey died from injuries received either from Wilson, or received through the accident with the motorcycle. The sequence of events seem clear enough, we have some circumstantial evidence, but no definite proofs," said Noble finally completing his report.

The Chief made a decision, "Well for the want of further factual clues, for the present we will just have to enter it as a case pending. A victim who is robbed of money that in itself seems to have been stolen, and as a result commits suicide, a robber, who himself is found dead from injuries suspected but not proven. It is all very unsatisfactory. But as we have no actual complaint, rather regarding the money or the corpse, except the agents Friedman and Schlebush, I must mark the docket pending with no further action at present," So saying, the Chief superintendent took up a red pen and scrawled N.F.A. Pending across the case folder. The Chief looked up at the two detectives and said," For the moment I want you both to concentrate on the other urgent work that is piling up. Both you and Blackie shelve it for the moment, and when and if preassure of work allows, you can go into it again."

CHAPTER 16

Others in the East Bay Metropolitan police organization were busy investigating the stolen motorcycle. They were intent in apprehending the perpetrator of the crime of vehicle theft. The fingerprint files had narrowed the search down to one person, William Broad, who already was on file as a petty criminal and had in the past been arrested in connection with prostitution an extortion. Further investigation showed that this individual worked in close association with another suspected criminal, one Jack Rose. Further collation of material elicited the fact that both these men were at present incarcerated on a disturbing of the peace charge. The report of these two men finally landed on the desk of the station chief superintendent. The police captain, upon reading the report, remembered the link between the military motorcycle and the incident reported in Noble's summary of the Nietrop case. He passed the report on to Noble's office for inclusion in the Nietrop file.

So it was that Harry Noble found himself reactivating the Nietrop case, albeit unknown to his superior officer. He now had a definite link between the motorcycle rider, the accident or attempt to kill, and probably the corpse found at Nietrop building, who had been identified as Grey of Castle Court. In perusing the dockets on Rose and Broad, Noble learnt the both Rose and Broad were on file as drug pushers who dealt in cocaine and heroin in a small way, and that Rose also ran a string of three prostitutes.

Both were known to the police vice squad and kept under surveillance by detective Richard Dlamini. Apparently Dlamini left these two loose on the off chance they would eventually lead the police to the big fry drug supplier. Not appearing in the report, and of course unknown to the police, was Dlamini's other agenda, which Dlamini kept entirely to himself.

Noble had Broad brought to the interrogation room, and he and Swart started the good cop, bad cop routine.

"You are in big trouble Broad, you know that don't you?" Noble started the proceedings.

"What do you mean? Me and Jack just had a scrap, that's all."

"I'm not talking about your fight with Rose, I'm talking about your deliberately stealing a motorcycle and running down and killing a man named Grey. I'm talking about murder, Broad, that's what I'm talking about," Shouted Noble.

"I never killed nobody, I don't know what you're talking about, I don't know no Grey. What do you mean murder?" Bleated Broad, thoroughly alarmed.

Swart broke in on his flurry of words, "C'mon Broad, make it easy on yourself. You were seen at the scene, your fingerprints match those found on the bike, we've got you to rights, so you might as well come clean, and maybe we can help you."

"Nonsense, we won't cut a deal with scum like this," threatened Noble, "It's the high jump for him that's for sure."

Swart intervened again, "C'mon Harry, maybe he didn't mean to kill Grey, maybe it was just an accident."

Broad quickly grabbed at this straw. "Yeah, that's right, you'se guys saw an accident with someone that looks like me. Fingerprints, I don't believe you've got prints. You're bluffing because I was with Jack Rose on Monday, I wasn't near any accident, so you'se can jump it, it's got nutting to do wit me." Broad was regaining some of his composure.

"Who said anything about Monday," Asked Noble triumphantly, "You've put your foot in it now, haven't you? C.mon man, admit it. You know you did it, you deliberately and with aforethought and intent rode down one Robert Grey, and he died from his injuries. You Mr. William Broad will be charged with murder of the first degree."

"You got nutting on me, I've got nutting to say. I want a lawyer," mumbled Broad.

"Have it your way," said Swart, coming into the interrogation once more," but you realise, don't you, that we have got the goods on you. You are going to be sitting for a very long time, unless—."

There were a few moments of silence while Broad savoured this possible alternative, then he asked "What you mean unless?"

Swart responded by saying, "You're going down for life, you know that don't you. But if you are reasonable, maybe we can make it easier for you. Like I say, help us and we help you. Tell us why you killed Grey, tell us about the money, tell us what is behind it all and we may get your sentence reduced. Notice, Broad, I said we may! It depends on what you tell us, and how much it is of use to us. If what you tell us is of use, then maybe, just maybe, you will get out of prison a relatively young man."

"It was all an accident, I tell you," whimpered Broad. Suddenly changing his tune, he continued in a subdued voice, "I didn't mean to kill him, I didn't even know that he was dead, or what his name was. We knew him as Wimpy, not Grey."

"Don't lie," snarled Noble, it's been in all the papers. Grey's name wasn't mentioned, but you knew all right. When you read about the dead man and the money found with him, you knew all right. So come clean Broad, if you want us to help you, start talking."

Now visibly shaking, his fingers picking at his buttons, Broad capitulated "O.K. I'll talk. It was like this, I hit a man with the bike sure, but I didn't mean to kill him. His death really was an accident; I was supposed just to hurt him enough to take him out of contention. I didn't know about any money till afterwards, when I read about it in the papers. I was scared, that's why I didn't stop. I don't have a license, and I thought that if I was charged, and the man sued me, well I don't have any money, and I was scared, that's why I didn't stop. That's the truth, I swear, it was just an accident."

"Who told you to take Grey out, was it Rose?" Asked Swart.

"Nobody, er, I don't know, I just wanted to."

"Rubbish Broad, someone told you to do it, you said Grey had to be taken out of contention. Now that is a word that I doubt you even know the meaning of, so who told you to take Grey out of contention. C'mon, you've got to do better if you expect us to help you," threatened Noble again.

"Yes it was Rose," admitted Broad sullenly.

Noble sent Broad back to his cell, they certainly could not pin a murder charge on him. The best they could hope for was a charge of culpable homicide, but Broad was not to know this, and a little brooding in his cell might cause his tongue to loosen a bit more. At least they had got a line on the reason for Grey's injuries.

They sent for Rose, and both men were surprised at his condition. The bulky Broad who looked like a well used punch bag at the best of times, had showed no obvious damage from the fight he had, had with Rose. Rose, on the other hand, limped into the room, his neck was purple with bruises, he had a black eye and a cut lip, that had since been stitched. He glanced at the two inspectors out of his one good eye and sat down, silently waiting.

"Your friend Broad has admitted to the killing of the man Grey, who was found at Nietrop building," began Swart, "so you might as well tell us your side of the story. We know most of it already and we know you are in cahoots with him."

"He's not my friend," stated Rose defiantly.

"O.K. Maybe not now," said Noble in turn, "So you had a fall out, but before that you were close. Admit it, I want to hear about then."

"Who is Grey? What about the money? When did you carry him to the offices of W.E.A.R., and why? Broad has admitted a lot to us, Rose, now we want to hear your side." Swart demanded.

"Broad is a bloody liar if he mentioned me in connection with the killing," blurted Rose, "Who's Grey anyway? I don't know any Grey. That is the truth, I swear."

"What about W.E.A.R. ? Do you know a man named Wimpy? Why did you take Grey to that particular office. Why was that money left behind? Answer me Rose," Yelled Noble.

"I don't know, I tell you, I don't know. I don't know Grey, I don't know about any money, about any office. It's got nothing to do with me. I don't know anything. I don't know Wimpy; I know nothing I tell you. That's all I've got to say." Rose belligerently insisted.

"What were you and Broad fighting about?" Asked Swart.

"We were drunk," was the surly answer.

"Nonsense. The police report of the incident said you had been drinking but were not intoxicated. What was the fight about, Rose?" Swart asked once more.

Rose remained sullen and silent.

"You know we will get to the bottom of this business, we always do in the end," Noble said, "It will go easier for you if you co-operate."

"I got nothing to say to you pigs. What are you going to charge me with? You got absolutely nothing on me." Challenged Rose.

"Take him back to his cell, we are just wasting time. He will find out soon enough how much we have on him." Noble said to the waiting warden.

Later that day, Harry Noble and Blackie Swart were again facing their Chief Superintendent.

"What do you mean by going against my strict instructions? I distinctly told you to shelve the Nietrop case. I instructed you both to get on with the other cases that are piling up. Did I not make myself clear? Maybe you are deaf, or just plain stupid." The Chief was livid, "Insubordination, that's what it is. I won't have it, do you hear. Well what have you got to say for yourselves?"

Noble and Swart felt like errant schoolboys, and writhed under the tongue lashing. They agreed with the Chief and humbly apologised. Harry tried to placate the Chief by telling him that their recent work had resulted in something more than just circumstantial evidence, and that at last they had certain new and hard facts that almost completed the case. They told how they had interrogated both Rose and Broad, and had managed to set them against one another.

Noble sought the Chief's approval to reopen the case officially, and further requested his permission to release Rose, but not Broad. By doing so, Harry hoped that Broad would be so incensed that he would tell the whole truth about their involvement in the case. The substantial information that the detectives had produced, and their intended immediate investigative procedures had mollified the Superintendent to some extent. He agreed to their re-opening the case, but warned them in no uncertain terms that he would in future not look kindly on their going against his orders.

Harry's plan worked to perfection. When Broad found out that Rose had been set free, and that he had been left to take the rap, he could not wait to tell the detectives the whole story. Broad explained how Rose had got to hear about Wilson's money through his girlfriend Noreen, and how Rose had planned for them to attack Wilson in his office at Nietrop building, tie him up and make off with the money. Broad also told of how the sudden and often appearance of Grey, known to them as Wimpy, had seemed to them ominous. How Rose had instructed him to temporarily remove Wimpy from the equation, with the resultant accident fiasco that the detectives already knew about. Broad completed his statement by revealing how he and Rose had watched how Wilson had been forbidden entry to Nietrop building on the fourth of September. That was the very date they had decided upon to attack Wilson for his money, and therefore had missed their chance.

Noble wanted clarification of Grey's supposed threat to their scheme if he was only a tenant of the first floor? Broad explained that they, Rose and Broad, did not know for certain if Wimpy, a.k.a, Grey knew about the money. But the fact that Wimpy, a.k.a. Grey was constantly in and out of the building at such odd times, and in addition he, Broad, had bumped into him on a number of occasions on the fourth floor, made them suspicious. They had decided to take him out so that they were assured of a free hand.

"O.K.Broad, here's the deal," Said Noble, "If we arrest Rose as an accessory to the killing of Grey, then you will automatically be for the high jump for the actual killing. We said we would help you if you helped us, so here is what we will do. We let Rose go free, and we book you for culpable homicide. That way you will get off with a sentence of five years. With good behavior, you can be out in a year or two "That's a bit hard. Me suffering for what was really Rose's plan." Grumbled Broad.

"That's the way it's going to be Broad You should be grateful that we are letting you dodge the murder one charge." Said Noble, terminating the interview.

CHAPTER 17

Harry Noble made a new list as a result of the facts they had recently acquired. The list now read:-

1   Grey, Wimpy, the dead man and the accident victim were one and the same.

2   Grey did not have the money with him at the time of the accident.

3   Or—Grey already had the money in the office when the accident occurred.

4   Or—Grey was not injured to the extent that he was unable to obtain the money after the accident.

5   Whatever the case, the money came from the fourth floor office leased by Wilson. As evidenced by the scaffolding found in the service shaft.

6   Wilson worked at the city council. Council denies any money loss. [However I personally am convinced that the money originated from the municipal source.]

7   Broad's confession implicated Rose as the mastermind behind their scheme. But apart from the accident sequence, Neither Broad or Rose had any further part in Wilson losing the money.

8   Broad's confession ends the case of the mystery of the death of Grey.

9   Obviously the money was the root cause of the chain of events.

10 The case can be closed once the ownership of the money established.

As far as Harry was concerned, the finding of the origin of the money was all that was needed to close the case completely. The only clue he had was the connection of Wilson to the City Council. He returned there to further his enquiry. It proved to be an uphill battle; the municipal authorities were not amenable to any suggestion of Wilson's wrong doing. In spite of the facts Noble was able to place before them, they would not consider any slight upon Wilson's good name. The praise for the man, his ethics, his honesty, his attention to detail, his expertise was too good to be true. No matter how persuasive Noble's presentation of the facts of the case, or the premis of Wilson's probable embezzlement, senior management refused to entertain any negative thought of the late Mr. Wilson.

Harry decided upon a different approach. He would tackle the female staff again, this time he would try and find a possible romantic link, or sexual indiscretion. Such a link might help to beak down the picture of the saint like character of Wilson, the management insisted upon.

He got half way through questioning the female staff, when one of the girls from accounts said she had often seen Wilson speaking to a filing clerk, which under normal circumstances, he, Wilson, would have no work related need to do so. This surprised Noble, as he had already interviewed a Mrs. Stannard of filing who had said she only knew Wilson by sight, and other than greeting him on occasion, they had no contact. Noble mentioned this to the girl from accounts.

The girl giggled and replied, "Oh, not Mrs. Straitlaced Stannard, I'm talking about Noreen Freebit."

No one had previously mentioned a second filing clerk, nor mentioned anyone named Noreen Freebit. Noble also remembered, Broad had mentioned, that Rose had a girlfriend named Noreen. This seemed a promising lead and further questioning produced the fact that Noreen had been off sick for two weeks, and no—one had thought to mention the fact. Noble obtained Freebit's address from personnel, and went in search of the missing woman. The address turned out to be a very seedy apartment in city central, but it was empty of any Noreen Freebit, sick or otherwise. Enquiries from neighbours elicited the fact that the flat had been close for about a week. Nobody knew where Freebit was to be found. Harry dragged his feet down the flight of stairs, and walked back to his car. "Who would want to be a police officer, what drudgery and tiresome work this was," grumbled Harry to himself.

Back at the station, Harry was sitting over a cup of strong black coffee, and chiding himself at his indulgence. He reckoned his normal intake of caffeine could not be good for his health, and that he must really cut it down. At a desk nearby two vice cops were discussing their recently completed shift. One was saying that he had better fetch the m.o. report on the o.d. they had found at the bus terminus toilets.

"Yeah," replied his colleague, then continued thoughtfully, "A pretty little thing she is. But she won't be for long if she carries on the way she is now. She is damn lucky she is still alive."

Harry ignoring his own advice was filling a second cup of coffee from the urn when the vice cop returned with the medical officers report.

"Here's Noreen Freebits m.o. report, Willy," he said to his partner.

Harry was not really listening, but somehow the name Noreen Freebit penetrated through the jumbled thoughts running through his mind at that moment.

"What!" he shouted.

The two vice cops jumped. Noble came over to them in a rush.

"Who did you say?" he demanded.

"What!" asked Willy, 'What !', asked the other vice cop.

"That m.o. report, whose did you say it was? Noreen somebody?" Harry asked breathlessly, shaking the vice cop by the sleeve.

"That's right," replied Willy Oosthuizen, "Some dolly named Noreen Freebit we picked up at the bus terminus toilets. Overdosed to the gills and in a very bad way. She's in hospital now."

Harry explained that he was in search of a Noreen Freebit in connection with his case, and this might be a stroke of luck. There might be many Noreens, but there could not be too many Freebits. Harry thanked them for the information and rushed off to the hospital.

On his way to the hospital Harry thought how ironical it all was. How often they would spend endless hours, sifting and searching for clues and links without success, then out of the blue, some chance remark made by someone not at all connected to the case in question would provide the missing link. The remark by the vice cop about Freebit for instance. And take the other night, when out if the blue, Harriet had brought up the subject of Grey being missing from his flat. Both those remarks had, in an instant, broken through the stumbling blocks that Harry, and his assistants, had spent hours trying to solve.

At the hospital the ward sister explained that the patient was incapable of being questioned at the moment. It would take a while before she would be competent enough to answer questions. Noble phoned for a constable to take up watch duty at the hospital. The constable was instructed to contact either Swart or himself, as soon as Freebit was able to respond to questioning. Another link in the chain of events, and Noble hoped it would not be a broken one.

CHAPTER 18

Harry's partner had been equally busy and had rounded up as many of Rose's girls as he could find. During the course of his interrogations Blackie found that the girls were somewhat jealous of a certain Noreen that Jack had been romancing.

"Who does she think she is, is what I want to know?" Complained one of the girls heatedly, "Here we are, on our backs for any Tom, Dick Or Harry, and she, high and mighty, only opens her legs for Jack."

"That's right," Interjected another, "You don't see him clipping her across the earhole, and sending her out on the streets to make him a bit of money. That little tart has got Jack round her little finger, or should I say round his little dick."

When Harry received Blackie's report he was elated, a further confirmation of a link between Rose and Freebit. At last the loose ends were coming together. For the first time in days he felt more relaxed and easier in mind, he phoned Harriet.

Harriet Noble picked up the phone "Oh, hello Harry, this is a surprise. I normally only hear from you when you confirm or delay our monthly meeting."

"Yes I know, sweetheart, that was our agreement, but forgive me please, I desperately need a distraction. You are the best distraction I know, and

I wondered, I hoped you might be free for an hour or so this evening?" begged Harry.

"Harry, I don't think it is a good idea. You know what will happen, if you and I meet tonight, only a day or so since our last date. Before you know it, there will be another meeting in another day or two, and soon we will be back where we were, permanently together and arguing and fighting once more."

"I am sure we are past that, Harriet, I'm sure we are more adult now. Would it really be so bad if we together again?" pleaded Harry. He remembered back when they were first married. He was a rising star in the police force then, they were so happy, almost twin souls, even their names were almost identical. Why did it all have to go wrong?

"Please Harry, don't make me feel bad. Your job hasn't changed. There are still the same stresses and strains. I don't think I could take it again, living under the same roof, and knowing your every move. Worrying again, as I used to do, remember, I nearly had a nervous breakdown at that time, it was terrifying."

"It can't be that bad now, can it?" Harry persisted, "quite a number of years have passed since then and I am still here, hale and hearty. So you see, you worried for nothing."

"No my dear, I am sorry, you know I love you, but when we are too close together, your job and the stress that goes with it, well it will just cause us to fight. I'll become a nervous wreck, resenting your job, and pestering you to leave the force, and before you know it, we will be back where we were when we first decided to separate. The present situation is far better. Our monthly get togethers are just perfect. We are always glad to see one another, we always enjoy ourselves, and we hardly ever fight or argue. You have learnt not to talk shop, and without the ever looming presence of your job, I am always left with a feeling of warmth and anticipation for our next meeting."

"I need you now, Harriet,I need to see you, to hold you in my arms. I love you so darling." Harry was feeling desperate, for the first time in days he was free of worry and strain. His progress with the case over the last day or two had left him with a feeling of euphoria, and he wanted to share it with Harriet.

"I know you do dear, but not tonight, my love. Save it till we meet at the end of the month. It is not too long to wait, and remember, I am waiting too. Goodnight Harry, be good." Harriet rang off. Harry Nobles feeling of gaiety and happiness collapsed like a popped balloon. Despondedly he hung up his phone in turn. For a moment a fleeting jealous thought crossed his mind. 'Was there someone else?' He fought the thought down as unworthy, Harriet was not like that. 'Being a damn policeman caused all this,' he thought, not for the first time.

Harry was at a loose end. He made his way to a nearby bar. He very rarely drank on his own. 'Strange,' he thought, 'how a man at a loose end gravitates toward a bar.' The barman welcomed him with his stock greeting, "What will it be, mister." A cold beer and keep them coming, I feel little down tonight, was Harry's request.

After three beers, Harry switched to brandy and water. He was beginning to feel a little better, and more than a little mellow. Other than the occasional red wine he shared with Harriet, he seldom drank alcohol and his system was not used to the mixing of drinks. Gazing inconsequently at the barman, Harry noticed his drooping Mongolian moustache seemed a little fuzzy. Harry blinked his eyes and peered a little closer and, yes, the moustache was getting fuzzier by the second, and what was more, the barman's head seemed to swell and shrink, come forward and then recede. It was most intriguing. "Strange," Harry mumbled aloud. His hand went up to his lower lip, it felt numb. Harry realized that he was more than a little tipsy. He mumbled goodnight to all and sundry, raised his hand in a sort of general salute and slipped off his barstool. He stood for a moment until the room stopped swinging round, and when it finally came to rest, he adopted a very studious and deliberate gate and made his way home to his flat.

Feeling somewhat queasy the next morning, Harry gestured to Blackie to answer the jangling and irritating phone on his desk. It was the constable on duty at the hospital reporting that Freebit was now capable of being questioned and that inspector Dlamini was with her at the moment. Harry was annoyed that the constable had allowed Dlamini in with Freebit before he himself had seen her. He realised, however, that Freebit was originally vices' problem and Dlamini had every right to be there. Noble and Swart left for the hospital.

Noble, nor anyone else on the police roster, knew that Dlamini was a crooked cop who took protection money from a string of minor drug pushers and pimps to turn a blind eye to their operations. Rose was one of these; it was therefore with an ulterior motive that Dlamini was visiting Freebit. When Dlamini first entered the ward Freebit was lucid, but a sniveling and shivering wreck. He knew the hospital would use a cold turkey treatment, to try and wean her of her need for drugs. He wanted her seeming as normal as possible, so that he could organize her transfer to a place of safety. To stabilize her he slipped her a line of cocaine to sniff to settle her nerves. With his contacts, once he had her transferred to a place of safety, he could arrange her release almost immediately. He knew of Rose's infatuation with the girl, and also the risk to Rose if she were to implicate him. Besides, his aid in getting the girl out of the reaches of his colleagues, Dlamini felt, could be worth a Rand or two more from Rose.

When Noble and Swart arrived Dlamini had not yet managed to arrange Freebits discharge. Harry explained his interest in Freebit in connection with the Nietrop case, and that he wanted to question her. The hospital doctor did not object to Harry's request, and nor did Dlamini for fear of tipping his hand. The three policemen went in to confront Freebit. Harry informed her that they required a statement from her, that it would be written down, and that she would be expected to read and sign it as true and accurate. By this time the cocaine had taken a calming effect upon Freebit and she was quite agreeable to comply with Harry's request.

Harry opened his questioning with, "Miss Freebit, I believe you knew Mr. Wilson who was a member of the city treasury department, and that you had met him in the course of your work.?"

"Ye—es, I knew him."

"Office gossip has it that you had more than just a casual acquaintance with him, that you were having an affair?"

"No. He was one of the bigshots. He wouldn't have been interested in me."

"Is it true that he gave you presents from time to time?"

At this question Noreen surreptiously covered her watch on her right wrist with her left hand.

"No he didn't give me gifts."

Harry had noticed her action with a policeman's trained eye, and drew his own conclusions.

"Did Wilson ever boast of having access to a large sum of money, or try to impress you, or attempt to buy your favour?" Was Harry's next question.

"Yes, he did try to impress me with his tales of how rich he was and what he could do for me, but I was not interested. I told him I already had a boyfriend."

"And did you tell your boyfriend about Wilson? What is your boyfriend's name, by the way?"

"His name is Jack Rose, yes I told him, and he said I was to play along with Wilson cause he was my boss, and if I didn't I might lose my job. Jack said I must be friendly enough to keep him interested, if you know what I mean."

"Is that all Jack said, just to keep him interested? Jack didn't express any further interest in Wilson?"

"Oh yes. Every time I saw Jack he asked me what Wilson had been up to, and what he said. And one time, Wilson told me he had money in cash quite nearby, ready for us when we needed it. Wilson was always promising me a good time and boasting about all his money, and Jack said to listen carefully when he spoke about money; he said men like that liked to impress girls, and one never knew when he might say something of interest."

"To true," agreed Harry, "and did he ever talk about where he kept this money? Did he keep it in a bank, or maybe at home, did he say at all?"

Noreen, now at ease and relaxed after her sniff of cocaine, was quite ready to talk. These policemen were nice and friendly and it was easy to talk to them.

"Yes he did as a matter of fact, he said something about having another place quite nearby at Nietrop building. He promised that when he retired in a few months, he and I would take the money and have a real good time. But of course, he died the other day, so I'll never know if he meant it." She lamented.

Harry and Blackie looked meaningfully at one another, and Harry said," Thank you very much, you have been a great help."

Blackie offered her the notes, and she read and signed them, and Dlamini signed as witness. Harry and Blackie took their leave of both Freebit and Dlamini. On their way out Swart said to Noble," Well I reackon that pretty well wraps it all up."

His partner agreed.

Jack Rose had left the police cells in a surly mood. The cops had nothing on him; he had not broken any law in this matter of Grey and the money. He was linked to the death of Grey only through his association with Broad, but no-one could prove he personally had anything to do with the accident that caused Grey's death. But the loss of the money hurt! Because of Broad and his damn motorbike, he, Jack Rose, had lost the money forever. Broad would pay, oh yes, definitely he would pay. Just wait until he gets out of prison, I will show him. Rose made his way back to the area around the bus terminus, where he conducted most of his business with his girls. Once he was back in his old haunts, he decided it might be wise to make himself less recognizable. He went to a men's hairdresser and had his hairstyle changed and his moustache shaved off. Then, with a pair of clear eyeglasses he purchased at a cash and carry store, Rose felt more secure. In his new guise he visited a number of rental agencies until he had found a furnished apartment reasonably priced and which was in a different neighbourhood to his erstwhile address.

Rose then went to Nesbit street, which was the heart of club land near the bus terminal, and where his girls had established their territory. He rounded up the girls and demanded their takings. These totaled to three thousand Rand.

"What is this?" He screamed, "I go away for a few days and this is all you bring in? Do you want to be slapped around again, is that it? C'mon cough it up".

Sheepishly the girls produced another one thousand five hundred from various hiding places.

"That a bit better, not good mind you, but better," grumbled Rose as he handed back a thousand Rand each to the three girls as their share, and kept one thousand five hundred himself.

"Seen Noreen lately?" He asked.

Shirley, who had given Noreen the fix she had desperately needed, told Rose that she had last seen her when she had left her at the bus terminus three days ago. She said she had given Noreen a jab of crystal meth. as she was so desperate. "She was heading for a real high when I left."

"Hells teeth, you gave her meths!! You idiot, she's only ever sniffed powder, and you give her a shot with a needle. Hell she must have passed out completely," railed Rose.

"She seemed o.k. when I left," mumbled Shirley defensively.

Dlamini had dropped Noreen off at her apartment, gave her a little more cocaine and said.

"Don't go off the rails again. Keep cool, and when Rose comes over tonight tell him I want to see him. I'll be at Francescos between eight and ten o'clock. O.K."

CHAPTER 19

It was the end of the month at last, and Harry and Harriet had arrived at Francescos that popular eatery, for dinner and dancing.

"It's very noisy tonight," complained Harriet," I wonder if there's a convention or something going on?"

"Yes it is. There is quite a crowd tonight, I suppose the service will be slower than usual, I hope not." grumbled Harry as he pulled a chair for Harriet at their table. By the purest chance they had been shown to the same table that had been occupied by Grey that fateful night of August the first.

They were enjoying a crayfish cocktail starter and sipping the complimentary glasses of semi-sweet wine, while they waited for their main course of king prawns they had ordered.

"Mm, the crayfish is very good," said Harry, "but will you mind if I leave this white wine, and wait for our usual cabernet to arrive?"

"Of course not, as you know I prefer red myself."

"But don't you see," said a woman's voice "it is absolutely not like her at all."

The sentence had been clearly uttered, just as if the speaker had been sitting between the two of them at their table. Harry and Harriet both sat bolt upright and looked about them, and before they could react, a second voice seemed to float in the air between them, it said;

"Oh I don't know. Phyllis can do some crazy things sometimes, she is such a scatterbrain."

The same phenomen that had amazed Grey on that night he had overheard the conversation between Rose and Broad, was now happening to Harry and Harriet.

"In all this noise, how could one hear a voice so clearly?" wondered Harriet.

"Yes, very strange indeed," agreed Harry as he gazed around the dining room.

After moment he caught Harriet's arm and whispered," I believe it must be those two over there, see them? Those two sitting two tables away from us over there." Harry indicated with a nod of his head.

"You can just see by their actions they are gossiping and spreading scandal," smiled Harriet. Then she had another thought. "I wonder if they can hear us as well. We had better be careful of what we say."

"It is strange that we can hear them so clearly from two tables away, in spite of all this background noise," mused Harry. Then suddenly, as if it had been announced over a loudspeaker, Harry knew how Grey had come to hear about Wilson's cache of money. Grey must have been sitting at this very table when Rose, and whoever he was with, probably Noreen, had discussed the matter whilst sitting at that table over there. Harry was dumbstruck, he was as certain as if it had been cast in stone, that this was the only possible explanation.

"Did you hear what I said?" Harriet's voice broke into his reverie "Your mind has gone off again, thinking of some case or another, I bet. Am I so unattractive that you can't pay attention to me for more than a minute?"

Harry saw the warning signs, pulled himself together and was immediately contrite. "I'm sorry love, my mind did wander a bit, it won't happen again, I promise. You know Harriet, that I love you more than the entire world. This job of mine, random thoughts keep thrusting their way into the front of my mind. I wish I could stop it. These meetings of ours are too precious to me, for me to willingly spoil them. I am really sorry, please forgive me."

Harriet leaned across the table, took his hand and squeezed, "I forgive you just this once. It is so disturbing to be telling you something that I was sure would be interesting, only to see your eyes glaze over, and your mind far away."

Harry felt guilty, he had almost spoilt their evening again, he must watch himself.

There was a smattering of applause as the evening entertainer mounted the small stage and sat down at the piano. He played an opening melody and it did not take long before the first couples were gyrating round the dance floor. Half an hour later, their meal finished, Harry held Harriet close in his arms as they joined the other dancing couples gliding across the floor to the strains of 'Fly me to the moon'

"You know inspector Noble," whispered Harriet in his ear, "I had forgotten just how well you dance."

Harry knew that if he could just keep the status quo, he and Harriet would make love this night.

CHAPTER 20

Dlamini, of vice squad, was off duty and he drove to Francesos restaurant in his Mercedes sport saloon. It was a car no vice squad officer could afford, but Dlamini did not rely on his police pay cheque as his only income; The hush money he received from characters like Rose and others who dealt in drugs padded his bank balance very satisfactorily. They paid him handsomely to turn a blind eye to their various nefarious doings, and hated him for the privilege. Dlamini, on the other hand, took great delight in putting the screws on them, and relished the pain they evinced each time he demanded payment.

He was at Francescos to meet Rose as he had arranged with Noreen. Rose would know to bring his payoff. A good percentage that Rose would be taking off his girls would now pass on to Dlamini. This month these overheads would make a big hole in his profits, in as much as he had spent almost a month in goal. His absence from his usual trading haunts would have left him somewhat short on funds and Dlamini knew that Rose would whinge bitterly about the payment. Dlamini smiled to himself in anticipation of the power he possessed to bend Rose to his slightest whim.

Rose had more than Dlamini's bribe to worry about, other dealers on whose turf he had been poaching lately were getting increasingly agitated. He would have to find someone to replace Broad who usually acted as his body guard. The weight of his worries hung heavily on his shoulders, as he slouched round shouldered into Francescos bar. With his new hairstyle, shaven features, newly acquired spectacles and hangdog manner, Dlamini did not at first recognize him. It was only when Rose slipped onto the corner seat alongside the inspector did he realise it was Rose. Dlamini ordered brandies for them both and waited for them to be served before he spoke.

"So how does it feel to be a free citizen once more and able to pay your way?" Asked Dlamini as he held out his open palm.

"Thank God that's over," answered Rose fervently as he passed over the bribe money.

"So why the new look Rose? It's no good trying to hide from us cops. I know so much about your operation and your contacts I can find you any time. What's more I've got so much on you I can pull you in when I feel like it, and you know that for a fact. I know that homicide have suspicions about you, and if I feel there is good enough reason, I can bring you in and hand you over to that department in a blink of an eye." Rose looked at Dlamini askance.

"Don't worry," Dlamini laughed," You are worth more to me on the street than in the cells. By the way, you know I got your girl away from the hospital, and away from the attentions of Noble and Swart. You know that don't you?"

"Yeah, Noreen told me, thanks."

"I reakon it's worth more than just thanks, Rose," Said Dlamini, holding out his palm again.

"Ah cheese ! Dlamini, have a heart," moaned Rose as he hesitantly handed Dlamini another fifty Rand note.

"So they couldn't tie you to those bags of money? Tie, get it, tie you in," Dlamini laughed at his own joke.

"What money?" Rose asked, all pretended innocence.

"You know as well as I do, the bags of money they say was tied to that stiff in Nietrop building."

"I don't know what you are talking about," said Rose, trying to evade the issue.

"C'mon Rose. We both know you had something to do with it", Dlamini insisted. "Anyway, I heard a couple of the murder and robbery guys talking about it the other day. Apparently all that cash is packed in boxes in the evidence room at the station. I just thought to myself that it should be easy to rip that off." Dlamini went on ruminatively.

Rose was suddenly all ears, "What's that you say?"

"I know just how much losing the chance to take that money is hurting you. Like I said, I know much more about you than you think I do, and I thought you might be interested, that's all" Dlamini hinted.

"What are you getting at?" prompted Rose.

"I heard all about the interrogation you underwent. You proved you could hold your tongue over the Nietrop business. Swart and Noble couldn't break you down, so I reakon I can trust you with an idea I have been considering. Besides, I've got enough on you to put you inside for a very long time if you don't tow the line," said Dlamini.

"Suppose I don't like the idea?" Rose objected half heartedly.

"If I say you will like it, you will like it all right, or I'll have your balls for breakfast, you understand. Anyway, as I said you have proved you can hold your tongue when necessary, so listen. Damn it," Dlamini threatened.

Rose was not about to tell Dlamini that he had not had to hold his tongue about anything, as there was really nothing he could have contributed to the solving of the Nietrop case. He was still feeling sore about the loss of the money, and the chance he and Broad had missed. Now suddenly, here was Dlamini with information that strangely excited and interested him.

"What I was thinking," said Dlamini,leaning confidentially close, "was that, now that the Nietrop case has been filed N.F.A., that means no further action, for your information. It will only be a week or two, before the evidence boxes with the money is moved to Police National Headquarters vault for safe keeping, until such time the ownership of the money is factually established, or the statute of limitations runs out. Which ever is the sooner. This plus the fact the Chief Superintendent is due for a months leave, and the guy who will be acting Chief in his absence is a dopey character, who only dreams of his retirement in the very near future. So you see, now is the ideal time to make a move on the money."

Impatiently Rose interrupted, "Cut all this crap and get to the point. I'm not interested in the cop shop's family tree."

"Listen Jackie boy, you've got too much lip, don't you get cocky with me. Just shut up and listen." Dlamini snarled, "What we need to do is to transfer that money to a safe deposit, our safe deposit, you get me? Now I cannot directly be involved, or seen to be involved in any way, but I can help to expedite the paperwork that will get the scheme in motion. I can organize that the goods be delivered to the right handlers, and receive a signed receipt for the goods in transfer, etc."

"So how do I benefit from all this?" Rose asked impatiently.

"You, my friend, will be a member of the armed guard who will arrive in an armoured van to remove the said evidence. Your immediate job will be to obtain a suitable vehicle, paint it with police markings and find two accomplices to complete the act. I will arrange for police uniforms for the three of you and arrange the necessary paperwork you will need. Oh yes, you must get hold of three automatic weapons, such as uzies or similar. It doesn't matter too much as to type, no ones going to notice that much."

"So, what's in it for me?" Rose persisted.

"All the past favours I've done you, I reackon you are the one that owes me. But I am a fair man, and a workman deserves his hire, so I will split with you on a fifty, fifty basis. There is too much risk to be mingy, and in any case there should be more than enough money for both of us," said Dlamini magnanimously.

"I seem to be doing most of the hard graft here, not to mention the risk involved," complained Rose, "how about a sixty forty split?"

"Fifty, fifty, take it or leave it," Dlamini flared, "You will never get a chance like this in your life again, and you know it. Don't you?—Don't you?"

All right, all right, o.k.," Rose agreed, he didn't really mind. He was only too pleased to have a second chance at the money he had given up for lost. They arranged to meet in two weeks and share notes on their respective progress.

Promising a thousand each for their share, Rose quickly found helpers from amongst his shady friends. It was just as easy for him to obtain from an indiscriminate gun dealer, and of course, at a black market price, three automatic weapons, each with a full magazine. These transactions cost Rose a good deal; the van however was priced beyond his means at present. Rose was sitting in his new apartment, trying to think of a way to beg, borrow or steal the hundred and sixty thousand he would require for the purchase of a suitable vehicle. It would not be wise to hi-jack a vehicle because the resultant hue and cry would jeopardize their plans. The telephone rang. Rose picked it up, "Hullo," he said cautiously.

"Rose, said the voice," I want the size of those men you hired."

Rose had never spoken to Dlamini on the phone before and did not recognize his voice.

The question was repeated "Rose, you there? Those helpers you hired, how big are they?"

It could only be Dlamini. Who else would know about the men he had hired. He wondered how Dlamini had got his new phone number, hell, you couldn't trust these police an inch.

"Oh," he said, "biggish guys, about your size I think, but with not such a big gut." Rose could not help taking a dig at Dlamini.

This remark passed right over Dlamini, a sense of humour he did not have. "Fine, two of my spare uniforms should do. You are the problem Jack; the police do not recruit runts like you.

The following day Dlamini phoned again saying he was unable to find a uniform to fit Rose. "You had just better wear a grey suit, can you do that? None of your spiv styles though. Make it conservative, another thing, what size is your head?"

"Six. Why?"

So I can find a suitable cap for you to wear." Dlamini rang off.

Rose still hadn't figured a way to get a van. He had knocked the living shit out of his girls again, telling them to move arse and bring in more cash. He knew though, that his income from this source, plus what he could realise from current drug sales, although adequate for his normal lifestyle, could never produce enough in the short term to procure a van. Desperately looking for a way and means out of this dilemma, Rose eventually came across a service station which had no vans for sale, but did have a service contract with the "Eversure Security Company". By chatting up one of the mechanics, he discovered that a security van came into the garage every two weeks for a service. The van due for service came in the morning, was serviced during the day and picked up the following midday by the security people. Rose made himself known to the garage night watchman, an elderly black man who proved amenable to Jack's suggestion of borrowing a van overnight, for which he, the night watchman would receive five hundred Rand in advance. His only condition was that the van had to be returned no later than five a.m. when he knocked off. All was set van wise, now he must get hold of Dlamini and apprise him of the situation.

One thing Rose did not like to do was contact the police in any shape or form. He had spent the greater part of his life avoiding the police, and it was so ingrained in his awareness that even though he knew that Dlamini was a crooked cop, he could not bring himself to contact him directly. Jacks fertile brain found the solution, his girls were so often arrested for soliciting that they were on first name terms with the vice cops, one of the girls was even friendly with some of the officers. All he had to do was to ask one of the girls to pass a message on to via the cops to officer Dlamini.

It did not take long for a response, "Listen here Rose, I don't take kindly to your sending me instruction via your prossies. It undermines my authority, so just don't do that, you hear. So what do you want?" Said the angered Dlamini.

"Sorry about that, but it was important that I see you urgently." Rose went on to explain his arrangements about the van. He pointed out that their plan would have to coincide with the vehicle service program. Dlamini was certain that, that could be arranged, but, he asked, what would happen if the van was not returned by five a.m.?

"Well, I guess the night watchman will shit himself right up to eight a.m. when the garage opens, then the shit will really hit the fan. But it will take time to sort out what had happened; I suppose it will be nine o'clock before they actually call the police. Then another hour or so for the police to take statements before a search is started.," suggested Rose.

"That's where you are wrong, the police will start an immediate search for the van. The statements and site inspection will be handled by a different team. Still we should have enough time, as long as the paper work does not take too long to process."

They established that the following Wednesday a security van was due for service, so Rose paid the night watchman the promised five hundred Rand and they arranged to pull off their heist on Thursday morning. Dlamini now had to set his part of the plan in motion. Dlamini's first step was to phone his brother-in-law, who worked in the reception office of a bus company, and instruct him to answer the phone on that particular

Thursday morning. Dlamini told his brother-in-law he did not know at
what time the call would come through, so he had better answer all calls
as Lieutenant Neethling. Any other caller would assume they had a wrong
number and would try again.

At nine a.m. on Thursday, just forty-one days after Noble had gazed at
the dead body of Grey, Wilson's millions were about to hit the headlines
again. An "Eversure Security Company" van pulled up at the entrance
of da Gama police precinct building. Two armed uniformed policemen
jumped out and took up positions on either side of the entrance. Both
men were large and grim, however a close observer might have noticed a
certain nervous anxiety about them. A third man dressed in a gray business
suit and wearing a peaked cap with some gold braid festooning the peak
entered the station carrying a clipboard of papers. These were the forms
Dlamini had previously typed out and handed to Rose the night before.
Dlamini, who had conveniently found time to loiter near the entrance,
took the forms from Rose, glanced at them and handed them to the desk
sergeant, saying the while," Something for the Chief, sarge."

The desk sergeant read through the forms which stated that evidence
packages ref. 6531 through to 6540 were to be uplifted to National
headquarters under guard. The forms had to be signed by the station
commander, countersigned by the evidence room duty constable.
Confirmation of the transaction had to be phoned through immediately
to lieutenant Neethling at 012-3203611. The desk sergeant was about to
stand up to take the documents through to the station commander when
Dlamini offered, "I'll take those through if you like?"

"Thanks Dlamini," The desk sergeant handed the forms back to
Dlamini.

The acting station commander, Captain Grant Fairweather was reading
the morning paper and enjoying a morning cup of coffee when Dlamini
knocked on the door.

"Enter," he barked, what now, this early? He hoped that it was not something to upset the quiet routine of his day.

Dlamini entered, stood to attention and said, "Morning sir, just a form that requires your signature, sir."

More red tape thought Fairweather, as he reached for the forms and perused them.

Fairweather looked up, "Get me headquarters on the radio, please Dlamini, I'll need to check this."

For an instant Dlamini's blood turned to ice, the last thing he needed, a call to headquarters would blow his scheme wide open. He pulled himself together, took a deep breath and said, "Excuse me sir, there is a number to phone sir, a lieutenant Neethling, sir."

'Ah yes, I see it," acknowledged the Captain, reaching for the telephone, "Yes, exchange, good morning, get me 102, 320, 3611. Yes that's right, thank you."

Dlamini's brother-in-law's phone rang, and he played his part to perfection.

'Yes," answered Fairweather, "all o.k. this end. I am signing the papers right now. Your van should be on it's way within half an hour, I should think. Good bye lieutenant."

Fairweather signed his name with a flourish and handed the forms back to Dlamini.

"Get this down to the evidence room. Make sure the driver signs a receipt for the goods, and make sure the evidence duty constable signs the release form with the date and time, will you Dlamini."

"Right away sir," Dlamini snapped a smart salute, accepted the forms, saluted again and marched out of the office.

Dlamini instructed Rose to accompany him to the evidence room. As they went down the passage, Dlamini placed his hand on Roses's shoulder and drew him to a stop and said in an aside, "Once you've loaded the boxes and got clear of the police station, drive to the corner of De'villiers street and Orpen avenue, you know where that is? I'll meet you there."

The Nietrop boxes, sealed with cellophane tape, were carried out to the van. One of the constables helping to carry the boxes chattily remarked to Rose that he had quite a long trip ahead, and asked how long did it take.

"Two days," answered Rose, "Its over twenty thousand kilometers, you know. I hope the weather stays cool."

Rose's two accomplices stood on either side of the back door as the constables loaded the boxes, there was a glimmer of a smile upon their faces. It was the first time in their lives that they had police under gunpoint, and although it was only a mock scenario, they enjoyed the feeling of power their borrowed uniforms and the automatic weapons gave them. Once the boxes were loaded, the two accomplices climbed into the back of the van, and Rose resumed the driver position. Just as Rose was slowly pulling out into the stream of traffic, another constable ran out of the station and called to him.

"Hey Eversure! We've just received a report that one of your vans has been stolen, not yours is it?"

Rose felt the colour draining from his face, but he had the presence of mind to respond with, "Very funny, sure I stole the van and brought it straight to you." With a laugh he managed to make sound less than a death rattle, he waved his hand and joined the traffic flow.

As soon as he had rounded a corner, Rose stopped the van once more. He did not trust anyone in the back with all that loot.

He opened the back door and yelled at his accomplices, "Hurry up now, everyone in front."

The corner of De'villiers and Orpen, being in a residential area, was quiet that time of the morning, most residents having left for work. Dlamini was parked, waiting for them. He had not used a police vehicle, it would have been too conspicuous, he had used his private Mercedes instead. Rose, his two assistants and Dlamini transferred the boxes to the Mercedes.

"O.k." said Dlamini, "Here's ten thousand, pay off the two goons, then dump the van somewhere and meet me at Francescos."

"No way," cried Rose, "I don't loose sight of that cash, where it goes I go."

"Don't be a fool," snarled Dlamini, "we've got to do it this way. Do as I say."

Rose reached into the van, grabbed one of the automatic weapons. "Just stay where you are."

"Hey !" shouted one of the accomplices, "What gives? We don't want any rough stuff. Just give us our money and we're out of here."

Rose threw the bundle of notes toward them without taking his eyes off Dlamini. Both goons started forward to grab the money, and one of them staggered against Rose. Dlamini acted instantly, drawing his pistol he loosed off a shot toward Rose and jumped into the Mercedes. Rose dropped at the sound of the shot and let fly with a burst of automatic fire. A line of bullet holes stitched across the side of the Merc. as it accelerated away, leaving a smell of burning rubber. The car suddenly swerved, mounted the opposite sidewalk and smashed into an ornamental tree. Rose's erstwhile helpers lost no time in grabbing the fallen bundle of notes and disappearing round the corner as fast as they could move. It was all over in a seconds, though to Rose it seemed as if all had taken place in slow motion. It was the first time he had fired a shot at any living thing, and although he was in shock, he experienced a strange sense of power. He wondered if Dlamini was dead, he knew he had to go over to the car and check, but for the moment he felt rooted to the spot, he could not bring himself to move. What if he had killed Dlamini, he had better make himself scarce. For the first time in a week he never gave thought to the money now lying in the back of the Mercedes close at hand

A few of those of the nearby population of this leafy, quiet suburb, who had not departed for work in the city, were alarmed by the sound of shots and the subsequent crash of tortured metal. A pensioner couple and two servant women were attracted to the scene. With hands clasped to mouths, and goggling eyes, they looked at Rose askance. The two servants in identical beige house coats were uttering a continuous high pitched whimper. The pensioner couple moved closer together and held each other in a nervous embrace. Rose with staring look, and still holding the weapon in his gloved hands, turned toward them with, what the onlookers took to be a threatening move. Panic set in and one and all beat a hasty retreat. Within a minute Rose found himself in sole possession of the area once more. The sudden appearance and equally sudden disappearance of the spectators shocked Rose out of his trance like condition. He would have to move quickly, someone was sure to phone the police.

The inbred fear of the police galvanized Rose into action. He rushed over to the car ; Dlamini was slumped over the steering wheel dead. The bloody mess that once was his dead testified to this. Rose's first thought was to pull Dlamini out of the car and drive away, however a glance at the front end showed the wheels badly askew. Rose pulled two of the boxes out of the car and ran to the van, hesitated a moment, then decided that using the van for a getaway was too dangerous. He looked wildly about the empty street lined with up—market private homes situated well back into their grounds. Most of the homes were bordered by high walls and, here and there, an occasional picket fence or hedge. All the homes boasted manicured lawns, flower beds and trees. Rose ran round the corner into Orpen avenue. A bus shelter stood some fifty metres from the corner. The bus shelter decided him and it took three trips to carry six cartons to the bus stop. Rose was about to fetch the another two cartons when a bus appeared a block down. He had no option, he would just have to be satisfied with what he had.

The bus conductor assisted Rose in loading the boxes onto the bus, and the bus moved off. At that moment a police car, with sirens blaring, came down the avenue at speed, and skidded round the corner into De'villiers street. Rose watched the car go by with satisfaction, he had pulled a fast one on the police again and he felt again that surge of power. Now that the immediate fear of imminent arrest had receded, he began to feel exhilarated. He remembered the feel of the weapon bucking in his grip as he had fired the shots, and it gave him a feeling of invulnerability. He had eliminated any need to share the money, he did not have it all, but at least he had the lions share. The money was his at last. He felt no remorse at the killing of Dlamini.

"How far are you going?" Asked the conductor, interrupting his thoughts.

"City terminus," said Rose.

"Three Rand please," said the conductor as he handed Rose a punched ticket.

CHAPTER 21

The robbery of the evidence boxes from Da Gama police station of all places was, to say the least, an embarrassment to the law department. The blatant daylight robbery followed by the discovery of Dlamini's bizarre murder stunned the entire precinct. The acting station superintendent, Captain Fairweather, was almost in a state of panic. How could such a disaster have happened to him on the eve of his retirement? He could see his retirement being deferred until this robbery and murder had been resolved, and the killer of one of their own brought to justice. For the first time in an uneventful and placid career, spent studiously avoiding any controversial issue, and always manipulating situations so as to appear in the best light, Fairweather found himself in the uncomfortable position of having to take serious responsibility. Inexperienced and unable to control such an emergency, he was issuing contradicting orders and making gross errors of judgement.

The only cool head at Da Gama was that of Harry Noble. He figured that the only person, other than Blackie Swart, the holidaying station commander, Captain Watson and himself, who knew the actual contents of the evidence boxes was Dlamini. This by virtue of his presence when they had interrogated Noreen Freebit. He remembered that he and Swart had discussed the case with Dlamini before they had confronted Freebit. He could not recall whether the contents of the evidence boxes had been mentioned at the time, but Dlamini certainly knew of the existence of the Nietrop case money. The ensuing event of the robbery, and Dlamini's actions during and just after the robbery had taken place, made him suspicious. Both he and Swart had been in their office at the time of the robbery, and he remembered noticing Dlamini hanging about the front office. Immediately after the robbery when the shooting at the corner of De'villiers street and Orpen avenue had been reported, the duty officers had mustered in the bull room to receive their orders. Dlamini, despite being on duty, was not at that meeting. It was shortly after that that Dlamini's death had been reported. Noble also remembered, from reading the Rose and Broad dossiers, that Dlamini had also known both criminals.

Noble tried to gain Captain Fairweathers attention to apprise him of these facts and his, Nobles, suspicions. Fairweather was in no state to listen to anyone and brushed Noble aside with," Not now Noble, can't you see we have a crisis on our hands. I've no time to listen to your theories at the moment."

Noble left the station in search of Rose. He thought a conversation with Rose might prove very interesting.

Jack Rose found himself standing on the sidewalk at the busy bus terminus, surrounded by the six evidence boxes, and feeling trapped by them. They were too bulky to carry together, and too valuable to leave unattended on the sidewalk while he searched for a taxi. It was a classic poor little rich boy situation, surrounded by millions, yet unable to do anything.

Noble was returning from Roses old address, Gardens, Gladhope road, Mountain view, where he had drawn blank. He was now in search of Rose's girls. Rose seemed to have vanished into thin air, and he thought that his prostitutes were certain to have an idea where he could be found. It was late in the day, but early for Rose's girls whose working day only started at nine in the evening. He would catch them at their most vulnerable time.

A person had to sleep, eat, buy the necessities of life, and to accomplish any of these one had to contact people. Besides which, Rose's girls were all users, and who better to supply them with their needs, than Rose. So ran Noble's thoughts as he turned into Terminus Street. Halfway down the street he noticed a man standing at a bus stop and at his feet a number of very distinctive evidence boxes. Rose he did not recognize because of his altered appearance. Harry could not believe his eyes. He instinctively braked his car, causing a moment of anguish for the driver following, The driver of this oncoming car cursed Harry roundly and hooted frantically. Harry pulled over to the side and double parked. This action caused a further upheaval in the traffic flow, but Rose, on the opposite of the street was so engrossed with his problem regarding the boxes, that he noticed nothing of the minor traffic drama.

Noble jaywalked across the busy street to the mans side, and only then did he realise that it was Rose himself.

"Mr. Rose, how fortuitously met. I've been looking for you for quite sometime."

"I've been around," said Rose, nervously edging in front of the boxes in the vain hope that Noble would not see them.

"You and I need a little talk, how about me driving you downtown for a little discussion," invited Harry Noble.

The last place Rose wanted to be was at the very police station that he, posing as a security man, had so recently left.

"Er, I,m waiting for a taxi," blurted Rose, "I've an urgent meeting to attend."

"I'm sure you have, but my need is greater than yours." responded Noble, "Come along."

It was then that Rose made a very rash move. In desperation he rushed at Noble and pushed him off the sidewalk and into the path of the oncoming traffic. Noble stumbled and fell; there was a screeching of brakes. Rose grabbed hastily for the boxes, trying to gather them all at once. One box slipped from his grip and landing on its corner on the sidewalk it, the adhesive tape burst loose, a selection of one hundred and two hundred Rand notes spilled out. Whereupon the perennial city breezes caught them up and sent a cloud of currency fluttering away. The passing pedestrians hesitated only a moment. They were quick to seize the opportunity. There was a rush to gather up as much money as quickly as possible.

Rose caught between his greed to rescue the spilled notes, his concern for the rest of the boxes, and his urgent need to escape, was unable to make a positive move in any direction. Noble recovering from his fall and near miss from being run over by a car that had just stopped in time, rolled over onto his knees, lurched onto the sidewalk and wrestled Rose down to the ground, and with police trained skill, handcuffed Rose's hands behind his back.

A certain amount of the loose money inevitably disappeared amongst the crowd. A few upright law abiding citizens gathered up the rest and brought it back to Noble. Harry confirmed his status by flashing his police badge and deputized two men to place the boxes into his car, while he manhandled Rose across the street and into the back seat.

'I say inspector, give me a break," Whinged Rose, "Let's make a deal there's plenty to go round. How about it inspector?"

"Shut up," shouted Noble, he had to think. He was bruised and sore, his clothes were torn and dirty and in a mess, was it all worth the candle? For the second time since the start of the Nietrop case he was in a position where there was a pile of unaccounted for money in his grasp. He remembered how he had been tempted the first time and how he had thought better of it, what of the present? The exertions of the past few minutes had left him tired and dispirited. He looked down at his ruined suit. Why should he have to run such risks? He had only just escaped with his life under the wheels of a car. This was the sort of risk and danger that had worried Harriet into making the break with him. How much better life would be with Harriet if he had the money and could give up this thankless job. 'Yes', he said to himself, 'I was once a keen and dedicated cop, but no more. The glamour has worn off, these days the job is just a drag.' This latter thought led him to a decision that was to regret in the days to come.

Unlike the spirit of urgency that usually attended a police car leaving the scene, Harry drove slowly away. An hour later they were still in the car, driving aimlessly round the city. The radio was squawking continuously about the ongoing search for Dlamini's killer while Noble, and the very killer the police were looking for, were idling away the hours. The fact that they had not gone directly to the police station had not missed Roses' notice. He began to have a glimmer of hope. Once it became obvious that Noble had something troubling his mind, the aimless journey they were taking confirmed this line of thought, Rose was even more certain of a chance to change his fortune for the better. Rose began again to broach the possibility of a deal, but received no response from the inspector. Finally Noble drove to a deserted stretch of beach on the outskirts of the city and parked.

For a moment Noble's mind shied away from the dangerous line of thought he had been thinking. Instead his mind brought to the fore the presence of the beach, and the sound of the breaking waves. It was strange how one's life was regimented. He had lived in this coastal city of East Bay most of his life and yet, after his teen years, he hardly ever went near the beach, or swam in the ocean. The only time he spent near the water when he and Harriet would on an occasional summer evening come and watch the phosphorus glinting and simmering in the breaking waves. Dear Harriet, oh how much he loved her. Could having the money bring her back to him?

This last fleeting thought brought Harry crashing back to the present. How could he keep Rose quiet if he turned him in and kept the money for himself? Rose would be certain to implicate him, what had he to lose; he was going to be charged with Dlamini's murder that was for certain. After all it was only he who could have killed Dlamini and left the murder scene with the money. He could possibly buy Roses' silence in payment for allowing him his freedom. But what would happen when Rose was caught again, as he certainly would be eventually? Would he then shop Noble for his action? He probably would, for once again, what had Rose to gain by keeping quiet? Then again, would anyone believe Rose, It would be his word against that of a police officer, an officer of good repute and in good standing. After all, if the whole city council could believe Wilson was incapable of any wrong doing, why should the police authorities think any less of a favourite police inspector? He had been a good cop all his life, risen through the ranks, but where had it got him? More than half his life was behind him and what did the future hold? At his age the best he could hope for was a promotion to chief inspector rank. Police work had already cost him his marriage, with little hope of reconciliation. That money in the back of the car could mean all the difference to him. He had let the chance slip before; he could not let that happen again. All this rationalization helped Noble make the move that would cost him his self respect and peace of mind. His desire for the chance to re-unite with Harriet and resume married life was the deciding factor. If he kept the money he could take an early retirement, but only in a year or so, it must not be too sudden, it might look suspicious. Of course it would be foolish to splash money around, but he could invest the money, live modestly, and maybe, no it would be a certainty. Harriet would come back to him if he left the force. A cold shiver crept down his spine as another thought crossed his mind. Harriet must never learn where the money came from.

Noble got out of the car and opened the boot. He opened the five sealed boxes, and the one that had burst open on the street. All, but the one that had broken open, were full, and even it was nine tenths full. Noble remembered, when he and Blackie had packed the boxes at Nietrop building, that there was four hundred and eighty thousand Rand in each box, and it didn't look as if the contents had been disturbed. That meant that there was approximately two million eight hundred thousand lying in the boot of the police car, give or take the thousand or two that may have blown away. It was a lot less than the original amount they had counted, and he wondered what had happened to the other four boxes. He gazed at what was left in the car. "It is more than enough for me," thought Harry. He finally made up his mind to keep the money, and now he had to decide upon Rose's fate. A sneaking thought crept unbidden into his mind, 'Shoot Rose. If rose was found head from a bullet wound, it would be thought that he had been hit in the shoot out with Dlamini and died from the wound whilst trying to escape.' Noble blanched at the way his mind was working. He could never stoop to killing; it was just not in his makeup. His subconscious mind struggled to force its way into the forefront of Nobles thinking, it told him that the wisest move was to hand the money and Rose over to the authorities. His own greed as he gazed at the money, overruled his rational thought, and Noble slammed the boot closed and went round to the back door of the car.

"Rose I've come to a decision that has been very difficult for me to make. Dlamini was no friend of mine and, for reasons of my own, I'm glad you killed him." Noble blatantly lied, "you know that if I take you in you will be charged with murder one. In other words you are facing a life sentence. Because it was a cop you killed the judge will pass a full life sentence with no chance of repeal or time off for good behavior. What is more, a cop killer is considered lower than the lowest scum, and the prison service will use the slightest misdemeanor on your part to increase your sentence. If I take you in, you will never be a free man again. Rose, you will die in goal, you realise that, don't you?"

Rose sensed from Nobles manner that some sort of offer was going to be made. He waited with bated breath. Maybe this would be his lucky day.

Noble said, "Because you did me a favour in bumping off Dlamini, I am going to return that favour, but with certain conditions. I will let you go provided you keep your mouth shut and provided you leave this city and never come back. Do you understand?"

Rose perked up, "Yes I understand, and thank you. I have enough money in those boxes—" Noble never got to hear what Rose intended to do with the money, he interrupted Rose. "Oh no my friend, that money is state evidence and stays with me."

Typical cop thought Rose, just as crooked as Dlamini. They are all the same the bastards.

"Have a heart inspector, you can't expect me to move without a penny," wheedled Rose.

Noble released Rose from the handcuffs.

"Now go!! And keep going or you will certainly end up as a permanent guest in the Presidents suite for life. The police don't take kindly to a murderer of a brother officer."

"So you think I should thank you. You and all cops are the same, all crooked, the lot of you," riled the unrepentant Rose, "You are stealing my money, you've got to give me some money so I can get away."

"Forget it Rose, get going I said," and with that Noble got back into the car and sped away.

In frustration and hatred Rose bent down and grasping a handful of beach sand, threw it fruitlessly after the departing car.

It was just getting dark when Noble arrived back in the city. He drove straight to his apartment and transferred the boxes to his bedroom, where he placed them temporarily in the drawers of a chest of drawers. He then went through to the kitchen, opened the refrigerator and took out a beer. In the lounge he sank into an easy chair and thought back over his recent behavior. He knew that he was by no means in an ideal situation, but eventually the furore of Nietrop case and the recent robbery would die down. Even at the moment the emphasis was on the Dlamini murder, and directed toward finding the killer rather than the theft of the evidence boxes, and the money contained therein. He just had to play it quietly and keep a low profile until things were quiet again. In the mean time he would invest the money; it should give him a return of about twenty eight thousand a month, he estimated. 'That should please Harriet,' he thought, little realizing that money was the least important item in winning Harriet back. Tired out after the incidents of the day, he fell asleep where he was in the easy chair.

The next morning Harry awoke stiff from sleeping in the chair, and full of aches and pains and bruises from his fall in front of the car. He took clean clothes from his wardrobe, and after a leisurely shower, he shaved and dressed and felt much better. He had awoken early, so had more than enough time before he was due at the station. While eating a breakfast of Wheatbix and milk, and sipping a drink of fresh orange juice, Harry thought once again about the money. He must find a more secure place to hide it, the chest of drawers was not a wise choice. It was remotely possible that Harriet may have some reason to fiddle in there, in spite of their separation; she still occasionally came to his apartment. He would do something about it when he returned from work this evening. Harry left for the police station.

The police station was still in a state of turmoil and confusion. Fairweathers hasty and confused orders were doing nothing for the morale of the station staff. Everyone was jumpy and irritable. Noble slipped quietly and unobtrusively into his office. His partner Blackie

Swart was nowhere to be seen. Harry glanced at his desk and found a note that Blackie had left, that said that Fairweather needed to see him. Harry went upstairs.

Fairweather was angry, "Where the hell were you yesterday, and why did you not keep the station informed of your movements? How can I be expected to run a station if I can't even contact my officers?"

Harry lied, "I am sorry sir, I tried, but could not get through on the radio. It was continually busy dealing with the search for Dlamini's killer." He told Fairweather that he had been out looking for a man named Rose in connection with the killing and the station robbery. Harry then explained his theory regarding the money, Dlamini's actions prior to his murder and the fact that Dlamini was privy to the information regarding the contents of the boxes, and the details of the Nietrop case. He described in detail what he knew about Rose's drug dealing and Dlamini's interest in Rose on this account.

"So you suspect that Dlamini may have been involved in the station robbery as an inside accomplice, do you," muse Fair-weather," Well put it on record in your daily report. And in future make sure you abide by the rules and correct procedure. In future report your movements at all times. I'll have something to say to your returning commander, you can be sure of that. He has been recalled from leave and will be back tomorrow. You are dismissed."

"Wow, Fairweather is in a stinking mood, isn't he?" Harry remarked to Blackie upon his return to their office.

"Sure is," agreed Blackie," You should have been here yesterday, he was really performing and causing chaos. He had everyone running this way and that over the Dlamini killing. I guess he is worried that it might have a detrimental effect on his retirement package. Anyway, thank God our regular chief will be back tomorrow."

"Yeah, so I hear. Thank goodness for that," was Harry's heartfelt reply.

CHAPTER 22

The day after Captain Watson returned to duty, he called together the entire station complement. The gist of his address was that the handling of the transfer of the Nietrop evidence to H.Q., though generally in accordance with normal procedure, was precedential in the use of a private security company van for the transport of the evidence. In view of this fact an internal departmental enquiry would be instituted. In the meantime, police work would proceed with diligence as usual, and the search for Dlamini's killer maintained as a priority. The Chief concluded by saying, "Last but not least, discussion of this matter will cease as of this minute, and that is an order. None of you will speak of this matter between yourselves, or with any outsider, unless it is pertinent to the case. You will certainly not speak to the press. Is that understood? Any public statement will made by me, and by me alone. Is that clear to everyone?"

"Yes sir," they all responded in unison, and they were dismissed back to their posts.

Harry was relieved to find that the death of Dlamini, and the concerted effort to find the killer was the prime interest of the station at the moment. The matter of the six boxes that had disappeared from the scene at Devilliers street and Orpen Avenue had not been mentioned at all. This suited Harry admirably; the lack of interest in the money gave him a false sense of security. But in his heart he knew he had betrayed his fellow officers and his calling. He tried to shrug away his guilt and get on with his work.

He asked Blackie, "Did the finger print people find any prints on the van, or the weapon that had been fired."

"They found plenty of prints in the van and on some weapons, but none on the steering wheel, or the drivers side. Nor on the weapon that had been fired, and found lying in the street. The desk sergeant reported that the driver had been wearing gloves when he delivered the paperwork. In view of this, it is assumed that the driver was responsible for the killing. The other prints probably belong to the other men that accompanied the van as guards. The prints that remained on the evidence boxes found in the back of Dlamini's car proved to be those of Dlamini himself, and of the constables that helped to load the boxes in the first place. Also, a few of the prints checked out with those found in the vehicle, probably of the guard assistants. There is no evidence pointing to the whereabouts of the missing evidence boxes." Explained Blackie.

"Uh—huh," muttered Noble absentmindedly as he wrote in his notebook.

There followed a silence as both men continued with their work. Fifteen minutes later Noble again asked Blackie if they had found any prints on the van or the gun.

"What's the matter, you o.k.?" Asked Swart.

"Why?" noble was surprised.

"Why! Because I told you, not more than a minute or so ago, about the prints. Don't tell me you didn't hear me!"

"Uh no—I don't recall you telling me. Did you? I am sorry, I am not feeling myself. I just can't seem to concentrate," Harry apologised.

Swart repeated what he had told him earlier, and Harry again apologised, saying his mind must have gone blank.

Later that day Swart noticed a further discrepancy in his partner's behavior Noble had passed a document through to records that should have borne his clearance signature. Noble again apologised for his error and carelessness. In the days that followed, Nobles carelessness, and normally meticulous work ethic, degenerated to such an extent that it became obvious. The chief superintendent finally had him on the carpet.

"I'm sorry Harry. You know we can't allow carelessness and slovenliness creep into departmental work. Maybe you are suffering from an overload. I am booking you off for a weeks rest, and I mean rest. I think also you should have a doctor give you a once over"

"No argument Harry", as Harry tried to refuse," A week off and that's final. Have a good rest," pontificated the chief.

Harry's drop in efficiency necessitated his weeks leave, but it transpired to be the worst possible decision. With nothing to do but think about the wretched money, and worry about his moral dilemma, Harry's nerves went from bad to worse. He had only been on leave for two days when tension and worry caused his following moves to border on the brink of insanity. The worry about the money so superficially hidden, forced him into action. He had to find an effective hiding place, but where? In his overwrought mind he saw the money as openly exposed in his apartment, and that all and sundry would know his secret by simply looking through his windows and know that he had hidden the money in his chest of drawers. This irrational fear of discovery led him to lock all his doors, even the inter-leading doors. Then he drew the curtains, and in addition, hammered some cardboard sheeting cross the window frames. All this, despite the fact that his apartment was on the first floor, and no—one could look into it from street level. With the windows blacked out, and all the doors locked, the apartment was as dark as a mine shaft. That his actions were strange in the extreme did not dawn upon Harry, as he switched on the lights.

He decided to hide the money in the base of his sofa. In order to do this, he had to unlock the bedroom door, remove the boxes from the chest of drawers and slide them into the passage. Then he locked the bedroom door once more. He slid the boxes along the passage to the lounge entrance, where he again had to unlock a door, slide the boxes into the lounge and lock the door again. Harry upturned the sofa, then realized that he would require a hammer and tool to remove the staples that held the hessian covering to the base of the sofa. He again unlocked the lounge door, passed through and relocked it, moved down the passage and unlocked the kitchen door. In the kitchen he first relocked the door, then pulled open the dresser drawer from which he extracted a hammer and a screwdriver. He then repeated the whole process on his returning to the lounge.

Noble pulled one of the boxes toward him, broke the sealing tape, and sat for a moment gazing at the exposed notes. His greed momentarily satisfied by the sight of the notes, he commenced knocking the staples loose and removed the hessian cover from the underside of the sofa. He stuffed the notes deep between the springs of the seat of the sofa. To his consternation he found that the seat would only hold the contents of three of the boxes, a total of one million four hundred and forty thousand Rand. He resealed the base of the sofa, righted it and pushed it back into its original position. 'What of the balance, the other one million four hundred thousand. No it wasn't that much, some was lost on the street, but near enough. Where do I hide the balance?' He sat with his head in his hands, rocking his body back and forth, as he wrestled with his thoughts. Harry's mind could not cope, he felt pressure building up in his skull, there was a severe headache, and a spasm of dizziness beset him.

What was happening to him, his head was pulsating, he desperately felt the need for fresh air. Starting up, he fumbled at the door lock, threw the lounge door open, and gaspingly made his way to the front door. The front door was also locked but the key was not in the lock. Harry shouted out in frustration," Where's the bloody key? I'm sure I had it a moment ago. Where did I put it?" He fumbled through his pockets and found his bunch of car keys. How could he have forgotten that, the front door keys was always attached to his car keys, had been for years. His mind really must be slipping. Harry opened the door, burst out into the corridor, rushed down the stairs and out into the open air.

Harry leaned against the side of the building, drawing in deep breaths of fresh air. Slowly his equanimity returned and the pressure in his head and the headache subsided. He thought,' The damn money, I wish I had never seen the damn stuff. Now I'm stuck with it, I can't hand it in without incriminating myself. I've chased Rose out of town, I won't be able to find him easily to re-arrest him, and so account for having the money. What a mess! ! Hell, I need a drink. 'His thought was father to the deed, and he moved off to a nearby bar without bothering to lock his front door. It was the second time in as many weeks that he had visited a bar, but Harry was beyond noticing the change in his habits, nor the fact that it was mid afternoon.

Through a fog Harry heard a persistent voice," Harry, Harry, wake up. Oh Harry please wake up. Come-on wake up."

He opened one eye a crack, and immediately closed it tight again. For some reason he was on a ship. He must be, why else was the floor swaying that way? He suddenly felt bile in his throat and rolling over, retched on the carpet.

"Oh hell, Harry," the voice said," What a mess! Come on, I'll help you. Lean against me and I'll help you up."

Harry knew that voice. Where had he heard it before? He wished it wasn't so persistent, he wished it would just leave him alone. He did not want to move, he just wanted to lie quietly in his misery. 'OO—OER, he felt terrible.'

Harriet managed to manhandle Harry up onto the sofa. Slipped off his shirt and wiped him down with a damp cloth. Leaving him comatose, Harriet next filled a basin with warm water, splashed in some Dettol disinfectant, and proceeded to clean up the messed lounge carpet. She then made herself a cup of tea and sat down next to Harry and gazed in wonderment at the blacked out windows and the evidence boxes lying on the floor. There was nothing more she could do at present, she would just have to wait until Harry had slept it off, then maybe she could expect an explanation.

She sat quietly and gazed sadly at the awards lining the mantle, most of them received by Harry as a young rookie cop. Flushed with enthusiasm for his chosen profession, Harry had won many awards for his keenness and ability at the police college. There were also one or two that attested to Harry's heroism for deeds above and beyond the call of duty. One photograph particularly stood out. It showed Harry standing at attention in full ceremonial dress, receiving a medal from the commissioner in chief of the National police force. Draped over the frame of the photograph was the actual medal he had received. Harriet wistfully remembered how proud she had been on that day. She turned and looked down at the sleeping form beside her and sighed. He looked a sorry defeated soul, so unlike the upright purposeful policeman that she knew so well. She wondered what could have caused this distressing and disappointing behavior.

Eventually Harry stirred and struggled to sit upright.

"So, inspector high and mighty," was Harriet's opening gambit, "do you mind explaining to me just why a man, who normally only occasionally drinks, suddenly ups and goes on a bender to end all benders?"

Harry looked at her blearily, "I must have got drunk—was I drunk? Who brought me home?—I can't remember a thing, was it you?" The confused inspector asked querulously.

"I'll say you were drunk! Absolutely stinking drunk! As to who brought you home, I've no idea. I happened to call here after work, and there you were, as it were. Actually you weren't there at all, you were entirely out. Will you, or rather, can you explain why all your windows are shuttered closed, also when I arrived, I found the front door standing wide open, but every other door in the place was locked tight?"

"The windows shuttered? What do you mean shuttered?"

"See for yourself," Harriet pulled the curtains aside, "And not just this room, the whole apartment."

"I don't know," ventured Harry. He sat staring into space for a while, deliberating his next words, and then said. "Darling, I know you won't believe this, but it was because of you. It's a long story."

"Sealed up windows! Because of me? What do you mean?"

The need to unburden himself, and the fact that Harriet was here with him, was enough to let the words come tumbling out. Harry told of the millions he had found at Nietrop building. How he had thought that with that kind of money he could give up police work and would be able to offer her, Harriet, the type of life she deserved. He told her how he had managed to overcome the temptation to help himself on that occasion. Then he told her about the robbery at the police station, and the subsequent death of Dalmini, of which he was sure she had read about. He told how Dlamini's actions that morning had made him suspicious, and how he knew of Dlamini's association with Rose. He covered the chance meeting with Rose and the fight that ensued in some detail, hoping that the description would gender some sympathy from Harriet.

Harry stopped for a minute before going further with his confession, and looked intently at Harriet from under lowered eyes, hoping to see some evidence of understanding. However there was no sign of tenderness about Harriet as she sat there, dumbfounded and horror struck, at the actions of the man she had always considered upright and steadfast.

Harry debated with himself if he should go so far as to tell Harriet of his releasing Rose, and finally surrendering to temptation and taking the money. Then he realized that with the three boxes right there on the floor in front of them, he had no option but to tell Harriet all. He blundered on with his tale, and in an effort to gain Harriet's support of his actions; he again explained that in taking the money he had hoped to be able to resign from the force and then persuade her to reconsider their marriage situation.

Harry spoke of the mental strain and worry his actions had caused him, his loss of concentration, his slipshod and careless work, that had resulted in his being sent home on rest leave. He explained how he felt as if he had painted himself into a corner, as it were, and now could not hand the money in without compromising his position with the police. Harry then tried to explain how the pressure and worry and guilt had led him to imagine that he was being watched from all sides.

Harry ended his torrent of words with. "All I remember was that I was in a state of panic by this time, Harriet. I remember thinking it was urgent that I hide the money. I vaguely remember doing something to the windows, but that's all. That's the last I recall. What happened next I can't tell you, the rest is blank? The next thing I remember was being surprised you were here."

Womanlike, Harriet had a feeling of guilt; her separation from Harry was probably the root cause of this mess he had got himself into. What Harry had done was shocking and inexcusable, but he had done it because of her. Men, no matter how proud and sure of themselves they were, were really such incorrigible babies and hopeless at looking after themselves.

"I can only think you must have had a breakdown," she said sympathetically, her motherly instinct coming to the fore," Relax now and try to pull yourself together. Don't worry; we will sort this out somehow."

Harriet's use of the word "We" was music to his ears, and for the first time in many days he had a glimmer of hope.

Harriet had taken down all the boards covering the windows and unlocked the inner doors. She took a curious glance at the contents of the boxes, and gasped at what she saw. 'Small wonder Harry was tempted,' she thought. Harry meanwhile had showered and shaved and generally made himself presentable. Harriet came in from the kitchen carrying a plate of sandwiches, saying that Harry must be hungry. The sight of food brought a squeamish feeling to Harry's stomach, but he forced it down as they sat down together to the light meal. After a while Harriet stood up full of purpose.

"Right, this is what we will do," said Harriet, all business, "I will take the boxes to my flat. They will be safe there and out of your way, and out of your mind. You use the two days left of your leave, plus this weekend to try and trace Roses' movements. If at the end of the four days you haven't found him, then you will return to work and throw yourself and your assistants into an all out search, as only you know how to do. Even if it means involving police from other centre's and cities. I am sure your chief will support you on this. Once you have found Rose, and I know you will, then you can hand the boxes in at the same time, and no one will know what you had done."

Harry knew that this was the right thing to do, though Harriet over simplified matters. He did not have the authority to order extra staff, nor direct any enquiry without his chief's sanction. Anyway there was an intensive search already underway at the moment. They would run Rose to ground if he was foolish enough to stay in the area. He would just have to be present at Rose's arrest if possible. It was also just possible that his chief would give him carte 'blanche on tracing Rose beyond the city limits if he could convince him of the need. He was not sure Harriet taking the money to her flat was wise, but he was grateful she was ready to help, and had not condemned him too much. He was not quite himself yet, but was only too pleased that Harriet had convinced him of the right way to go. He didn't know why he had been unable to figure it out for himself. There was no doubt that his mind had been confused lately.

In spite of his coming to his senses regarding the money, Harry realized that he had not mentioned the money he had hidden in the sofa. Harry wondered at his motive for this, and was secretly pleased that he still had this cache. 'Out of sight out of mind, and what Harriet doesn't know won't hurt her.' Harry rationalized. Subconsciously he still wanted to be in a position of financial independence, though not for himself, it was all about Harriet.

Harriet picked up two of the boxes and said, "Let us get these over to my flat as soon as possible." She hefted the boxes, then said, "This one feels empty." She put them down on the floor again and opened the empty one. "Did you know that this one was empty?"

Harry hesitated a moment, then recovering his wits, he said, "Yes, two of them are empty. Remember I told you about Rose dropping them and they broke open. The contents were blown down the street and I was not able to recover the loose notes. At the time I thought I had better hold the boxes as evidence."

"Yes, I remember, but I thought you said only one box had broken open?" queried Harriet.

"Yes," answered Harry, "but afterwards I found that another box was empty."

Harriet excepted Harry's explanation, she had convinced herself that she was the cause of Harry's predicament and did not want to entertain any further doubts regarding his actions. All she wanted at the moment was to help Harry clear up the mess he seemed to have got himself into, and get him to pull himself together and once again become a positive and self confident man. She had suffered a severe shock in discovering Harry in this state, and even though she was naturally strong and self reliant, this episode had really unsettled her more than she cared to admit.

It was evening by the time Harry and Harriet had completed transferring the boxes to Harriet's flat, and she had no difficulty in persuading Harry to stay over for supper. All this attention from Harriet was to Harry as a dream come true. He began to feel as if his irresponsible actions had been worthwhile after all, and worth all the trouble and anxiety he had been through. He felt he could now confidentially face what ever the future might bring.

CHAPTER 23

Rose sat on the beach, staring moodily at the ocean, and weighing up his options. He looked at his watch, it was a shade after three thirty and it must be all of twenty kilometers back to city centre, he had better start walking. As he walked he felt through his pockets, expedient anonymity had demanded that he left his identity document and his bank card at his flat that morning. All he had with him was four hundred Rand in twenty Rand notes. He had enough for a taxi if he could find one in this godforsaken neck of the woods. He was not sure where he was, it was part of the city he had never visited before, but he knew that if he walked in a North westerly direction he would eventually reach his destination, but "Phew", it sure was hot.

Three and a half hours of unaccustomed shambling along the hard surfaced sidewalks, and now the heat of the day changed to the cool of the evening, exacerbated by a chilly coastal breeze. Rose pulled on his jacket once more, stopped and looked toward the loom of the centre city lighting now appearing in the darkening sky. It was still a long way to go. 'At least in the dark of the night I won't be recognized. Just you wait you bastard,' Rose ruminated as he trudged along, his thoughts erratically jumping from his present situation to the anger he felt at the loss of the money. 'Leave the city huh! No way was he leaving until he had evened up matters between himself and that blasted cop.' The further he walked and the more discomforted and footsore he became, the more his lust for revenge. 'Besides, he reasoned, he had a better chance of hiding out there in a place he knew well, than in some strange environment. Anyway, all the money the cop had stolen was somewhere in this city, he was certain the cop meant to keep it for himself. The four hundred bucks in his pocket would not last long, he must retrieve his bank card first. He had a few thousand in the bank that would keep him going while searched out the cop and got his hard earned cash back.'

At last he came to a suburban corner shop which was open. He entered and asked the Lebanese proprietor if he could use his phone. The Lebanese refused, saying that his was not a public phone, but if he walked further along the road he would come across a public phone kiosk. Rose asked to change a twenty Rand note. With much grumbling about himself being short of small change, silver was handed over. Rose continued on his weary way, hopefully looking out for the phone booth. At last it loomed out of the darkness. Rose opened the door and found the cord dangling. The hand piece had been removed. "Typical," he muttered as he looked at the vandalized phone. He doubted there would be a working public phone in the confines of East Bay City.

There were few cars about in this part of town. He did try to hitch a lift from the few cars that were going his way, but no one was willing to stop. He looked at his watch again, only half an hour had passed since he last checked the time, he could have sworn it was later. He looked about him but could not recognize the area. The large oak trees lining the avenue cast deep shadows limiting the light from the spaced street lighting, and there was not much he could discern, it became quickly dark these winter evenings. Most of the houses were large and situated well back from the avenue; all he was able to determine was that they were sumptuous in appearance.

What he did see looming out of the gloom was the entrance to a public park and he suddenly realized how thirsty he was. He went through the gates and into an ablution building, where he drank thirstily from a tap. Along the wall of the room was a bench, and Rose thought he would just rest awhile. He subsided upon the bench. 'Ah! What bliss.' He lay down, and just as he drifted off to sleep the sleep of exhaustion, the park superintendent, his working day finishing at six thirty p.m., was walking round the perimeter of the park locking the gates for the night.

Rose awoke and gazed about him, for a moment he was disorientated, and then he remembered where he was. It all came back to him. He was a fugitive from justice, wanted for murder. He had to get out if sight, find a hideaway, but first he had a score to settle. He had thought little or nothing about the death of Dlamini, it had been necessary at the time. It had been his first killing, and strangely, it had given him an extraordinary sense of power, and even pleasure. If only he could deal with that bloody cop, who had robbed him, in the same way. The treatment he had received from that cop was the turning point. In the past Rose had always been against killing, reckoning it caused more trouble than it was worth. But since the killing of Dlamini he had felt the power of a gun, and he wanted nothing more than to treat that cop with some of the same medicine. Somehow, he would trace that particular cop and deal with him. He had killed once, it had been easy, and if he was ever going to get caught, well it might as well be for two murders as for one. 'One thing was for certain, the cop would tell him where his money was before he died, yeah, that was for sure.'

He stood up from the bench and made his way to the gate of the park. It had been locked for the night. Iron palings, one point eight metres in height, stretched away into the distance and were too high for him to scale. Rose proceeded to walk the perimeter hoping to find an opening. He had covered about a hundred metres when he came across a section where three palings had been prised away. Rose angled his way through the gap, but tore his jacket on a rusty bolt, leaving him looking more disheveled than ever. He commenced his hike toward the centre of the city.

Finally he arrived at an area he recognized and where he felt more at home. Here the shops were beginning to open for business. People were moving about in the streets, traffic lights winking, controlling the early morning traffic. The buzz and activity was an environment he understood, and he felt less exposed. That was until he noticed the heavy police presence. Police constables paraded the sidewalks in pairs, examining every passing face. It was a known fact that police hated a cop killer, and obviously the search for Dlamini's killer had been intensified. What was he to do? Rose shrank back into a doorway. He couldn't now go to his apartment, and he daren't go to his girls, or to Francesco's, they would be concentrating on those places for certain. The only place of safety he could think of was his supplier of drugs. The police suspected his drug pushing, but they had not found his source of supply. The old Jew, Meier, was the only connection he could think of that was known only to himself. He was a good customer of Meier's, surely he would help him. It meant another long walk. This time in daylight, and fraught with the danger of discovery by these many watchful policemen who were parading the streets.

Keeping to the back streets, huddling in dark corners, or behind bus shelters, or refuse dumpsters whenever there was a doubt of the safety of the moment. Rose made a circuitous course to the seedier part of the city. Along the way he came across a fast food outlet and he bought a much needed hamburger. It was the first meal since yesterday's breakfast, and it lifted his spirits somewhat, but did little to fill the void in his stomach.

Rose was not a man who spent much time walking; his usual mode of transport was by taxi or bus. Now forced by circumstance to get from place to place on foot, he realized for the first time just how large a place was East

Bay City. The necessity to duck and dive to avoid patrolling policemen was very tiring, and time consuming, and it took many hours to reach his destination. It was past five o'clock that afternoon when a tired out Rose arrived at Meiers shop. It was already closed with the shutters up; he would have to wait till morning.

Meier's pawn shop was a front to his much more munificent trade as facilitator to pushers such as Rose. The cheap gents and ladies watches, the dusty secondhand clothing that filled the shop window were only a façade to hide the main source of business. Meier during business hours, managed to look as seedy as his shop. His usual dress comprised a skull cap, a long stained blue overcoat, covering a shabby grey suit. His feet were shod with an old pair of carpet slippers. Such was the man known to Rise. But once the business day was over, Meier retired to an area of affluent homes in the very suburb that Rose had shuffled through on his weary Odyssey to the city.

Rose was hungry again, but there was no food outlet at this part of the city, he would just have to tighten his belt. There was no one about, other than the occasional black men who carried out night watchmen duties. At the moment they were all busy stoking their kindling and coals in the perforated drum braziers, which served to warm them through the long night. Rose had nowhere to spend the night, so he ingratiated himself with one of these night watchmen, and joined him at his warm and glowing brazier, which would keep off the nights chill.

He would just have to sit it out until daylight, waiting for Meier to open his business. He found himself feeling drowsy from the heat of the burning coals, and within a quarter of an hour he was fast asleep. Pasted on the wall behind the sleeping man was a large wanted poster with a police artist's representation of Rose. The night watchman had thought Rose looked familiar, and now that he had a chance to study him, he noticed the similarity between the sleeping man and the picture on the poster. The hair style was different and the moustache was missing, but that it was the same man was of no doubt in the watchman's mind. He let Rose sleep on.

"Baas, Baass, word wakker, wake up." The words finally penetrated Roses' deep sleep and he started awake. The coal brazier had long since burnt itself out, and Rose was stiff and cold as he struggled to his feet, The friendly watchman of the night before had suddenly adopted a menacing mien in the morning light.

"Jy moet wag tot my baas kom." He said.

"What? I don't understand Afrikaans." Said Rose.

The watchman took Rose by the shoulder and turned him to face the poster. He said," My Baas kom, him bell polisie nou, nou."

Rose could not understand Afrikaans, but the message glaring at him from the police poster was enough to clarify the watchman's meaning.

"Wait, wait a minute. I will give you money,O.K.? You not tell policeman o.k., I give you money then I go, o.k.?" pleaded the shocked and alarmed Rose.

"How much?" was the pragmatic rejoinder.

"Twenty Rand."

"Haugh! You wait for baas."

"O.K. I'll give you forty Rand, that's all I've got." Lied Rose, as he reached toward his pocket, breathlessly and hopefully waiting the black man's agreement.

The watchman stepped forward and thrust rose against the wall, and while threatening him with his traditional night stick, a knobkerrie, he pushed his hand into the pocket, that Rose' involuntary movement had indicated, and brought out three hundred and Eighty Rand, leaving the silver.

"Haugh !" the watchman exclaimed again, he gawked at the money for a moment, then he thrust Rose away, saying, "Go, go now. Now you go."

Rose tried to remonstrate," C'mon, that's all I've got. You can't take it all."

The black man raise his knobkerrie in a threatening manner, saying again, "You go now. I call polisie."

Rose had no option but to move on, and he did so with alacrity. He made his way back to Meiers shop. It was still early, he could not expect Meier to arrive before eight o'clock. Where to wait in safety? The street was lined with shop fronts none offering any suitable hiding place. Rose looked left and right, at this hour the street was comparatively empty, but he was certain it would not be long before the inevitable constable would heave in sight. With his unshaven scruffiness and his slept in and torn clothes, Rose felt extremely conspicuous.

There, he knew it would happen; two policemen came ambling down the opposite side of the street, looking carefully at the few early pedestrians. All Rose could do was move as unobtrusive as possible in the same direction, and stay ahead of them. He reached the end of the block and gratefully turned the corner out of sight. Rose increased his pace, almost running at times, until he had covered another street block. He looked left and right, all was clear, he turned right and went up the street that was at the back of Meier's shop, then another right turn, another street block, and with one more right turn, he was back in the street from which he had started. Rose looked thankfully at the distant and receding backs of the policemen. He went back to Meier's shop.

Meier had arrived during this interval, and he was busy wrestling aside the mesh screen that protected the door. Meier was unaware of Rose's presence as he opened his shop door and he received a frightening shock as Rose pushed past him and hurriedly entered the shop.

"Mensch ! You can't come in here, "raged the startled and angry Meier, "The vorld, he looks for you. It is in all the papers and you come in here. No, no, out, go avay, I don't vant to know."

"Please, for God's sake, please Meier, I'm desperate, you are my only hope. I'm your good customer of many years, you know me. Help me please," pleaded Rose.

"I know you, yes, when you were a business man. Now you are a vanted man, I don't know you, I'm sorry." Was Meier's adamant reply.

Rose grabbed the old man passionately by his coat collar. "Please Meier, you are my last chance, you've got to help."

"I vould help you if I could, Meester Rose, but you know my position. I don't vant the police interwention. You understand Meester, its nothing personal, its just business. I'm sorry."

"At least let me wash and shave, please Meier. Also if you have some other clothes you can let me have from your stock. I need to change my appearance. At least help me that much."

"To change your appearance a plastic surgeon you vill need, not clothes." Quipped Meier, then he hesitated. His remark had prompted another thought. Always quick to seize an opportunity to make a quick buck, he said, "Maybe I can help you. I know a man; he is a doctor, a cosmetic surgeon. He is also a customer of mine. Maybe I can persvade him to help you change your appearance so your Momma, she vould not knowing you."

"Really? Asked Rose in sudden desperate hope," You could arrange that for me?"

"Come back here in this storeroom. You hide vile I make phone call, yes." Ordered the now motivated Meier.

Rose sat in the musty, dusty, dirty storeroom, nervously hoping and waiting impatiently for Meier to bring him news that would guarantee him avoiding detection, and grant him freedom from police persecution. It seemed hours before Meier eventually put in an appearance.

"Yes," Meier said. "I can arrange it. It vill cost you one hunnert and sixty thousand bucks."

Rose would have had that kind of money if that crooked cop had not interfered. He had about fifty thousand Rand in his bank account that was if he could get his bank card from his apartment. However that did not stop him taking a chance on Meier's gullibility. 'Get the job done,' he thought,' I'll worry about paying later, once I get my money back from that copper.'

"O.K." he said," Go ahead and arrange it. The sooner the better."

"No problem," Meier was not about to be bulldozed. "Cash up front," he said laconically.

"Have a heart Meier, you know I can't get near my bank at the moment. You know me, you know I will pay you as soon as I can move about in the open again. I need that op. to be free again."

"Yes, and you can also easily disappear. Mr. Rose, me I am friendly mit everybody, but trust anyone, I do not. Cash I say. No cash, I cannot help you."

Meier was not one to waste time on lost causes. From past experience, Rose had always had the ability to produce cash when required, but he saw that this time it would not be readily forth coming. He decided not to waste further time on a project that was not immediately profitable.

"You get the money and I help you," asserted Meier. "Now you must leave. You cannot stay here."

Rose found himself unceremoniously pushed out on the street once more. Ravenously hungry, still shabby and dirty, Rose crept fearfully along the canyons of the city. His hunger drove him into a delicatessen, but as he was about to make his selection in accordance with the few coins left in his pocket. The manager accosted him. He was hustled outside again accompanied with the comment that they did not tolerate beggars, and to get moving. Try the Salvation Army, he was advised. 'Yes why not? That is a good idea, the Salvation Army. They are down in the harbour area. I hope I can make it there,' thought Rose as he moved off in that direction.

He was so tired hungry and thirsty that he was becoming light headed. So much so in fact, that he walked right past a uniformed policeman without noticing. The policeman, in turn, looked at the rundown and disheveled Rose and dismissed him as just another of the city's many vagrants. In fact this situation was to occur a few more times during Rose's attempt to get to the Salvation Army, without him, or the police realizing that his disheveled and unkempt appearance was serving as a very effective disguise.

Still keeping to the less frequented streets, Rose moved slowly, dragging his weary and footsore body in direction of the harbour. At one stage his throat was so dry, and he so desperately thirsty, that when he came upon an air conditioning unit which was spewing excess condensation out into the street, he cupped his hands under the condensation pipe, collected the drops of moisture and licked them fervently from his palms. He plodded on, now a blister had developed on his heel, causing even more discomfort, would the journey never end.

CHAPTER 24

End it did. But it was not the end of the journey Rose had intended. It ended in the back of a police van. He had not been picked up because he had been recognized, but because his weakness and exhaustion had caused him to stagger and weave as he shuffled along. The occupants of the police van had thought he was a vagrant and drunk. They were going to place him in the cells at Point road police station to sleep it off, for it was the harbour precinct jurisdiction area that Rose had reached at last.

The police on their routine patrol thought nothing of it, a loitering drunk was a common enough occurrence in their area. He would be discharged again in the morning, once he was sober. After shoving Rose in the back of the van, and climbing back into their seats, the driver said, as he let in the clutch, "Come to think of it, I didn't smell any liquor on him, did you?"

His companion agreed that that was the case, and ventured the opinion that it might be drugs.

"Anyway he is not fit to be on the streets. We'll take him in anyway and the district surgeons people can decide if it's anything serious."

Rose refused to speak, and they found no I.D. on him, neither was he recognized as one of the usual riff raff that hung around the harbour environs. The desk sergeant simply took his fingerprints, booked him as John Doe, and locked him in a cell that was occupied with three other equally distressed individuals. The desk sergeant also could not smell any trace of alcohol on Rose that could account for his staggering and uncontrolled movement. He thought it might be a case of weakness and hunger, or, as the patrol men had surmised, a case of drug addiction. While he phoned for someone from the district surgeons office to check him over, Rose's likeness looked down from a wanted poster pasted on the wall behind the desk sergeant, who, not being involved with the crisis at Da Gama precinct, or the follow up search, never gave it a thought.

The cell contained four steel stacked beds, a stainless steel wash hand basin affixed to a wall, a cold water tap and a loose toilet bucket. The visiting doctor found all the occupants lying on their respective bunks, and he had to ask the warden which was Rose. He was pointed to one of the bottom bunks. The doctor took Rose's blood pressure, and with his stethoscope listened to Rose's heart and chest. He pried open one of Rose's eyes and shone a pencil torch beam at the pupil. Pulled Roses mouth open and gazed at his throat. Pushed and pulled at Rose's stomach area, spent some time examining Rose's inner elbow and thigh areas. Satisfied with his examination the doctor banged upon the cell bars and was let out into the free world. The doctor reported to the desk sergeant, "Nothing much wrong with your latest guest sergeant. A bowl of soup, some staple food and a cup of coffee, plus the good sleep he is enjoying at the moment, and he will be as right as rain. He is neither on drugs nor drunk, simply dehydrated, exhausted and hungry. You can do more for him than I can, see to it, won't you sergeant."

"Sure, we will feed him as a guest of the state, offer him a nights lodging, and if his fingerprints show up clear, we will let him go in the morning. Thank you for your trouble, doctor."

Though Dlamini, when he was alive, knew of Rose's drug pushing activities, he had never booked him, preferring to let him practice his dealings, and exhort protection money from him instead. He had mentioned to other members of the vice squad, that he was hoping Rose would lead him to the source of the drug supply route, but he had never submitted an official report. Therefore the only record against Rose was one of disorderly conduct arising from his altercation with Broad. Other than that there was no official record against Rose that warranted the police holding him further. With regard to his being wanted in connection with Dlamini's murder, as mentioned before, the police staff at point road precinct, were far removed from the situation at Ga Gama precinct, and rightly or wrongly were not as vigilant as they should have been. The following morning, Rose was fed breakfast, his pocket contents were handed back to him and he was free to go.

Now that he had had a full nights sleep and been fed, he had no further need of the Salvation Army. Rose was amazed at his luck and could not understand how no one had recognized him. As he walked down the street he happened to glance at his reflection in a plate glass window. He almost did not recognize himself. The scruffy, unshaven, wild haired individual, dressed in rumpled and stained clothing bore scant resemblance to usual suave appearance, or to the image portrayed on the wanted posters. "This is all very well,' thought Rose,' but I cannot go on for ever and a day without bathing, shaving or wearing the same shoddy clothes, no matter how good the disguise.' For the moment he strode on with a greater sense of invisibility.

Unaccustomed to the exercise the long walk had forced upon him, plus the two nights of sleeping on the hard bench in the park in the first place, and the second night on the cold sidewalk respectively, Rose had suffered extensively from physical and mental exhaustion. Had he but realized it, his arrest, resulting in a good nights sleep on a mattress, albeit on the thin side, plus the supper and breakfast he had received, had been extremely beneficial. He had been on the verge of mental and physical collapse when he had been brought in, and had degenerated to a degree of irrationality.

This morning, however, he was feeling lucid and able to think clearly. He came to a bus stop shelter and sat down to plan his next move.

Rose thought back over the sequence of events. Only Dlamini had known of his change of address, and he was dead. He had not yet told any of his girls, so the only address known to the police was the one from which he and Broad had been emoved the night of their fight. The chances were that his present apartment was inviolate. If he could get there undetected, he could shower and change his clothing. He decided he would not shave; the image in the window had reflected a satisfactory change in appearance. If he could buy a bottle of hair dye, and again resort to wearing those spectacles he had bought, he should be able to evade detection. His recent experience with the police had shown him that they were not all that vigilant.

Rose caught the next bus to the city. He sat at the back of the bus, thus ensuring that the other passengers were facing forward and away from him. His far from salubrious appearance guaranteed him a seat away from the other occupants. In fact a woman, who had been sitting in the aisle next to him, rather pointedly stood up and moved indignantly three seats further up the aisle. Alighting at centre city, he was pleased to note that the earlier heavy police presence was now no longer evident. It looked as though the intensive search had been called off. The police must have reasoned that if, in the five days since the murder, they had not fund him, then he must have either left the city, or found a secure hide-out. He had no doubt, however, that the search for him was still ongoing, albeit less intense. He still moved with care, and to day found no difficulty in reaching his apartment.

All Rose's clothing tended to be on the flash side, and his normal style of dress was familiar to the vice squad at least. Rose chose the least obvious pair of slacks he possessed and a plain pink shirt. It was the best he could do at present. Wearing his glasses and dressed thus, and with his bank card safely in his pocket, he braved the gaze of the outside world once more. He went to a nearby automatic teller and drew a substantial sum. At least it was apparent they had not been able to freeze his account. Again in funds Rose purchased an unobtrusive grey suit, a plain blue tie and a hat. His next stop was a pharmacy for the hair dye. As his hair colour was brown, he thought it would be sensible to choose blond dye.

In his subdued grey suit and with his newly dyed blond beard, eyebrows and hair, and wearing his new hat and spectacles, Rose felt very secure as he stepped out into the flow of pedestrians. All this fuss and bother, the discomfort of the last few days, all was the fault of that bloody cop who had diddled him out of his money. The thought was constantly in the front of his mind. And his only motivation at present was to exact revenge. He was not sure how he was going to find that particular cop, but bloody well find him he would, and then he had better watch out. First he had to get a pistol. The same dealer who had provided the automatic weapons would help overcome that problem. His old squeamishness about killing was a thing of the past; his shooting of Dlamini had taken care of that, in fact, now that he thought about it, it had given him quite a thrill. Once again the thought crossed his mind that if he had one murder against him, what mattered a second. As Rose made his way to the gun dealer he continued his daydream, one thing was for certain, before he put a bullet in that cop's brain, he would make sure the bastard would tell him where he had stashed his, Rose's cash. That the cop still had the cash he was certain, else why had the cop not driven straight to the police station.

On his way to the gun dealer Rose had to pass close to the area where his girls normally plied their trade. They usually didn't appear on the streets till after dark, but he thought it would be a good idea to test his disguise if he happened to meet one or more of them during daylight hours. Rose altered his route to encompass the streets where the girls usually operated. His luck was out however, none of them were evident at their usual street corners. Somewhat disgruntled he moved on his way. Amongst the crowd on the streets he did notice a few casual acquaintances, and he was pleased to see no startled glances as he passed them by. He was becoming more confident, and instead of skulking along as he had been doing the last few days, he began to strut with his old aplomb. Rose certainly did not look like Rose any longer, but his gait resumed the old Rose arrogant swagger.

CHAPTER 25

The last few days of his rest leave, and during the weekend that followed, was spent by Noble revisiting all Rose old haunts, but to no avail. It looked as though Rose had taken him to heart and really left the city for good. This was the situation Noble originally hoped would occur, but it was now becoming a hindrance to his getting himself off the hook, allowing to whitewash his conscience.

Upon his return to work Noble read all the recent reports pertaining to the case in order to bring himself up to date. These reports mentioned the additional police that had been seconded to Da Gama division to assist in the search. That in spite of the additional assistance, Rose had continued to evade capture. The reports further mentioned that due to budget constraints, the use of the additional task force had to be curtailed, but that Rose's description had been circulated nation wide, and all points of exit from the country had been alerted. The general consensus was that Rose had left East Bay City. The most recent addendum to the report was that Dlamini had been accorded a police burial with honours.

The gist of the reports, together with his own failed search for Rose, brought home to Harry that the albatross of the money would remain firmly round his neck. He consoled himself with the memory of Harriet's return to his side and her support; selfishly he congratulated himself that his actions had at least achieved that much. An unsolved murder investigation is never put to rest, but it now had been placed on back burner, and normal police routine was back in place.

The station commander called Noble to his office. As he entered the chief stood up and shook Harry's hand and said, "Harry, I trust your weeks leave finds you ready and able once more. Did you consult the doctor, as I suggested?"

"I'm fine thank you sir," said Harry, "As a matter of fact I did not see a doctor, but you will be pleased to hear that Harriet rallied round and looked after me. Her presence was just what I needed to get me going again."

"Well that is good news. I'm delighted that you and Harriet are becoming closer once more. I sincerely hope that you can finally overcome your past difficulties. I am also glad to see you are ready for work again." Superintendant Watson resumed his chair, shuffled some papers around and said, "As you will have read in the reports, we had a considerable drive, at considerable expense, in trying to apprehend this Rose individual. The only success we attained was the apprehension of the men who masqueraded as police guards during the robbery of the evidence boxes. Under intensive interrogation they revealed that Dlamini and the driver resorted to the use of firearms, but claim they fled the scene as soon as the shooting started. They claim ignorance of the actual killing, or of the disappearance of the evidence boxes, or the contents thereof. As you know, four of the boxes were found at the site and since returned to the station. Where the other six boxes are, I have no idea, nor how Rose, if it was him, managed to remove that many boxes without transport, unless there are other miscreants involved."

"You have had a clearer insight into this matter from the inception of the Nietrop business, and I know you are convinced that there was collusion between Dlamini and this Rose character. In fact it was on the strength of you report to Captain Fairweather of your suspicions, that this whole intensive search for Rose was mounted, unfortunately later than it should have been." The superintendent sat back in his chair and folded his hands across his belly. He continued to speak, "The station has a mounting backlog, and perforce I have to call in the men that were allocated to the search. In any case they were not making much progress. Harry, I want you to hand all your present work over to Swart, and I want you to personally and exclusively concentrate on this case. The killing of one of our own is always a serious matter, but apart from that, if there is more than just the suggestion that Dlamini was a dirty cop, as you suspect, then I want the matter cleared up as soon as possible."

"O.K. chief, but it might mean I will have to travel out of the city if there is any indication that Rose had decamped."

Superintendant Watson agreed, "If it is necessary to do that, so be it and I will sanction your out of pocket expenses, but remember the state is not Bill Gates or Donald Trump, keep the costs down. And Harry, I want this matter cleared up quickly, don't waste time."

"I understand Chief," said Harry. He saluted and left the Chief's office.

Harry drove to Harriet's florists shop to apprise her of the situation. Harriet was busy with a client when he arrived, so he waited in the shop and stood looking at the myriad of blooms arranged in the shop window on display.

Rose now feeling completely inconspicuous in his blond disguise, hat and black rimmed eye glasses, was nonchalantly strolling along the street past Harriet's shop, which was situated close to his new apartment. Since taking up residence at his new address, he had often passed this way and had noticed the extremely attractive woman that worked there. As he passed the shop he glanced in, in the hope of seeing her. Rose broke his stride and stopped, his jaw dropped open in surprise, there right in the show window area was his nemesis. The blighted cop who was the cause of all his woes. He reversed a few hasty steps beyond the edge of the window and out of sight and paused. At last luck had played into his hands, if he could help it; he would not lose sight of the cop again. He crossed to the other side of the street and waited. The other customer in the shop completed whatever business she had and left. Rose saw Noble go up to the woman he admired and kissed her. They retired into an office. Rose waited; sooner or later the cop had to leave. Rose had his recently acquired pistol stuffed into his trouser belt, he was ready. He wasn't sure how he would go about it, but somehow, do or die, he would have his reckoning with the shit who had caused him so much misery.

Rose had to wait three-quarter of an hour before he saw Noble leaving the florists and walk toward a car, parked strangely enough, right outside his own apartment block. Rose rushed forward to overtake the policeman, but crossing the street against the traffic slowed him down, and this allowed Noble to reach his car and climb into the drivers seat. Noble looked over his shoulder at the oncoming traffic, judging the moment to pull away. Rose reached the drivers door and pulled his pistol freeing it from his belt. Just as Rose pointed the pistol at the back of Nobles head, Noble still looking toward the traffic, released the clutch and accelerated into the traffic stream. The sudden acceleration of the car threw Rose off his balance, and his opportunity was lost. He had taken too long to cross the street to reach Nobles side.

Rose was furious, so near and yet so far, he stood for a moment cursing his luck. Then he realized that the suddenness of Nobles appearance, and his own unbridled hate, had almost caused him to shoot the man in uncontrollable rage. Had he done so, he would never have found the whereabouts of the money. He controlled his anger, took a deep breath or two and felt more in control. In retrospect he had been lucky; he had almost committed another murder in a busy street, with little or no chance of making a getaway. He replaced his pistol in his belt and looked around, nobody appeared to have noticed his recent actions. He breathed a sigh of relief; he really must control his emotions and not act so spontaneously. Rose crossed the sidewalk to his apartment.

Rose sat in his apartment and re-assessed his position. It occurred to him that the woman in the florists had obviously been on intimate terms with the cop. She more than likely could tell him the cop's name and where he lived. Rose returned to Harriet's business.

"Good day madam," He politely greeted her, adopting his most cultured voice. "Just as I approached your shop just now, I noticed a gentleman leaving. I was sure I recognized him, an old friend I have not seen in ages."

"Really?" Harriet replied, "An old friend you say?"

"Yes, as a matter of fact, quite good friends indeed at the time. But as I say, I've not seen him in a long, long time and I'd love to catch up with him again. The trouble is, and I know it's terrible to admit it, but I've quite forgotten his name, although I remember his face so clearly. You would'nt by any chance know his name would you?" Rose asked hopefully. Harriet, re-assured by the smart and conservative appearance of the stranger, said, "Yes, as a matter of fact I do. His name is Harry, Harry Noble, and he is my husband."

"Of course, that's right, how could I have forgotten!" exclaimed Rose.

Harriet paused a moment then said, "It must be a very long time since you knew him. We have been married for over ten years, and I certainly don't remember you at all."

"Oh yes, it must be much more than ten years. It is astonishing how time flies. To be honest, I hadn't given him a thought for years, but catching a glimpse of him again prompted memories. I thought. how much fun it would be to chat about old times. Would you mind if I called?" Rose requested in his most charming manner.

"No, I suppose not, but actually we are not living together at the moment." Harriet suddenly wondered why she had volunteered that information to this complete stranger. Well it was out now, nothing she could do about it, but it was embarrassing none the less. She found a sheet of paper and writing hurriedly, she said, "Here, I'll write down his address for you."

"Thank you so much, you are most helpful and kind." Said Rose at his gallant best. He bowed gracefully to Harriet as he left the shop.

What a strange co-incidence, quite a dandy in his manner, hardly the sort to be a friend of Harry's, she thought to herself as she walked to the shop entrance, and watched as the man walked down the street and entered an apartment block two buildings further along. Harriet reasoned that Harry would not yet be back at his office, she would give it a moment before she phoned him to warn him of his possible visitor. The rest of her day was a busy one, and she forgot entirely about the mans visit, and also her intention to phone Harry.

Harriet closed the florist at the end of the day, and, walking home, she passed Nietrop building as usual. The sight of the building brought Harry to mind, and then she remembered about the strangers enquiry. She chided herself for her memory lapse and decided to go to Harry's flat after supper, rather than phone him about the man claiming to be a long lost friend. If she was to be honest with herself, she was curious about this strange friend, and wanted to question Harry about him, and she could do that better face to face rather than over the phone. Harriet smiled to herself over her curiosity.

Shortly after leaving Harriet, Rose went to the address in River Kloof road he had been given. He established that Noble's apartment was on the first floor. Rose grinned to himself, "So Mr. Noble, I'll get you now for sure."

CHAPTER 26

Carrying a T.V. meal of precooked Lasagna, just warm and serve, Harry slipped it into the microwave. He poured water for some instant coffee, and while waiting for the water to boil and his supper to warm, he went to the bathroom to wash his hands. Returning to the kitchen, he removed the heated Lasagna from its packet, placed it on a plate. He then spooned instant coffee into a cup and added boiling water and added some milk and sugar. Carrying the plate, a fork and the cup into the lounge, he placed them on to an occasional table next to his favourite "Lazy boy" easy chair. He switched on the T.V. kicked off his shoes, and settled back in the chair to enjoy a leisurely supper. While he ate this austere bachelor meal, he gratefully remembered that if all went well, he would soon be enjoying a home cooked supper with Harriet once again.

He was swallowing the last of his coffee when there was a knock at the door. He glanced at his watch, eight o'clock, who could this be? He seldom had visitors and Harriet had her own key, she simply would have walked in without ceremony. Harry got out of his chair, slipped into his shoes and went to answer the door.

A smallish, dark skinned and surprisingly blond man, wearing black rimmed spectacles stood at the entrance. "Hullo Harry old man, how are you? I suppose your wife mentioned I'd be calling. Well here I am, it's been a long time no see eh?" The man held his hand out in greeting.

"No. My wife hasn't mentioned anything. Should I know you?" Harry was nonplussed as he warily shook the strangers hand. Something about the man seemed vaguely familiar.

"Sure you do, we were bosom chums, it must be ten or twelve years ago," said the man, pushing his way into the apartment.

Rose was gratified. If a cop who had spent the better part of a day in his, Roses' company, could not recognize him now then his disguise was better than he had hoped. He took a vicarious thrill in flaunting his false identity to Noble's distinct mystification.

"Nice place you've got here Harry, show me around."

Harry was completely taken aback, he followed the strange man into the kitchen. "Yeah, it's not bad, this is, er the kitchen." The man was definitely familiar, Harry thought, but not ten years ago. I'm sure that is I had ever met him, it was sometime more recent.

"I don't recall your name," Harry ventured, "You say you know my wife?"

The man ignored Harry's question and walked down the passage and into the lounge. He looked at the sofa, the two matching easy chairs and Harry's favourite "lazy boy". The stranger spent a moment studying Harry's trophys on the mantle over the fireplace, and even pulled aside the floor length curtaining, but made no remark.

'He obviously knows that I am with the police,' thought Harry,' he has shown no surprise at seeing the awards.' Harry followed the strange being as he presumptuously continued his inspection of the bathroom. Returning to the passage, the man asked, "What are these?" gesturing to the two closed doors, Bedrooms I suppose?"

"Yes, but I only use one, the other is empty," answered the flummoxed host. 'Maybe he did know Harriet, but really ! this was a bit much.'

Nothing deterred, the stranger opened the door of the empty room, walked in and opened and carefully inspected the empty built-in cupboard.

Leaving the cupboard door open, he retraced his steps to the passage and opened Harry's bedroom door and entered. The bewitched Harry watched dumbfounded as the man opened the bedside cabinet, glanced inside seeing only a tin of menthol rub. He then kicked the divan base, saying." Solid base, wise choice, a bed on legs always attracts dust underneath."

When the man opened the wardrobe it was more than Harry could bear. Nothing like this had ever happened to him in his life before and he had been nonplussed, but now he finally remonstrated. "I say, this is too much, you come barging in here saying you are my long lost friend. You snoop through my flat as if you owned it, you do not even extend the courtesy of giving me your name. On the strength of your supposedly knowing my wife, you expect me to welcome you with open arms!!! I think it is high time you offered me an explanation. Just who are you, and what do you want?"

It had been fun while it lasted, and he had, had an opportunity to have a cursory look for signs of the boxes, but his bluff could not last forever. Rose faced Harry, suddenly producing a pistol fitted with a silencer. It dawned upon Harry at last,' Ruddy Rose, how could he have been so stupid, no wonder the face had looked familiar.'

"I don't see them. Where is the cash? I'm not leaving without it, cough it up or I'll swear I'll shoot." Rose aggressively gestured with the gun.

"Don't be a fool Rose, you'll never get away with it." warned Noble.

"Ha! That's what they always say. I got away with Dlamini's killing, and I'll get away with your's, don't think I won't. I've killed before, you better believe it, it was easy, and I'll kill again if you're not quick about producing my cash." hissed Rose. Harry could see that Rose was working himself up into a dangerous nervous rage. His gun hand was shaking, and his finger whitening on the trigger.

"Calm down, take it easy, it's no use threatening me, its not here, I took it to the police station, you're wasting your time, I say. Come on now, don't be a fool, you're making things worse for yourself. Hand me that gun Rose," urged Noble.

"Ha! Likely story, you kept it for yourself. Just like Dlamini, crooked to the core. He also tried to do me out of my share, and look where it got him. I shot him through the head, killed him, just like I'm going to kill you if you don't produce my money right now." Rose was losing control, "Noble!! What a name for a crooked cop. Now do as I say at once" A spark of insanity gleamed in Roses eye as he raised the pistol menacingly.

It was at that moment that Harriet appeared in the doorway. She said, "I thought I heard voices when"—That was as far as she got, there was a "Phut" from Rose's silenced gun and Harriet sank to the floor. "Nooo!" Harry's cry echoed in the room, and he threw himself wildly at Rose. Harry's momentum carried Rose and he toward the bed, where it caught Rose behind the knees. They crashed together; falling on the bed, there was another "Phut" as a second shot was fired. Harry was the heavier man, but Rose was desperate and he fought like a tiger. Harry had to concentrate on the pistol, he grabbed at Rose's wrist with both hands and squeezed as hard as he could, numbing Rose's grip. Squirming and rolling, Rose slipped a hand into his pocket and pulled out a bunch of keys. Gripping the key ring in his fist, and with the keys pointing through his fingers, Rose went for Noble's face. Harry sensed his intention and turned his face away just in time, the keys raking searingly down his cheek and neck and onto his shoulder.

As they wrestled, they and the bed were smeared with blood. Neither opponent was consciously aware of this fact, but as the blood got onto their hands, their grips became slippery and less secure. Noble realized that he was losing his firm hold on Rose's pistol hand, and with a desperate lunge upward. He managed to raise himself into a kneeling position, straddling Rose. Noble pulled Rose's arm upward and trust with all his might, bashing the knuckles of the gun hand against the wall. The impact loosened the gun, which fell onto the bed. Both men made a concerted grab for the pistol. Winning by a fraction, Harry grabbed the pistol by the silencer. Moving away from Rose he rolled onto the floor into a crouching stance. He raised himself shakily but quickly, and with the butt of the pistol hit Rose hard on the temple. Rose lay still.

Harry took a hurried step toward Harriet, his leg collapsed under him and he fell heavily on the floor. He looked down stupidly at the blood gushing from his leg, where the second shot must have hit him. He felt no pain, but the adrenalin that had surged through his body subsided, and he started to feel dizzy. He could feel a weakness coming over him. Harry knew that his weakness was from the loss of blood, and he had better call foe help before he fainted.

His major concern was to get help for Harriet. He didn't know if she were dead or alive, he only knew that he had to get help urgently. He dragged himself back to the lounge, leaving a trail of blood behind him. He crawled to the phone beside the TV., and through a red mist he struggled to reach for it. In what seemed to be slow motion he managed to pull the instrument down to the floor, and dialed the police emergency number.

"Help," he whispered weakly, "Harry Nobles flat. Ambulance, police hurry."

"Speak up please, I cannot hear you," the operator responded.

"Police inspector Noble." Harry muttered a little louder, "My home, emergency. Send ambulance, hurry, please hurry." Harry's voice faded away as he fainted.

The telephone operator called the police night duty staff. "I've received an emergency call for an ambulance to go to inspector Nobles residence, give me his address, hurry." Receiving the information the operator called the hospital ambulance services. "This is Da Gama precinct. This is an emergency; send an ambulance and paramedics urgently to 14 Woodrow heights, 65 Kloof road. A police contingent will be there momentarily."

Immediately the operator had finished his call, his internal phone buzzed. "What's this about Harry?" Was the puzzled query.

"The caller was very faint. All I could make out was that an ambulance was required at Nobles place. Someone better get out their pronto, somethings up I reackon."

The paramedics arrived shortly before the police officers. They found Noble, a woman and a man still lying where they had fallen. Harriet was found to have a graze across the left top of her skull where the bullet had passed, cutting a path through her hair. There was no doubt she was suffering from concussion. The other man was equally unconscious, a reddish blue contusion centered about his temple. He had no other injuries despite the bloody clothing and bedding. Noble was semi conscious but unable to speak. A bullet wound was found in his leg where major damage had occurred, causing a serious loss of blood. In addition he had an abrasion on the side of his face and neck.

The ruckus in Harry's flat had not disturbed the other residents of Woodrow Heights. But the sirens of the arriving ambulance and police vehicle certainly had. A curious inquisitive crowd, in various states of dress, from suits to dressing gowns, and pajamas gathered round the doorway to Harry's flat, as the injured were carried out.

The police without comment dispersed the crowd ; locked Harry's flat and left in their turn. At Woodrow heights rumours were rife, conjecture and discussion abounded, but eventually the subject was exhausted and the complex settled back into its usual complacent lifestyle.

CHAPTER 27

Rose was still unconscious, and two constables had been detailed to stand guard in his ward on a rotational basis. The doctor had said that it was a wonder Rose was still alive after receiving such trauma to his head.

Harry, with his neck bearing a 'Betterdine' and plaster dressing, and his leg, now encased in plaster of Paris from hip to ankle, having undergone extensive surgery, was not surprised at the doctors remark. Killing Rose had been foremost in his mind the instant he had seen Harriet fall from Rose's shot. His enquiry after Harriet had elicited the news that she was fine, but still l little woozy from the concussion and experience. His request to be taken to her side was gently denied owing to the serious injury to his leg. He was told that Harriet would be visiting him before he would be in a mobile state. He just had to be content that Harriet was fine, and patiently wait until the doctors gave him the o.k. to move around.

Harry's colleagues all paid him sympathetic visits, including his superintendent, Chief Watson. After commiserating with Harry over his injuries and Harriet's misfortune, Watson was not long in getting down to business. He congratulated Harry on his speedy apprehension of Rose and then came the question Harry was dreading. How did it come about that Rose had been in Harry's flat the night of the shooting? Harry pleaded weakness, he said, "I'm sorry Chief, I don't feel up to talking at the

moment. I still feel too nauseous and weak from the anesthetic to be able
to concentrate right now."

"Of course Harry, silly of me to worry you with questions at the
moment, sorry. You rest now. Soon as you feel up to it we will talk again."
The chief gave Harry's arm a reassuring squeeze, and left him to his own
tumultuous thoughts.

On his rounds the next morning, the doctor brought Harry the good
news that Harriet was to be allowed to visit him for a short while. He said
that Harriet needed to see him to satisfy herself the he was alright, hut she
was not to stay too long, as she herself was far from over her experience
and had to take it easy. Her visit was a joyous occasion for both Harriet
and Harry, but the nurses cut it short after only fifteen minutes. They
were worried that the excitement, both parties had evinced, would have
a detrimental effect on their recovery. In spit of their protests, the nurses
were not to be denied, and both Harriet and Harry had to comply with
their orders.

Harry's agile brain soon came up with a plausible explanation for
Rose's presence in his flat, but it would require Harriet's agreement and
participation. He was impatient to see her, and kept nagging the nurses to
allow him to use a wheelchair. Not yet, the nurses kept stalling, it is not
Harriet that was the problem, she was progressing very well and he was not
to worry. The problem was with him, and only the doctor could say when
he would be allowed up. 'Oh well, he would just have chance Harriet's
agreement with his story if the chief happened to ask him again before he
had a chance to brief Harriet,' thought Harry resignedly.

Harriet was discharged before Harry had a chance to see her again.
The doctor told Harriet that she was not to worry about Harry, but to
be assured that he was fine. He did not want her to visit Harry for at
least a week. Both of them needed to relax and rest completely, and the
excitement of a visit between them would not be advisable at present. The

doctor added that she could go home and rest, but under no circumstances was she to go back to work for at least two weeks.

Regrettably, the doctor added, her hair would not likely grow where the bullet had scored its path across her skull, but if it did recover its growth, it would be white. It was a shame, but she should at least be gratified she was still alive, that bullet could have easily killed her. They sent her home in an ambulance and she did not have a chance to see Harry.

Harry's leg was not responding to treatment as well as the doctors had hoped. They were worried that it may remain permanently stiff. Harry was placed under a strenuous physio therapy schedule, and although he had graduated to the use of a wheel chair, he was still hospital bound. The doctors were keeping the wound under close observation, and until they were certain the physio was helping, he would have to remain in hospital.

Harry was sitting in a wheelchair reading when Harriet breezed in on her first visit a week after her discharge. She had changed her hairstyle, and there was no sign of the bullet scar. She looked beautiful, bright and healthy, and there was no evidence of her recent traumatic experience. She had brought Harry a packet of shredded biltong and a bottle of orange squash. These she placed on the bedside cabinet before leaning over and giving Harry a loving kiss on the lips. She told him he looked fine and asked how things were going. Harry was overjoyed at her surprise visit and her wonderful appearance. He reached for her and they kissed once more.

Harriet told him that she had, had no after effects. She mentioned she had been booked off for two weeks recovery rest, and that she had asked a friend to watch over the florist while she was away. She said that contrary to the doctor's warnings of possible negative reactions, she felt as well as ever before, and so full of energy.

Harry was eager to place his solution regarding Rose's visit to his flat, and so he interrupted Harriet's flow of words. "Please darling, slow down a minute. There is something important I have to discuss with you."

"What is it Harry, bad news about your leg?" Harriet was instantly concerned.

"No, the leg is coming along slowly, its nothing like that. It's about Rose and the Chief. He was at me the other day about how it was that Rose happened to be at the flat. I managed to gain a bit of time by telling him I was too weak to answers questions at that time. Up to now he hasn't raise the question again, but he will sooner or later, and I want to tell him something plausible, to do that I will need your help, will you help me?"

"You know I will sweetheart, How can I help?" Harriet responded immediately.

Harry then went into some detail in explaining the story he had concocted to tell the superintendent.

After hearing Harry's plan, Harriet was less inclined to help. She did not take kindly to lying outright to Chief Watson, and said as much.

Harry was very persuasive, saying he would do all the talking, and he doubted if the chief would ask Harriet anything. He just wanted to be sure that, should there be any questions, they would be able to co-ordinate their answers.

Harriet finally agreed, she realized it was the only way Harry would escape being implicated, and she suppressed her scruples. Harry pulled her close and kissed her again in relief.

The discussion about Rose had temporarily displaced Harriet's great surprise. She reached out and took both of Harry's hands in hers, and with a happy smile told him she had spent yesterday cleaning up the mess in his flat. She said the place was as good as new except for the bloodstained bedding and mattress. These, she said, were beyond redemption, and she had asked the building janitor to dispose of them. She handed Harry a set of keys she had found next to the bed, she thought they must be Roses.

Harriet then broke her great surprise. "Darling," she said," when you are discharged from hospital you won't have to go back to your bachelor existence. You can give your landlord notice; you are coming home with me. I've decided we will give our marriage another go."

"Do really mean that Harriet? Are you absolutely sure? I mean you have just been through a graphic and harrowing experience of what a cop's life can be like, in case you had forgotten," said Harry, hoping against hope that what Harriet had said would actually come to pass.

"Harry, I am so certain that I even phoned a second hand shop and sold all your old furniture. Now you have no option, theres no way you can escape, you'll just have to move back in with me." She gazed lovingly at her dear and wonderful husband.

"What !" exclaimed Harry in alarm, "everything."

"Just about. I did keep a few items, such as your awards, your clothes, and of course I didn't part with your favourite old "lazyboy" chair. Every thing else went; it would have clashed with the furniture in my apartment. In any case, there would'nt have been the room." Harriet told Harry happily.

"The sofa? You didn't sell the sofa did you?'

"Yes, of course I did. What's so special about that old thing? I didn't think it was so important, was it? Any way I couldn't separate the sofa and the matching easy chairs, they formed a suite after all. The "lazy boy" I can just live with, it's neutral beige leather. But the other stuff, upholstered in that autumn shade floral linen material, with the old fashioned wingback style. It would have just clashed with my furniture. You don't really mind, do you?" Harriet was so excited and effervescent, bubbling with enthusiasm, she felt sure Harry would be happy with her decision to restart their marriage. The experience she had just survived brought home to her just how short life could be. She was determined that Harry and she would not miss another minute of it away from each other.

The sofa and the money were gone. Harry was shocked and aghast, and his mind took a moment to absorb and adjust to this latest state of affairs. He gazed at Harriet wide eyed and with his jaw sagging open. With his decision to return the other four boxes as soon as possible, and with his return to grace in the chiefs' estimation, Harry had become inured to the money hidden in the sofa. As the days had gone by he had felt less and less guilty, even rationalizing that he was entitled to that share of the money in lieu of the risks he had run. Particularly since this last fracas, and the danger and injuries both Harriet and he had suffered. Now Harriet had unilaterally sold the sofa. One thing was certain; he would never be able to tell Harriet about the secret of the sofa. She would never condone or consider hanging on to any portion of the money. All this passed through Harry's mind in a few seconds before he answered Harriet's question of, "Harry you don't look happy. Did you not want me to sell your stuff?"

"No I'm fine. It was just so sudden. Of course it's o.k. Thank you, thank you for having me back in your life on a full time basis. The rest is not important at all." Harry silently philosophized,' Oh well, although the money was in my possession, I never really had it to spend. Maybe it is all for the best.' Suddenly Harry felt free and relieved; it was as if a heavy load had been lifted from his shoulders. The metaphorical albatross that had hung about his shoulders had lifted and flown away.

After the excitement of Harriet's announcement had subsided, their conversation moved on to more mundane subjects, and in passing Harry asked what had made Harriet come to his flat that particular evening. Harriet explained how Rose had come to her shop pretending to be Harry's long lost friend. She mentioned that, she had thought at the time, the bearded stranger was not the sort of man she associated as Harry's typical friend. She told Harry how she had followed the man to the door when he left and saw him go into a residential block just down the street from her shop.

Harriet went on to say she had intended to phone him and warn him of the mans probable visit, but the shop had got busy and she forgot. She only recalled her intention to phone on her way home. Harriet admitted to her curiosity, and had decided to pop round to his flat after super rather than phone. When she arrived at the flat she heard voices, and followed the sound to the bedroom. She said she could not remember being shot. That information had only been forthcoming after she had regained consciousness and been told so by the doctor.

Harry in turn told her how he had thought she had been killed, and how murderously he had attacked Rose. He added in a subdued voice, "I thought I had killed him, and I was glad."

Harriet hugged him, "It's all over now. I understand what you went through, but relax, don't think about it, he got what he deserved."

Speaking of Rose reminded Harry of the keys Harriet had brought; also he recalled that she had said she had seen him go into a residential block near her shop. These two facts gave Harry the solution of what to do with the remaining boxes Harriet had taken to her apartment.

"Harriet, I have just thought of something, and unfortunately I have to ask you to become involved again. Because of this gammy leg of mine I won't be able to carry those boxes you took to your flat, but this is what I have in mind. We remove the boxes from your flat and place them in Roses apartment. Then when I return to work I hand in the keys and explain they were found in my bedroom, and must belong to Rose. I can also explain how you learned of Rose's address. There's bound to be a search of Rose's apartment which will result in the finding of the money. But, as I say, I will need your help to carry the boxes. What do you think?"

"Good idea Harry, certainly I will help. I helped carry them to my flat didn't I, so I can do it again."

He was on crutches, but at least he was mobile and at last the doctors decided he could be discharged. The doctor's prognosis was for a ninety percent recovery, provided he continued with the exercise program they had worked out for him. He would be left with a permanent limp, but physio therapy should help to return some flexibility to the damaged knee.

Almost before Harry had become accustomed to living in Harriet's apartment, he was busy reconnoitering the means of transferring the money to Rose's apartment. He spent two days at Harriet's shop, and from there watched the traffic in and out of the building in which Roses had lived. He decided that ten a.m. was usually the quietest, and he decided that that was the most auspicious period to carry out the deed.

He first went there alone to familiarize himself with the layout. Rose's flat turned out to be situated on the top floor of the building. Fortunately there was an elevator; else the stairs would have defeated Harry on his crutches. He let himself in using the keys Harriet had found, and carried out a thorough inspection. He was looking for a suitable hiding place. He knew from personal experience just how exposed the possession of such a large sum of money made one feel, and there was no doubt that Rose, had he had the money, would have not left it in an obvious spot. He discovered a trap door in the ceiling in the bathroom and he decided to stash the boxes there.

Waiting for a quiet spell in the traffic, Harry led the way and Harriet followed holding three boxes in her arms, her chin pressing down upon the top box to keep them steady. Once in the flat, Harry directed Harriet to drag a kitchen chair to the bathroom.

While Harriet returned to her shop to fetch the remaining Box, Harry Poked the trap door open with one of his crutches. It hinged upward and fell with a crash in an open position, sending down clouds of dust. Harry swung himself out of the falling dust cloud, but not fast enough, and he was seized with a violent sneezing spell. When Harriet returned Harry, helped her up onto the chair and held her steady, while she pushed the boxes into the ceiling space. As Harriet stepped down Harry folded her into his arms and gave her a resounding kiss.

"Why! Inspector Noble," Harriet exclaimed, "You do pick the strangest places to become amorous."

"It's just so good to be with you again and to be doing things together." explained Harry. They locked the flat and with Harriet holding onto his arm, they left the building.

The chief was delighted to welcome Harry back to work, and of course immediately requested to write up a report on the occurrence that had taken place at his flat. This gave Harry the opportunity to record the scenario that he and Harriet had agreed upon. The report he produced for the chief's edification mentioned that he had perchance noticed a bearded fair haired man wearing spectacles passing in the street outside Harriet's florists. He wrote that he had thought it was Rose in disguise, but was not certain. As he did not want to be embarrassed should it prove to be a stranger, he had prevailed upon Harriet to approach the man with flirtatious advances, the idea being to trap the man into making a date with Harriet. She would then invite the man for a drink that evening at Harry's flat, pretending it was hers. The ploy worked and the man had agreed to meet her that evening.

Harry had cleared all his photographs and awards from the mantle in his lounge and placed them on the bedside cabinet in his bedroom, where he himself hid when the man, he suspected of being Rose, arrived. After Harriet and Rose had, had coffee, he tried to make love to Harriet and she knew that it was time to lead him to the bedroom. When Rose saw Harry, he realized he had been duped, and he pulled his pistol and fired at Harriet in rage. Then the whole situation got out of hand resulting in the episode of which the chief was aware.

Chief Watson humphed and hawed as he read through Harry's report, while Harry stood in front of him and squirmed uncomfortably in trepidation of the dressing down he was sure was coming to him. Finally the chief finished reading and looked up at Harry. "Highly irregular Harry, and very foolish of you to place Harriet's life in danger like that, but what's done is done. Just don't ever let something like this happen again, do you hear. I know Harriet is your wife, but that doesn't make her a member of the force, and you know as well as I, that it is not done to endanger the life of a member of the public unnecessarily. Having said that, Harry, I must congratulate you on clearing the case up so quickly. You did a magnificent job. I asked you not to waste time, and you certainly did not do that. By the way, I am delighted that Harriet is o.k. and suffering no ill effects. It is also tremendous news that you two are together once more, and just to give you something else to celebrate, I am happy to tell you that I recommended your promotion to chief inspector, effective as from the first of the month. Congratulations again, Harry."

Harry was completely taken aback and inordinately pleased. "Thank you very much, sir," he said as the chief reached out and shook his hand.

"Well," said the chief, all business once more, "Back to work. I see that you are still walking with the aid of a stick. I suppose I will have to find you a desk job until that leg is fit. Come along with me." As they walked along, Harry reached into his pocket and produced Rose's keys.

"By the way sir when we cleaned out the flat we found these keys. They must belong to Rose. The name of the building is on the tag, and co-incidentally enough, the building is close to Harriet's shop."

Oh, Is that so" answered the chief, "I will return them to the landlord, but before that, I will get someone down there right away and perform a thorough search."

The chief was pleased at how the case had panned out. The search of Rose's apartment had yielded the four evidence boxes which had been returned to the evidence room. True two of the boxes were still missing, probably spent on bribes or similar. The serial numbers of the notes should have been recorded when the boxes were originally sent in. That they were not was another piece of rank carelessness. Now they would be impossible to trace. For that mistake he must take the blame, for he was in charge of the station at that time. The robbery of the evidence boxes was due to the carelessness of Fairweather, nevertheless, in spite of the many mistakes and false starts, a satisfactory ending to the affair after all.

Though Dalmini's crookedness as a cop had been revealed and his actions denounced, the authorities felt strongly about a cop killing, and Rose had been charged with aggravated assault and first degree murder. He was sentenced to life imprisonment plus twenty years. All through the trial he had tried to implicate Noble, accusing him of taking the six boxes of money. The finding of the four boxes in the ceiling of his flat caused his claims to be treated with disdain. Many prisoners made accusations and threats when they were sentenced, and these were taken from whence they came.

Harry's promotion to detective chief inspector meant a considerable jump in his pay packet. It went a long way to dull Harry's guilt regarding his erstwhile questionable behavior. Harriet was also extremely pleased with the added finance. The added imcome made it easier to start a home together once more. If Harriet had only known how much easier it would have been if she had not sold the sofa.

CHAPTER 28

East Bay Auction Mart, boasting the logo 'Why buy new when used will do', was Mr. Levy's pride and joy. He prided himself for, what he felt, were fair prices he paid for the secondhand furniture he purchased for stock, and equally for the value for money of the goods he offered for resale. He was particularly pleased with his recent purchase of the wingback styled lounge suite. The Saunderstown linen upholstery was in exceptionally good condition, and since he had gone over the suite with Vanish Foam upholstery cleaner, it looked as good as new. He had paid four hundred Rand for the sofa and three hundred Rand for the chairs. Mr. Levy estimated he could ask One thousand two hundred Rand and nine hundred Rand respectively for the pieces. He rubbed his hands with satisfaction, a nice three hundred percent profit, and still a good buy.

A young couple, just married, was window shopping for their new home. They had received a double bed and curtaining for a wedding present from her parents, while various friends and relations had provided cutlery, crockery and curtaining. There were still many things they required, hence the window shopping. They had been lucky in renting a recently vacated flat in Woodrow Heights, River kloof road. The rent was rather steep, but in East Bay City accommodation in the middle class range was at a premium, and they considered themselves extremely fortunate to have signed a lease for number fourteen Woodrow Heights. It did mean though they would have to settle for secondhand lounge furniture instead of the new suite they had hoped to purchase.

The young wife pointed to the chairs and sofa in the window of East Bay Auction Mart, she said, "Look at that suite honey. Won't it match the curtains, mom gave us, perfectly."

"You are right, darling," he agreed, "I wonder how much they want for it, shall we go in and enquire?"

Mr. Levy's large frame clad in an open neck, short sleeved white shirt, the collar pulled slightly askew by the yellow shoulder braces that strained to hold his creased khaki trousers in place over his abundant stomach. His iron grey hair, brush cut, made his head seem to be sporting a steel helmet. His beady brown eyes, glistening with avarice, his fleshy lips wreathed in an ingratiating smile, formed a perimeter surrounding his prominent nose, which like his stomach, led the way as he moved forward to greet the young couple.

"Good day young missus, good day young chentleman, how can I help you?"

"That suite in the window, what is the price please?" asked the young man, his young wife squeezing his arm in anticipation.

"Ah yes. I can see you have a good eye for fine furniture, young sir. An excellent choice, I Mr. Levy can assure you. You will not be disappointed, like new they are. Missus, feel the comfort, sit here in this chair please, and you sir, sit on this sofa. How does that feel, good eh?, like sitting on a cloud." Mr. Levy beamed down upon them enthusiastically.

"Yes they are very comfortable, but how much does it cost?" asked the man anxiously.

"Two thousand five hundred and, sir, and cheap at the price," said Mr. Levy, trying the market.

"Oh!" sighed the young couple, drooping in despair. The young man said sorrowfully," It is more than we anticipated." They turned sadly away.

"Wait, wait," Levy cried, as he shuffled round, blocking the couples intended exit. "Such a young couple, you start life together, no? It is hard, yes? I Levy will help you."

Levy's smile disappeared, and what he thought, was a look of solicitude spread over his mobile features. He looked instead as if he was about to burst into tears. "Come sit in my office, we talk this over, not so? Maybe I can help." Levy led the way into a smallish alcove in which there was a desk and three barrel chairs. The desk was cluttered with pamphlets, invoices, scrap paper, a telephone and an old fashioned crank type adding machine. Against the wall was a bookcase filled with files and bearing a price tag showing it was also for sale. Levy ushered them to seats and with a grunt, eased himself into the protesting chair behind the desk.

"Opening proceedings he asked," How much did you wish to pay, Mr. eh?"

"Roberts, our name is Roberts. This is my wife Sheila, and they call me Robbie. We only have fifteen hundred Rand," Roberts ended lamely.

"Mm, hmmm," muttered Levy as he pilled a sheet of paper toward him and scribbled some figures, pretending to be earnestly trying to help. For five minutes Levy contorted his features into various configurations of pain and sorrow. Finally he leaned back, his chair creaked alarmingly in protest.

"Mr. Roberts, I'm a fair man, I say I will help you, and I will help, but you understand I must also make a living. The best I can do is two thousand one hundred Rand," offered Levy, reverting back to what he had originally intended asking for the suite.

Roberts looked at his hopeful wife, shrugged his shoulders in disappointment, and said," I can only manage fifteen hundred, it's all I have." He stood up," Come dear; we will just have to keep looking."

"Mr. Roberts, don't be in a hurry, please sit again, let us discuss this problem. I can see your lovely wife is very disappointed, so would I be also if I were to lose such a bargain. You are such a nice couple, I would be sorry if I cannot help you. You give me Fifteen hundred as deposit and pay the balance off in three months. Would that make it easier?"

Roberts was hesitant, he looked at his young wife. She in turn looked pleadingly at her husband. "They will go well with our curtains," she hinted.

Levy struggled out of his chair, "I will give you a moment to talk it over," he said, moving out of the alcove. He was not worried; he had seen the looks that had passed between the two young people. The hook had been set, left to themselves they would reel themselves in.

True to Levy's instinct, within a short while Roberts came out of the office looking for the owner of the business. Levy was standing on the other side of the showroom, and seeing Roberts made his way back to the office in a surprisingly short time, considering his bulk. Rubbing his hands together, his face wreathed in smiles once more, he settled into his chair again. "Ah! I can see by your smiles you have decided to buy, yes?" Levy opened a drawer in his desk and brought out a pink form. He looked questioningly at the couple, and Roberts proffered him the fifteen hundred Rand. Levy took the money, slipped it into his pocket, filled in the pink form and handed it to Roberts for his signature.

"What is this, my receipt?"

"No, it is just a form to say you have paid a deposit of one thousand five hundred Rand and agree to pay the balance in three months from this date, that's all. Please sign at the bottom."

Roberts filled in his address and signed, without reading the fine print, that recorded the fact that the balance was subject to an interest of twenty percent. Mr. Levy did not enlighten him.

"Thank you so much," gushed Mrs. Roberts, taking Levy's hand. "When do you think you will deliver?"

"This very day, yes, this very day, I promise you," answered the complacent Mr. Levy.

That evening the young couple sat together on their newly acquired sofa. Each pondering silently the pains of buyer's remorse, though neither would admit the fact to the other. They had spent rather more than they could afford at present, and the rest of the month would be lean pickings for them. They sat watching the weekly National lottery draw on television. "Wouldn't it be nice if we were to win, what a way to start our married life," mused Sheila Roberts, unknowingly sitting upon the fortune that was hidden in the springs of the sofa, "Then we could pay cash for everything and not have to worry about monthly payments."

"Never mind love, three months is not too long. We will still have it all paid for," said her husband.

Young Mr. Roberts was hard working and ambitious. He looked forward to the years ahead and was certain the fortunes of the Roberts family would prosper. There would come a time when they could afford to upgrade their lifestyle. When that day dawned the lounge suite would probably for sale once more, and he would at last buy a brand new suite for his dear wife.

But long before that day would arrive, a strange incident occurred. The young Mr. Roberts had left for work that one particular morning, and his wife had cleared the kitchen table of the breakfast things, and started the daily round of dusting and sweeping their apartment. Whilst sweeping out the lounge she noticed a one hundred Rand note lying near the base of the sofa. She picked it up thoughtfully, looked wonderingly at it as she turned it round in her hand. 'It must be Robbie's,' she thought,' It certainly is not mine, I can't remember when I last had one hundred Rand. For that matter, I'm surprised that Robbie would have a hundred Rand and not tell me.' She took it through to the kitchen and placed it under a door magnet on the refrigerator

That afternoon when Roberts returned home, his wife met him at the door with a welcoming kiss. She asked him if he had missed anything lately.

"No sweetheart, why do you ask?'

"Are you absolutely sure?" she insisted. Robbie felt through his pockets, "I seem to have everything. What do you mean?"

"O.k. then, can I keep what I found," and his wife led him through to the kitchen and proudly showed him the one hundred Rand note.

"Good Lord," exclaimed Robbie, "Where on earth did you find that? It certainly is not mine."

His wife explained the circumstances, and try as they might could not account for the money. In conclusion they decided that it must have got stuck in his clothing at some time unknowingly, and then fallen unnoticed onto the floor. Robbie assured Sheila that he could not recall ever having had a spare hundred Rand, but, as he said, they should not look a gift horse in the mouth. Just on the off chance that there might be more lying around, Robbie lifted the end of the sofa and looked underneath.

"Don't be silly," his wife chided him "We don't have that kind of luck."

"No, I guess you are right, still one never knows. By the way, I noticed that the hessian underneath had pulled away a bit. I had better get a few tacks and knock it fast before it goes further." So saying he fetched a hammer and tacks and tipping the sofa on its back, he pulled the hessian into position and tacked it fast. Had he looked under the hessian during the process, their lives would have taken a very different path.

CHAPTER 29

The country as a whole, and East Bay City in particular was experiencing a boom period, the public had more purchasing power than years previously, and young Mr. Roberts was revelling in these conditions. Like many others, he found that selling was not difficult in this economic climate. He was an insurance salesman, and of late had written many worth while policies. His commission from these sales added to his basic salary, had allowed the Roberts family improve their lifestyle considerably.

Robbie phoned home. "Sheila, guess what? I've been speaking to our manager and guess what?" Robbie, beside himself with excitement, never gave Sheila a chance to answer. He rushed on, "He says that now that I have reached the levels of sales that I have, my earnings qualify me for a home loan if I so desire. If I can pay the deposit, they, the company will assist me with a home loan of up to eight hundred thousand rand. Isn't that good news? So when do you want to go house hunting?"

"Yes, oh yes, darling, that is wonderful news. We can start a family once we have a home of our own. I'll phone some estate agents right away, shall I?"

"Yes, do that. The sooner the better." Robbie rang off, thrilled at the thought of becoming a land owner.

It was not as easy as they had anticipated, and three weeks later they still had not found a suitable home. The eight hundred thousand Rand loan they qualified for did not give them a wide range of dwellings to choose from. To them it seemed like a fortune and they had visions of four bedroom, two bathroom homes, with eight hundred odd square meters of property. In reality they found that the best on offer in that price range were small two bedroom, single bathroom starter homes, with a maximum of six hundred square meter erven. As one estate agent explained, building costs to day were prohibitive. And it was impossible to build a home under six thousand Rand per square meter. The agent persuaded them that even although it was small, a starter home was a sound asset. Investment in property was generally sound, and property values seldom if ever dropped. It was not the size that counted, but the location. If they decided to buy they must only buy in the best locality they could afford. With these wise words firmly imprinted on their minds, Robbie Roberts and his wife finally became owners of a rustic, two bed roomed cottage with a pretty established garden at 111 River Kloof road, not far from their recently occupied apartment. "Well at least the removal costs will be minimal, it's only a skip and a jump from our old place," philosophised Robbie, as he wrote out one cheque to cover the transfer fees, and another to pay the water and electricity connections.

During the course of one weekend, Sheila and Robbie Roberts employed a private lorry owner to help them move, their now well used furniture, to their new home. After a concerted effort of cleaning and dusting, Sheila took off her house coat, hung it on a hook behind the kitchen door, and washed her hands. She put the kettle on to boil and set cups for tea. She shouted to Robbie, who was outside painting the side door to the garage, to come in for tea. Sitting down to well earned refreshing cups of tea, they gazed around at their surroundings.

"Yes, I must say it all looks very, and homely and comfortable. Well done Mrs. Roberts", complimented Robbie.

"Thank you kind sir. It's the best I could do with what we've got."

"Never mind sweetheart, the very next thing we are going to do, as soon as I bring in a few more commissions, is get ourselves our long promised new lounge suite to do justice to our new sitting room."

CHAPTER 30

Two years had past and the Roberts were sitting together on their old sofa. The sales commissions had not come in as fast as Robbie would have liked this last year or so, and so they had not been able to change the furniture as Robbie had hoped. The cost of living had gone sky high, and people were struggling to make ends meet. Personal insurance had been put on a back burner, and sales of policies had fallen right off.

The Insurance Company's staff who were lucky enough to deal in business and company insurance were still doing all right, unfortunately, in spite of all his hard work and past good results, Robbie had not yet been promoted to corporate sales level. If sales did not improve soon, Robbie wondered if he would ever reach those imperiam heights. He looked toward his wife as she sat quietly reading, he knew she wanted to conceive, and they had tried consistently ever since they had moved into their own home, but with no luck as yet. In a way he was glad, two might live as cheaply as one, but a third demanding mouth to feed, not to mention the clothes and baby things and whatever, well with one thing and another, it was just as well.

Robbie did not want to worry Sheila, but lately he had borrowed more than he could repay, and that was just to live. The company automatically deducted his bond payments on a monthly basis, and when, as had been occurring lately, he had been unable to make any commissions, they had just lengthened his bond period with a resultant increase in interest. He had done his best to honour his bond repayments, but often he had found himself short in meeting their living costs. So far the firms accountant had been helpful, saying, as he advanced Robbie a few hundred Rand, that now and then these down turns came about, next month would be better, you'll see.

The next month, however, did not improve, and the constant shortage of money did nothing to boost Robbie's confidence. His sales fell lower and lower, his debt load got larger and larger, and his bond payments fell even further behind.

One Monday morning the firms sales manager called Robbie into his office.

"Sit down Robbie, we have got to have a little talk."

The sales manager sounded friendly enough, but not enough to allay Robbie's growing fear.

"Robbie, As you are no doubt well aware, there has been a downturn in business these last few months. I have noticed your personal turnover is way below par, and under the circumstances I think you'd be better served in some other line of employment. Robbie, I'm afraid we will have to let you go. In accordance with company policy, I am giving you one months notice. I am sorry it has come to this, more especially with regard to the money you owe the company on your house payments. You realise that money will have to be paid back. I strongly suggest you try to arrange for a building society to take over your bond; otherwise you will have no option but to sell your house to meet your obligations. I am sorry it has come to this, but I am afraid the company cannot carry you any longer. I am sure you understand the situation, and I wish you luck in your future endeavours."

Robbie found himself standing in the passage outside the manager office, he was in a state of shock, his face drained of colour, and he was near to tears. Not only had he lost his job, but they would also take his house, his company car and his petrol allowance. What was he to do, what could he tell his wife?

He went to the accountants office, "I say Mr. Fuller, I'm a bit short again. Do you think you could give me an advance of about twenty Rand?"

"No, I'm sorry Robbie, but the news had already filtered down. I can no longer subsidise you, I'm sorry. Here, take these, they are two referrals that have come in. See if you can turn them into signed contracts. Good luck."

Robbie looked at the referrals with a sinking heart. In his present frame of mind he doubted he would be able to convince anybody into the wisdom of taking out a policy. Still a referral was better than a cold canvass, he better give it a try.

The first address was a Mr. Whistler of "Pool For You", swimming pools and accessories, situated at 120 Main Street, Central. Robbie drove to Central and called on Mr. Whistler, Unfortunately Mr. Whistler was very busy at the moment, could Mr. Roberts set another appointment? How about tomorrow? No tomorrow was not suitable. Wednesday then? Wednesday was his golf day, sorry. Well what day would be suitable Robbie asked.

"Oh, I don't know," answered Whistler off handedly, "I'll tell you what, why don't you leave your card and I will call you the moment I have a free moment."

Robbie despondently handed over his business card, "Sure thing Mr. Whistler, look forward to seeing you, good bye for the moment."

'Just as I expected,' thought Robbie negatively. Then he shook himself figuratively,' Don't get depressed, the next one is sure to be better."

The next address was fairly nearby, but as it was almost lunch hour, he thought it would be better to make the call in the afternoon. He drove back to his office where he decided to phone the prospective client and try to make a firm appointment. If the client was prepared to accept the time strictures of a firm appointment, then he had a good chance of making his sales pitch with less pressure and making a good presentation. This time he was lucky, the woman who answered his call thanked him for his prompt response to her enquiry and would be pleased to see him at two o'clock.

Promptly at two p.m. Robbie arrived at "Natures Gift Florists". "Good afternoon Ma'm, my name is Roberts from"—

"How do you do Mr. Roberts, thank you so much for coming," said a glowing and very pregnant woman, "I am Harriet Noble, I am the woman who phoned your company. I hope you will be able to help me."

"I am sure we can Mrs. Noble, what did you have in mind?" asked Roberts, this sounded more promising, he exulted.

"Well Mr. Roberts, as you can see, I am expecting, and as I am already past thirty, there could be some risk at my age. I don't want to sound negative, and medicine had made huge strides these days, and I'm sure everything will be alright, but I just wanted to be on the safe side should anything go wrong. I want some sort of policy on my soon to be born child so what ever happens to me, at least he will be taken care of."

"Congratulations Mrs. Noble, I'm sure you will have nothing to worry about, but in any case a policy for your child is a wise move. I suggest an endowment policy in your childs name to be taken out by your husband, so that should anything happen, God forbid, to your baby, we could incorporate a codicil to change the beneficiary to either you or your husband, as required. They discussed various options that were available at length, and in the end Robbie was assured of a very reasonable commission. Robbie went home in the happy frame of mind which was the usual effect one experienced after making a policy sale. He felt up to the task of telling Shiela his bad news regarding his job termination at the end of the month. If he could pull of a few more sales, similar to the one he had written for

Mrs. Noble, then, maybe his boss would reinstate him. It was amazing how just one sale could inject a feeling of optimism once more.

It was coming up to the end of the month, and Robbie was no nearer earning enough to meet his bond payment, let alone housekeeping money. He had made two more sales since the Noble policy, and in terms of his housing contract with the firm, his bond payment would be deducted first, and he would receive the balance if any. The way things were going, he did not think there would be a great deal coming to him in the way of the balance of his commissions, with which to supplement his basic salary. Sheila had managed to get a job as cashier at a local supermarket, and although helpful, it was still not enough to meet their necessary commitments.

Robbie was always depressed these days, but still undaunted, he worked hard at trying to make worthwhile appointments, both to sell insurance and to arrange job interviews. His main problem was lack of skills. The only area in which he had experience was sales, but almost all the sales positions he had applied for, required not only the ability to sell, but also an understanding of the product he was to sell. Robbie found it hard to understand how employers expected him to know about their product without giving some sort of training, but this seemed to be the case at every interview. He had, had so many failed interviews that he knew the stock rebuttal by heart. "I'm sorry Mr. Roberts, but sales experience is not enough. Ours is a specialist product, and as your experience in—X, Y or Z, depending upon the firm and their product where he happened at that moment to be applying for a job,—I am afraid we cannot help you."

Other insurance companies also had no openings; the best they could offer was a job on commission sales only. As he could not make the grade in a job that commanded a basic salary plus commission, a commission only situation served no purpose. He did at one stage get a job as a barman, but that had not lasted long because of his inability to quickly calculate change. Many of the bar clients never ever looked at the change they received, but enough of those who were short changed, complained, and of course one never heard a peep from those who happened to be undercharged.

Well this was the end of the line. This month end he would be on his own, he had come to the end of his notice period, and he would finally be totally unemployed. He and Sheila discussed their plight that evening over a supper of rice and boiled chicken. Robbie sadly explained to Sheila that as he now had no regular income, and as her salary was so low, their funds were insufficient for their bond to be taken over by a building society. They had no option but to hand their house back to the firm. In the mean time to give them a little capital to carry on with, they had better see if they could sell some of their furniture. The only items they might get a worthwhile price on were their fridge and the lounge suite.

Mr. Levy, when he called the following day at Robbie's request, was very sorry to hear of their misfortune. Yes, of course he would help. The fridge? He would happily give them five hundred Rand. Yes he knew it was a little low, but they must understand the risk he would be taking. Today the fridge is in perfect working condition, but what could happen tomorrow? Refrigerators', as he was sure they well knew, had a habit of breaking down without any warning. Yes, Mr. Roberts, I am sure that it has given you no trouble over the years you have owned it, but you see, that was then, and this is now. The same refrigerator is now many years older, and could break down at any minute. The lounge suite, well that was another matter, yes he could see that it was still in a very good condition, but the style, you see, it is no longer popular, too old fashioned. The best he could do there was four hundred Rand for each piece, a total of twelve hundred Rand and plus the fridge, that would be seventeen hundred Rand. You accept my offer, good, there you are, cash on the barrel as they say. No don't mention it, my pleasure I'm sure. My truck is a little busy at present and I will only be able to collect tomorrow some time, if that's all right with you. Fine then, I'll trot along then, at least you can enjoy one more night with your furniture free of charge. Levy chuckled at his own joke, but the humour of it was lost on Sheila and Robbie.

As Levy was about to leave, Robbie made a forlorn attempt to improve his situation. He asked Mr. Levy if he might need a salesman, or maybe even a lorry driver perhaps. No, Mr. Levy replied, he did all the sales himself, as for a lorry driver, even if he could, he would not insult such a fine chentleman as Mr. Roberts by offering such a menial job. With a final wave, Mr.Levy left them.

Robbie handed the money over to his wife, keeping back only twenty Rand. Sheila did not query why he had held back the twenty Rand, and Robbie was grateful for that trust. It happencd to be Sheila's birthday the very next day, and although he knew he would not get much for twenty Rand, he also knew he could not hold back any more money in their straightened circumstances. He hoped that at least he could buy her some flowers, just to show he hadn't forgotten. He knew she would understand and would be happy that he had remembered her birthday.

CHAPTER 31

Sheila had to be at work, and ready at her till at the supermarket by eight a.m. She kissed Robbie goodbye as she left, and he told her he would again pound the pavements in the hope of landing some kind of work. Sheila wished him luck as she went off; not mentioning that it was her birthday. Robbie also had deliberately failed to wish her. He knew she was disappointed and hurt, but he wanted to make the most of his surprise later when he presented her with the flowers. He intended to leave immediately after Sheila and hurry down to "Natures Gift Florists" and buy the flowers.

Mrs., Noble recognised him the minute he walked in at her door. She gave him a warm smile of greeting and said how nice it was to see him again, and had he been keeping well?

Robbie said he was reasonably well and asked after Mrs, Noble's health and baby in return. Harriet said she was fine,and she knew that Mr. Roberts would be pleased to hear, that Young Harry was absolutely blooming. The social pleasantries completed, Harriet asked how she could be of assistance? Robbie explained that it was his wife's birthday and that he wished to buy her some flowers.

Harriet said she knew just the thing and retrieved from the back of the shop a gorgeous bouquet priced at three hundred Rand. Robbie blanched at the price and Harriet could see that he was crestfallen. She said, quickly and tactfully, that if he found that particular bouquet a little gaudy, maybe he would like to walk around the shop and pick something out himself that he felt might be more suitable. All the flowers were price marled, she added, and he could mix and match at a price that suited him. Robbie thanked her and proceeded to walk around the various flower displays.

It did not tale long before Robbie was back in front of Harriet, looking very hangdog indeed. He looked so sorry for himself and disappointed, that Harriet's heart reached out to him.

"My dear Mr. Roberts, whatever is the matter? You look positively pale, are you feeling all right? Can I get you some water?" Said Harriet with concern.

"Oh, Mrs. Noble, I've made such a fool of myself. I never realized that flowers were so expensive. To tell you the truth, things haven't been going all that well with me lately. The down turn in the economy has knocked the bottom out of insurance sales, and things got so bad that I lost my job. I've been trying to get some other job, but so far, no luck. As I told you, today is my wife's birthday and although she understands our predicament and doesn't expect a present, I thought I would surprise her with a bunch of flowers just to show I hadn't forgotten.

I thought that twenty Rand would be enough, it's all I have. I see now I was mistaken. I'm sorry Mrs. Noble; I'll just have to give it a miss."

Harriet was at once concerned, from the first time she had met him she had immediately liked the young man, and she was really sorry to hear of his situation. She said, "No you won't, young man. I will not hear of you giving your wife's birthday a miss, as you put it. You take this Three hundred Rand Bouquet as a gift from me, and go and make your wife's day."

"I couldn't Mrs. Noble, not in a million years. I couldn't accept a three hundred Rand gift like that." Robbie remonstrated.

"Don't be silly, Mr. Roberts, I insist, and if it will make you feel any better, you can pay me back when you get a job. I'm sure it won't be long before you are on your feet again. Please take the bouquet."

"No, Mrs. Noble, it's not just the cost of the flowers alone that's the problem. You see, if I present Sheila with such a magnificent bouquet, she will immediately fly off the handle, and rightly so. She will accuse me of wasting money on unessential things which we can ill afford at this time. The whole purpose of my surprise will be spoilt. Believe me, I am absolutely grateful for you kindness, but you can see it wouldn't work."

"Yes. Of course, silly of me not to realise that. But let me at least make you up a neat and pretty little posy. You simply must give her something, and I am sure you will not object to what I have in mind."

"Thank you Mrs, Noble, you are very kind indeed. At least let me give you this twenty Rand toward the cost. I know it will be not nearly enough, and I promise to pay you the difference the moment I get work."

"Not in the least. I absolutely refuse to accept any money. It is my gift to you and your wife. I am very sorry to hear of your bad luck, I wish there was something more that I could do." In the end Robbie accepted the gift of flowers, thanking Mrs.Noble again profusely. He could see at a glance the so called posy Mrs. Noble had put together was worth at least fifty Rand, if a cent. Robbie left "Natures Gift Florists' delighted with the thought that Sheila would at least have her birthday remembered in style.

Roberts had hardly left the florists when Harry Noble turned up. He had an hour or two to kill before he had to appear in court as a prosecuting witness, and he thought he would drop in on his wife and beg a cup of coffee. Harriet was pleased to see him and she busied herself at the percolator for a moment, then produced steaming cups of cappuccinos for Harry and herself.

"MMM ! Just what the doctor ordered," murmured Harry in appreciation as he pulled up a chair in front of Harriet's desk.

"Guess what happened just a moment ago?" Harriet asked conversationally.

"You sold a dozen Roses to the Presidents wife?"

"No, you fool, but it was something almost just as unlikely. You remember my telling you a year or so ago about that nice and helpful insurance agent who helped me choose our son's endowment policy. Remember, I couldn't get over how he had spent so much time and trouble explaining the best possible policy to suit our needs at the most competitive rate. Remember also I told you how he had spent hours explaining all the fine print and all that legal gobbledygook you get with these policies."

"Yes, I remember," said Harry, "I also remember telling you not to be fooled, that being extremely nice and helpful was an insurance agents stock in trade. The nicer they were, the more likely you would buy a bigger and better policy, and in so doing, guarantee a bigger commission for him."

"Oh, you are always so pragmatic. Well anyway, that same Mr.Roberts was in just a moment ago, and I was shocked to see the change in him. He has lost his job due to the weak economy and as yet has not found another. He didn't say too much, but reading between the lines and just looking at his condition, I could see that things were far worse than he made out. Harry, I was thinking, you know a lot of people, maybe you could put in a good word and help him get some work?"

"Woah Girl! Don't you go placing your lame ducks in my care. I'm no nursemaid. In any case it was not so long ago you rescued me from disaster, remember. You are much better at this sort of thing than I will ever be." Said Harry, trying to avoid being involved. He should have known better, he was no match against Harriet once she had a bee in her bonnet.

"C'mon Harry, do it for me please. Just pop around to his house and introduce yourself, and you will see for yourself what a nice young man he is. Please Harry, he did help us get a first class cover for young Harry, and I sort of feel responsible for him somehow. Once you have met him you will see for yourself that he is far above the average in presentation and ability I am certain that, once you know him, you will also want to help him if you can. You said yourself you had an hour or two to kill before you had to be in court; in what better manner could you spend your time. Please, pretty please Harry."

"O.k., o.k., I can see I'm not wanted here, I might as well go and see this paragon of virtue of yours. What is his address by the way?" Harry said, capitulating.

"That's another co-incidence," said Harriet, "It's 111 River kloof drive, not far from your old flat."

"Oh yes, I know the place, a little two bed roomed cottage, quite a nice place actually. Well I'll pop along there shall I?" Harry kissed her and left to get his car.

Harry rang the front door bell with no result. Probably a dead battery, thought Harry, and he pounded on the door instead. After a while he knocked on the door again, but still without a response. He decided that no one was at home and with a sigh of relief at being getting let off the hook, he turned to go back to his car. Just at that moment a young man came shambling along the path toward him. He wasn't looking where he was going as he walked head down, and moved in a very despondent manner. He almost collided with Harry, and jumped back startled.

"I am terribly sorry" Robbie apologised, "I wasn't looking where I was going. Roberts is the name. Were you looking for me?"

"Not at all, I am easily overlooked," answered the brawny Harry humorously, "And I can probably help you more than you can help me, at least I hope I will be able to. My name is Harry Noble, Harriet's husband."

"Oh!" exclaimed Robbie in surprise, "What a kind and nice lady your wife is. You have no idea how she helped me this morning, and she hardly knows me from a bar of soap. Did Mrs. Noble send you here?"

"But don't let us stand here, please do come in." At this invitation Robbie unlocked the door, and stood aside to allow Harry to enter. "Why did you have to come all this way. Did I leave something at the shop?"

Harry Noble started to say that his wife had asked him to come, but that was as far as he got, because it was at that moment that he saw the Saunderson linen covered wingback sofa that looked just like his old one. Harry stopped in mid stride, then after moments pause, went toward the sofa and had a good look at it, felt it, walked round it, and was as sure as ever he would be that it was in fact the sofa he had once owned. Roberts meanwhile stood nonplussed. 'What was going on here?', he wondered. Then he remembered his manners.

"Please sit down Mr. Noble. Can I get you something to drink, something to eat maybe?" Robbie hoped against hope that the stranger would refuse as he knew they had nothing to eat or drink in the house.

"No thanks, I'm fine," said Noble, much to Roberts relief, "You will pardon me, and tell me to mind my own business if you feel I am being impertinent. My wife sent me along to meet you, and see if I could be of help. She tells me you are having a bad time of it lately and that you have lost your job."

Harriet's' sympathy and willingness to offer help was just boo much for Robbie in his weakened and depressed state. Tears welled up in his eyes and he turned aside to hide his embarrassment. "Your wife is too kind, and you too, sir for taking interest in our troubles. Yes it is true we are having a bad time of it lately, in fact it couldn't get much worse for my wife and I. But we will survive somehow, we simply have to. There is nothing anyone else can do for us, we are too deeply in debt, and stand to lose everything within days."

Harry felt very sorry for this young man in his misery, and could understand his wife wanting to do all she could to help. Even at so short an acquaintance, one could see that Roberts was a well brought up young man. He was likeable, polite, and respectful and looked supremely honest. Harry, through his long training as a police officer, could accurately gauge a mans character.

Harry said, "Come sit down here and tell me about it. Maybe we can help or maybe we can't. I make no promises, and anyway it usually helps to talk about your problems to someone outside your immediate family."

Robbie sat next to Noble and told of his sad tale of woe from the time he lost his job to the present. Harry asked, "Let me get this straight. You say that the house is due to be repossessed imminently, and from then on you will be out on the street. You also told me you had sold your fridge and lounge furniture to a Mr. Levy from whom you bought the suite in the first place."

"Yes that's right, at least it's right regarding the lounge suite. The fridge I bought from someone else previously. Mr. Levy gave us seventeen hundred Rand for the lot, and believe me, we needed the money badly."

Suddenly Roberts jumped up. "Good Lord," he cried in panic, "I'd completely forgotten. I have been out all morning and Levy was supposed to collect the furniture today. I hope he hasn't been here already and found me gone. He will think I'm trying to crook him."

"Let Mr. Levy stew for awhile, sit down again," said Harry soothingly, "There are one or two questions I have to ask. Firstly, when exactly did you first buy the lounge suite from Levy?"

"Let me think, we have had it for quite a while. It must have been at least three years ago, maybe more, I'm not exactly certain."

"Secondly. Was there ever a time, since that purchase, when you came across a large sum of money by some strange circumstance? If so, what did you do with the money?"

Robbie gazed blankly at Noble, "I don't quite understand, how do you mean, come across a large sum of money? How much Money are you referring to, and where was it supposed to come from?"

"Mr. Roberts, let me be frank. I am meeting you for the first time at me wife's insistence. Both Harriet and you have told me of your unfortunate circumstances. Certain observations I have made since I walked in at your front door have made me wonder if you or your wife are hiding something from the public eye. I have to know if at any time you were in possession of a large sum of money, and what happened subsequently? You have to be honest with me or I cannot help you."

Roberts looked at Harry as if he had taken leave of his senses. He was bewildered and not a little afraid.

He did not know how he was supposed to answer Nobles strange question. He said, "Well yes, I suppose so. Up to two years ago I was doing really well. I had a company car, petrol was paid for by the company. My policy sales were very good and I made good commissions. I wouldn't call it large sums of money in the sense that one thinks of big money, but I was doing well So well in fact that the company was even prepared to grant me a bond to buy this house, that's how we managed to buy this house in the first place. I was meeting mymonthly bond payments with ease."

"That is until I lost my job when the economy got tight and insurance policy sales dried up. As I told your wife earlier, the boys who were doing corporate insurance were better off, but unfortunately I had not reached that level yet."

"I see ", said Noble, "And at no time, since buying the lounge suite, did either you or your wife have any access to any other monies whatsoever."

"I don't quite understand you, but no. We had no other form of income until my wife got a cashiers job at the supermarket."

"I see," said Harry Noble, "and you have no relations who could help you."

"Unfortunately, no, My parents have been dead many years, and both Sheila's parents died in a motor accident not long after we were married."

"One final question and I repeat myself," said Harry earnestly, "Since you bought the lounge suite, neither you or your wife, purely by chance I might add, come into a large sum of money. by finding it lying around for instance?"

"No, of course not. Well to be absolutely honest, we did once. Not a large sum, but large enough for the likes of us. One day my wife found a hundred rand note lying on the floor, just where your feet are resting now. Neither of us remembered having had or lost a hundred Rand. Until this day that business has been a bit of a mystery. We were thankful for it nevertheless, I can tell you."

"And that's it? That's the only extra money you ever had? Did you look under the sofa to see if there was more where that came from?"

"I certainly did," laughed Robbie, "but zilch, zero, nix, unfortunately."

"Well thank you very much Mr. Robetrs. Your story is very interesting, and you certainly have had a tough time of it, and there is a faint chance I may be able to help you. I will leave you now; there are one or two things I have to check. I want you and your wife to stay put for the moment. Should Mr. Levy arrive, stall him. You can tell him your affairs have become a police matter, and you have been forbidden to dispose of any of your furniture. If he complains about the seventeen hundred, tell him he will be reimbursed within the day. If he still is not satisfied refer him to me, Chief inspector Noble. Understand?"

Roberts did not have the faintest idea what was happening, but the goodwill exuding from Harry Noble, together with the assurance of likely help in some form, relieved his anxiety. For the first time in many months he felt a sense of freedom from worry. He followed Noble as in a trance, and stood gazing after him in wonderment as Noble walked to his car.

Noble returned at once to Harriet's shop. Harriet could tell from the expression upon Harry's face that he had been impressed by Roberts and she smiled and said, "He's really a nice young man, isn't he? Do you think you can find him an opening somewhere?"

Harry said, "It was the strangest thing. You know my sofa you sold, well it turns out that the Roberts bought it. I just saw it as large as life in Roberts lounge. Roberts told me he bought it from a Mr. Levy. Was that who you sold it to?"

"Yes, that's right. Mr. Levy of East Bay Auction Mart. My goodness that is really interesting." Said the amazed Harriet.

"Anyway, I think I will be able to help them, but I have to move fast. I've only got another half hour before court, and I have to withdraw seventeen hundred Rand to start the ball rolling. I haven't time to explain now, I'll tell you about it later. I just wanted to be sure that it really was my old lounge suite they had bought. Cheers, I'll see you later."

Noble withdrew the money from his bank and sealed it into an envelope together with an explanatory note, waylaid a passing constable, and asked him to personally deliver the envelope to Mr. Levy at East Bay Auction Mart. Harry then had to appear in court.

After the court session Harry went directly to East Bay Auction Mart and approached Mr. Levy. Mr Levy said he had received the money and had not gone to fetch Roberts's furniture, but he complained that was not the way to do business. He said he had paid a fair price for the furniture and was entitled to earn a profit upon his investment by resale. Harry had to resort to flashing his badge before Mr. Levy accepted the money as settlement. Levy noticed the name on the police identification wallet Harry had shown him, "Why it's you officer Noble. I remember buying dat very same suite from your good wife originally. It is a small world isn't it?" gushed Levy.

Noble brushed Levy's attempt at friendliness aside.

He asked Levy in a stern no nonsense voice. "Tell me this Mr. Levy. Did you at any time tamper with that suite before you sold it to Mr. Roberts?

Before you answer, think carefully. Your immediate future hangs upon your answer."

Levy was now suddenly alarmed. What is this all about? What had Roberts been up to? He hastily assured Noble that all he had done was clean it with upholstery cleaner. Not that it was in any way dirty, he was quick to assure Noble, it was simply a matter of policy. He cleaned all stock before resale.

"Now tell me this, Mr. Levy, did you have it cleaned by an outside cleaner, or by your own staff?" Levy told Noble that his own staff had cleaned the suite under his personal supervision. Noble pressed further, was Levy certain he had been present the whole period the cleaning was carried out? Levy assured Noble that that was the case, he had no idea what Roberts had been up to, but there was no way he wanted to become involved if he could help it, and he answered all Nobles questions truthfully. Good said Noble finally, now just one more question. Since my wife sold the suite to you, had you sold it to anyone else and again repossessed the suite before you finally sold it to Roberts. No said Mr. Levy, as a matter of fact Roberts came in and bought the suite in a matter of days after he had originally bought it from Mrs., Noble.

Harry was satisfied, he thanked Mr, Levy for his help in accepting the payback money, and for the information supplied. Noble left East Bay Auction Mart, much to the relief of its owner.

Harry sat in his car and thought about this strange turn of events. Harriet had never ever known of the money hidden in the sofa, and must never know. His superior, the station superintendant had been satisfied with the return of the bulk of the money, had accepted the loss of the one million nine hundred thousand odd as money spent by Rose in bribes and suchlike, and the Nietrop Case had been closed. Now once again there was this huge sum of money up for grabs, but as far as Harry was concerned, once bitten, twice shy. Never again would he willingly put himself through the torment and guilt he had felt when he tried to pocket the money himself. The only good that had come out of his slide into lawlessness was the return of Harriet to his side and their resumption of their marriage, and for that he had no regrets at what he had done, but that was enough. His recent promotion had not only given him a decent rise in salary, it had caused him to be raised above the front line and dangerous police work. Now that he was detective chief inspector, he was more a director of operations, and a behind the scenes operator, much to Harriet's delight. His rise in salary, together with the nice steady income Harriet made from her business allowed them to live in modest comfort. No, he decided, he was no longer tempted. He could not conceive what had possessed him, to even consider taking any of that money for himself at that particular time. A cold shiver caressed his spine, and he shook himself involuntarily, as he thought how close he had come to ruining his career. Suddenly here was the possibility of the money again coming to haunt him. Young Roberts needed the money far more than he did, so let some good come out of it after all. Just as long as he could steer clear of the money. He would have to do some explaining to Roberts and also convince him to act with discretion. Harry let in his clutch and drove back to Roberts home.

Robbie Roberts opened the door to Noble with a blank expression on his face, He had no idea what Noble had been up to, nor what was in store for him and Sheila.

He only knew he was not too thrilled at the solemn expression on Nobles face, and he expected the worst. Nobles opening remark caught Roberts by surprise.

"Mr. Roberts, I think I would like that drink you offered me earlier. I think I need it, and so will you in a minute or two. A beer would be nice if you have one?"

Robbie's face fell, he didn't like the sound of Nobles warning in the first place, and secondly he had no beer to offer. He apologised profusely for this lack of hospitality. Noble brushed his apology aside, "Never mind, not important. Have you a hammer and a screwdriver handy?" At Robbie's nod Noble requested that they be fetched. Robbie returned with the tools requested looking more stupefied than ever.

Noble took the tools from Roberts hand and placed them on the floor next to the sofa. He sat down and said, "What I am about to relate to you is stranger than fiction, and within the contents of what I'm about to tell you lies the solution to your problem. Listen carefully. A year or two ago a large sum of money was brought to the attention of the police. In tracing the origin of this money the police found it led to an important organization. The organization concerned denied any knowledge of the matter in spite of there being very clear, if circumstantial evidence, of their connection to the money. Without going into to much detail, it was decided that the money be placed in Police headquarters vault for safekeeping, until such time a legal action was instituted by the rightful owners to claim it, or the statute of limitations ran out. Do you follow me so far?"

"Yes I think so, but what has all this to do with us, my wife and I, I mean." Queried Robbie

"I think it will, let me finish".

"Sorry, please go on," said Robbie, ashamed at himself for rudely interrupting the Inspector.

"Now this is where the story takes a strange twist. In transferring the money to the state vaults, a robbery occurred and the money was stolen. You may remember the case from the newspaper story about the robbery at Da Gama Central Police station. Subsequent police work resulted in three quarter of the money being found. One quarter was never accounted for, and it was assumed that the robber had used some of the money for his own ends. On the other hand it may still be hidden somewhere. This is important, do you understand what I am saying when I say it may be hidden somewhere?"

"Yes, I think so", answered Roberts, still not sure what all this was leading up to, he however tried his best to concentrate on what Noble was telling him, no doubt it would become clear in time.

"In another three or four year the statute of limitations runs out, and unless claimed, the money in the state vault will become the property of the state in its entirety. On the other hand if a portion of the money that had mysteriously disappeared was to suddenly appear, it would become the finder's property as its rightful owner has never been established. In any case it would be near to impossible to prove any connection between the money found and that of the original money in police custody as there are no records of the serial numbers of the notes. Should you, for instance come across this money, your financial problems would be immediately solved."

"It sure would," interjected Robbie fervently.

At this point Harry reached down and picked up the screwdriver and hammer in one hand, and tapped them against the palm of his other hand, and looked intently at Roberts, and said, "The interesting thing about all this, Mr. Roberts, is that all I have told you occurred at about the time you purchased your first furnishing. The very pieces of furniture I managed to forestall Mr. Levy removing from your home."

Robbie Roberts wondered, not for the first time, if Noble had taken leave of his senses. Being the gentleman that he was, he had sat silently, as he had been requested and, without undue interruption, listened to Noble's story. However, he could neither make head or tale of it, nor figure out how it bore any connection to his person dilemma. And why had Noble requested the screwdriver and hammer? They obviously were an important clue if only he could figure it all out. The only thing that was abundantly clear to him was that Noble had purchased his furniture back from Levy at his own expense. To Roberts this was a situation that had to be clarified immediately, and something he had to redress somehow. He said, "I'm sorry Mr. Noble, er sorry, inspector Noble, I'm afraid I don't quite understand what you are trying to tell me, except the fact that you must have repurchased my furniture from Levy. I doubt that Sheila will have much of the seventeen hundred left, but of course we will re-imburse you. What ever is short on the seventeen hundred, you have my earnest assurance, that I will pay it back as soon as I possibly can."

Harry was exasperated, how could he get his message across without acknowledging the fact that he was instrumental in hiding the money in the sofa. He had decided that he personally did not ever want to see or touch the damn money again in his life. He was not superstitious, nevertheless he retained a sneaking feeling that the money had somehow cursed him once, and he never wanted to go through that experience again.

"Forget about the seventeen hundred, it's not important. If you are worried about it, you can pay me back once you are on your feet again. What is important is that you think very carefully over what I have just told you. Work out the clues I have given you, and showed you, and act accordingly. You do not have much time, they are about to repossess your home. Mr. Roberts, one final clue, think about that one hundred note your wife found on the floor that day. I can do no more. But with what information I have given you, can, if you have the sense I have credited you with, solve all your problems." Again Noble smacked the hammer and screwdriver in one hand against the palm of the other. "There is only one final warning I must give you. When you, and I am sure you will, eventually find your solution, I ask you to act at all times discretely and not go crazy."

With these final remarks, Noble took his leave of the bewildered young man. As he left Roberts home he wondered how he could have made the situation any clearer, short of telling Roberts outright about the money hidden in the sofa. Well only time would tell if he had been successful in helping Roberts as much as Harriet had hoped he would.

CHAPTER 32

Month end again, and Harry was busy going through his bank statement, checking their monthly expenses when He noticed a money transfer to his account in the amount of seventeen hundred Rand. He leaned back in his chair with a smile of satisfaction on his face.

"You look like the cat that stole the cream," Remarked Harriet, "What is so amusing?"

"I was just thinking," replied Harry, "of the young Roberts family."

The end.